Spoonin'

Spoonin'

Kimberly T. Matthews

www.urbanbooks.net

Urban Books, LLC
97 N18th Street
Wyandanch, NY 11798

Spoonin' Copyright © 2011 Kimberly T. Matthews

ISBN 13: 978-1-60162-418-5
ISBN 10: 1-60162-418-2

First Mass Market Printing July 2014
First Trade Paperback Printing June 2011
Printed in the United States of America

10 9 8 7 6 5 4 3 2 1

This is a work of fiction. Any references or similarities to actual events, real people, living, or dead, or to real locales are intended to give the novel a sense of reality. Any similarity in other names, characters, places, and incidents is entirely coincidental.

Distributed by Kensington Publishing Corp.
Submit Wholesale Orders to:
Kensington Publishing Corp.
C/O Penguin Group (USA) Inc.
Attention: Order Processing
405 Murray Hill Parkway
East Rutherford, NJ 07073-2316
Phone: 1-800-526-0275
Fax: 1-800-227-9604

Acknowledgments

Novels are hard to write. Acknowledgments are even harder. So many people have added so many pieces, both great and small, it's hard to collect and compile them all. There are so many that lurk in the shadows of this novel coming to fruition—family members, friends, coworkers, strangers, business colleagues, other authors; the list could go on for a full page. At the beginning and end of the day, God gets the thanks, the glory, and the praise for all things. Without Him, I could do nothing.

Dedication

To every woman who has sought intimacy in the arms of the wrong man—and survived it.

I've heard it said that the journey from the wilderness to the Promised Land should have only taken eleven days. But instead of getting there on schedule, the people stumbling, fumbling, and misguided by their own ways turned what should have been a few nights of journeying into forty years of wandering.

Each time I've heard that, I've always thought that I would have been the one person in the group wise enough, keen enough, sharp enough, or just have the plain common sense enough to recognize that I was walking in circles. I'd be the one to say, "Hey! The way out is *this* way!" I'd be the one to recover from the mistakes early, recognize familiar signs, and take the necessary actions that would get me to my destination quicker.

Funny, how I'd always thought that—until I found myself in the wilderness.

Chapter One

Nobody had been excited when I thrust my hand out on Thanksgiving Day over the pan of baked macaroni and cheese and announced, "I'm engaged!" My smile couldn't have been bigger or brighter in expressing my zeal for Sydney's proposal. With star-filled eyes, I wiggled in my chair as I looked around at my momma's face first; then at Gene, my stepfather; then at my older sister, Andra, and her husband, Coleman. I don't even think they stopped eating long enough to look up, but Coleman did sit back in his chair with a grin. He wiped his mouth with a napkin first, then raised off his chair just enough to reach out for Sydney's hand.

"Congratulations, man." They slapped and shuffled hands, following the unspoken brotherly handshake code. "You going in for the lockdown, huh?"

"Yeah." Sydney nodded coolly. "It's that time. She's the one." I rubbed his leg under the table, and he turned to me and pecked my cheek quickly. "She's the one."

"You hear that, Big G," Coleman asked, looking at Gene. "You're getting a new son-in-law." Gene just grunted and filled his mouth with more fried turkey. Andra kept right on eating, but she'd always been a hater, anyway, so her opinion didn't matter to me. Momma cleared her throat after a few seconds and managed to say, "Oh . . . well . . . uh . . . I guess congratulations are in order. Congratulations." She spoke with absolutely no conviction, then nervously shifted her eyes over to Gene and nodded her head a bit, prompting him to say something. "Gene?" she finally said when he didn't say a word. "Gene, did you hear Kareese?"

When Gene did look up, he stared intently at Sydney while he slowly chewed a mouthful of food. I could have sworn I could hear that whistling sound they play on the old cowboy western show *Bonanza* or *Rawhide* when there is about to be a gun showdown. Sydney met his stare, but he could only take a few seconds at a time before looking randomly at anything else besides Gene's eyes. I almost expected him to say, "You eyeballin' me, boy?" But instead he said, "If you ever hurt my daughter, you won't live to tell about it."

"Gene!" Momma whispered, but he paid her no attention.

"You hear me?" he asked, demanding Sydney's verbal confirmation.

"You don't have anything to worry about, Mr. Watson," Sydney respectfully answered, folding his bottom lip into his mouth and resting one arm across the back of my chair. "I love Kareese with everything in me, and I see the example you set before her of what a man is supposed to be and how he is supposed to take care of his woman; so I already know what you expect, and I already know what she expects."

Gene said nothing while he tapped his fork against his plate, which made me uneasy. He must have stared for another fifteen seconds and was only distracted when my baby, Casey, began banging on the tray of his high chair with his sippy cup, sprinkling apple juice all over the place.

"Get him, babe." Sydney nudged me, although Casey was closest to him. I saw Momma twist her lips and roll her eyes as I pushed my chair back to get my baby. I know what they all were thinking; and, honestly, I was thinking it myself. Sydney should have taken care of him. He was sitting right there, but I acted like it was nothing. I'd mention it to Sydney later.

"Come on, Booka-boo." I unlatched the tray and lifted my pride and joy up from his seat, and Casey wrapped his short arms around my neck and laid his head on my shoulder as he crooned his own little song.

"Look at my little nephew." Andra grinned, getting up to follow me out of the room, but I knew her motive was not her intrigue in Casey. We had barely made it to the den before she started on me.

"Girl, you're actually gonna marry him?"

"Uh, yes—duh!" I threw my hand up to display my ring a second time.

"Why?" She scrunched up her face like she'd just bitten into a lemon.

Truth be told, Sydney had his faults, but he could put it down like nobody's business. He knew how to work me over real good. And I mean *real* good. I knew how dim-witted I would sound if I said I was getting married for sex, so I kept it to myself. Besides, that wasn't my *only* reason. I did love Sydney. "Don't start, Andra."

"I'm just saying. I don't think you should do it," she advised, following me through the den and upstairs to what used to be my bedroom.

"And why is that? So you can keep the one-up on being married and building a family the 'right' way, while you continue to look down on me about being an unwed baby momma?" I couldn't count the number of times Andra had made throw-off comments about me becoming a statistic and how she saw single mothers on her social services job every day who had picked no-good men to father their children whom they wouldn't be able to feed without government assistance. "You're so self-righteous."

"Self-righteousness has nothing to do with it, but using good sense does, and you're about to do something stupid."

"Who are you calling stupid, Andra!" I snapped. "You get on my damn nerves thinking you're so perfect!"

"I'm just trying to keep you from making a mistake, being all excited about somebody who doesn't even really care about you. I don't know why you can't see that." She yanked at my left hand, only to look disapprovingly at my ring. "What is this cheap Kmart mess he put on your finger? Is that all you're worth? A $39.95 half-price Blue Light Special?"

"Just because he couldn't afford a ten-thousand-dollar ring doesn't mean he doesn't love me." I snatched back my hand, feeling both anger and embarrassment wash over my face; the ring was rather small and I couldn't argue that point. "I'm marrying a man, not a ring. It's not your place to manage my life."

"Well, if you don't care, then I don't care." She waved her hand and plopped down on the bed just as Momma walked in.

Momma's mouth didn't move, but her face—slightly contorted and raised brows causing rows of wrinkles in her forehead—said it all. She held out her hand, which meant *let me see the ring*. I gave her my hand and she did a two-second inspection.

"What, Ma?" I prompted. "Go ahead and say it."

"I don't have to say anything. You want to lock yourself up in a cage, go right ahead," she answered, backing up a bit to lean against the wall.

I had made the mistake of sharing with my mother the details of some of my and Sydney's arguments, one of them being about me not allowing him to open my car door, which I saw as pure gallantry.

"Ma, it's so nice that he always, always opens my car door. He even gets offended if I don't let him," I'd gushed.

Momma had folded her arms across her chest, unimpressed. I should have stopped then, but I didn't. Sydney and I had just started dating, and things were going so well, I couldn't hide my excitement.

"That's like the only thing we ever argue about."

"You better make sure that man is not trying to control you," she stated flatly.

"Control? Ma, he's just being chivalrous," I'd defended. "He's a gentleman."

"You keep on believing that," she'd said. I dismissed it. She never liked anybody I dated, anyway. I could have brought the President of the United States of America home, and she would have found something wrong with him, too.

"Can't y'all just be a little bit happy for me?" I almost begged.

"Don't look to us for your happiness. You're all grown. You wanna get married, get married," Momma said, sounding like any mother character played by actress Jennifer Lewis. It was almost like she'd said, "When times get tough, don't come over here crying to us. You grown. You want to be miserable, be miserable."

"So when is the wedding?" she asked next.

I'd already picked a date, but I didn't want to say because I knew that they didn't—and wouldn't—approve. "We haven't quite decided yet. Probably in the next few months." Really, I was thinking in a few weeks. Had I said that, Momma would have gone into a whole speech about rushing into marriage.

"Mmph, mmph, mmph!" Momma shook her head and walked out, leaving a trail of silence behind her.

I wasn't expecting cheers and champagne but it hurt my feelings just the same. I did have a small ray of hope that my mom would be an excited mother of the bride, and would take joy in helping me with the planning.

"The next few months, when?" Andra asked, filling the dead air. "What kind of wedding are you going to be able to put together in less than a year?"

"What difference does it make if you're not invited?" Her eyes popped open in shock. "We've decided that we don't want anybody there who is not truly happy for us, so that kinda scratches you off the invite list, but I felt like the least I could do is tell y'all about it."

"Which part do you want us to be happy about, Kareese? You might be the one for him, but he ain't the one for you," Andra expressed. "He ain't got nothin' to offer you."

"He has a job. He pays the bills. And he is Casey's father, or did you forget that? It seems like somebody would be happy about the fact that he wants us to be a family."

"He only has a minimum-wage, part-time job!" she yelled. "And it's a miracle that he's been there for three months now, from the way he likes to job hop. How is he gonna support you and the baby on that?"

"Sydney has a good heart," I said, taking up for my soon-to-be husband.

"What the hell is a good heart gonna do if he doesn't have the money to put a roof over your head and food on the table? Use your head, Kareese!"

"Like you did by having two abortions just so you could get your degree on time?" I spat, without regret. "You're always bragging to people like you did the right thing by waiting until you got married before deciding to have kids, but we both know that ain't true. If you asked me, you don't even have a damn heart." My words had cut Andra to the bone, snatching away her look of pride and replacing it with hurt and shame.

"You didn't have to go there," she uttered, rising to her feet and storming out.

"You're so quick to judge other people, but I didn't think you'd have anything to say about that," I finished, chasing her with words.

My face was warped into a scowl, but when I looked at Casey and he began smiling at me, my frown disappeared. So what if I hadn't finished college? I had a beautiful baby who was worth much more than a piece of paper that would only prove that I'd passed an economics, an English, a few business, and a couple of science lab classes at some overpriced school. I could go back to school any old time. But for right now, I had a man who wanted to marry me. Love was knocking on my door, and I was answering with or without my family's liking.

I met Sydney during my sophomore year at Wake Forest University when Yalisa and I stopped in a KFC to grab a two-piece snack in between studying for exams. I found Sydney to be charming, although he was serving chicken in a box. He was neatly groomed—as much as he could be in a fast-food uniform—had beautiful white teeth and an outgoing personality. He made no secret about his interest in me—stuffing my order with extra wings, then writing his phone number on the box.

"Here you go, miss," he said, licking his lips seductively. "I hope you enjoy it."

"Thanks," I answered, reaching for my bag and the change. He purposely let our hands touch and gave me a half smile.

"What's your name?"

"Kareese."

"Miss Kareese, I hope you call me so we can get to know each other better."

"We'll see."

It hadn't taken me long to call him, go out a couple times, and then start officially dating; which we did for a year before my education came to a screeching halt by my unplanned pregnancy. I cried for two weeks straight, feeling like a failure, feeling like I ruined my life, feeling like I'd wasted my parents' money and my time. Then I cried for two more weeks when Sydney told me he wasn't ready to have any kids and he thought I should terminate my pregnancy.

"We're not seeing eye to eye on having no baby," he'd said, but what hurt more was when I suggested we keep the baby and get married. "And we *definitely* ain't seeing eye to eye on no marriage!" he'd exclaimed.

It was hard for me to see myself having a baby for a man who didn't love me enough to marry me, but after doing a bit of research on pro-choice, I definitely couldn't take a baby's life for a man who didn't love me enough to marry me. I'd have to tough it out as a single parent and hope for the best. There were plenty of women before me who'd been faced with the same situation and went on to be successful, and if they could do it, I could do it too. At least, that's what Yalisa kept telling me.

"You're not the man I thought you were, Sydney," I had managed to choke out through tears, snorts and sniffles. "Don't worry about me or the baby. Just know that in seven more months, you will have a son or daughter somewhere on God's green earth." I hung up the phone, then deleted his number from my contacts list although it was well programmed in my memory. I watched my phone for the next twenty-four hours hoping that Sydney would call to tell me that he loved me, he couldn't imagine living his life without me, and he would never in his lifetime allow his baby to be born and not be apart of his or her life. I wanted him to say he wanted us to be a family, even if we did put off the marriage part for a little while. When that didn't happen, I dolefully accepted the fact that I'd have to go it alone, and in my anger and disgust I changed my phone number. I didn't see or hear from Sydney again until six months later when I could no longer see my toes, had a million, zillion stretch marks on my belly and a face as fat as Porky Pig. I was out shopping for more baby clothes when I bumped into him in the food court of Crabtree Valley Mall as I sat enjoying a Chick-fil-A sandwich with a large sweet tea. Engrossed in the latest issue of *Baby Talk* magazine, I hadn't noticed when he walked up to the table.

"Kareese," he called, his tone even and low. He didn't wait for me to respond before he pulled out a chair and sat. "Wow. Look at you." His eyes lowered to my swollen abdomen, while my brows rose in annoyance.

"I didn't ask you to sit down."

He bit into his bottom lip, still fixated on my stomach. "Look at my baby."

Studying his face, I watched his mouth tighten into a ball, with his bottom lip still tucked inside. He dropped his head in what looked like shame, but I wasn't sure. With his thumb and forefinger, he rubbed his eyes before he looked up at me again.

"Kareese, I'm sorry." He swallowed hard, then spoke again. "I know that 'I'm sorry' don't fix the hurt I must have caused you, but it's the least I can say."

Weak. My lips twisted to one side. I was unmoved by his apology.

"I can't blame you for cutting me off after the way I acted." He shook his head at himself. "I was just being stupid and selfish, but I haven't stopped thinking about you and the baby since that day. When you wouldn't take my calls, I felt like someone had snatched my heart out of my chest," he said, placing a hand over his heart like he was about to say the Pledge of Allegiance.

"I spent a lot of time thinking about you, about us, about the baby, and how I was just being a sorry man. I couldn't even look in the mirror at myself, knowing that I was on my way to being a deadbeat dad."

"Whatever, Sydney. You're not on your way to being a deadbeat. You are a deadbeat," I clarified.

He nodded. "I deserve that." He pressed his lips together and gazed across the court. "I know you don't believe me, but I miss you and I want to be a part of your life and my baby's life."

"And just when did you have this great epiphany?"

"The day after you hung up on me, then changed your number. The day I went to your dorm and found out that you'd dropped out of school. The day I went to your sister's house and she told me to stay the hell away from you."

Andra did let me come live with her and Coleman after I told my parents I had to leave school. Of course they were furious and told me to make it the best way I could. In other words, I wasn't welcome back home as a form of punishment. Andra had also told me the day Sydney showed up on her doorstep looking for me that she'd given him a good piece of her mind.

"And that's all it took, huh? A little tiny idle threat from my sister was enough to chase you off."

"She told me that you'd gotten an abortion."

Internally I gasped, but a different expression fell from my lips. "That must have been a relief for you, since that is what you wanted in the first place."

"That's what I thought I wanted, until she told me that." He grabbed at his face, squeezing his eyes and nose. "But when she told me that . . . I don't know. Like I said—it felt like somebody had taken my heart away." He hesitated a bit, then continued. "I spent a lot of time praying after that. I mean a lot of time. I felt so guilty, because I knew you wouldn't have done that if I had just stepped up to the plate and been the man I should have been. I just asked God to let me see you so I could just say 'I'm sorry' or something. When I saw you sitting here today, still carrying my baby, I just started crying." He chuckled a bit. "A grown man, standing in the doggone food court crying"—he pointed toward a strip of wall between Moe's Southwest Grill and Crisp Salads—"standing right over there."

I began to believe him.

"I don't know if you will ever give me a chance to redeem myself or not, but I'm just so thankful to God that He let me see you one more time and that my baby is still here. I know I don't deserve you, Kareese, and I will have to accept it if you don't want nothing else to do with me, but please let me be a father to my child."

How could I have said no to that? I cussed Andra out for trying to control my life by lying to Sydney about the baby and moved out of her house, going to live with Sydney in a small one-bedroom apartment. A month later, with him by my side coaching, holding my hand, and feeding me ice chips, we welcomed Casey Romelo Christopher into the world. I'd considered Sydney to have redeemed himself, but as for my parents and my sister—they weren't trying to hear it. Not then, and not today.

Chapter Two

Sydney, Casey, and I left my parents' house shortly after and drove the next ninety minutes to his parents' house.

"Show me that rock, girl." Sydney grinned, then winked seductively.

With a giggle, I placed my hand into his; he kissed the back side, then centered it on his crotch and I began fondling.

"Mmm," he moaned. "Yeah, that's it. Work that thing, baby."

We'd played "show me the rock" eight other times since he'd dressed my finger with his commitment. I'd show him the rock on my finger and he would show me the one in his pants. Once I got him to full attention, we would find somewhere to pull over and get our freak on. Didn't matter where; sometimes it was right on the side of the road, as long as one of us kept our eyes open just in case a police cruiser rolled by. Other than that, every other driver on the highway was too busy trying to get to where they were going to pay much attention to us.

The first time we played, we made sure Casey was asleep. Then we turned on a narrow little dirt road between some cornstalks; which was the perfect place for me to sit on the hood of the car, open my legs, and show him how much I was looking forward to being his wife. For this round, I got on my knees turned toward the driver's seat while he stood in the passenger door behind me, gripped my hips, and laid his pipe. Woooo! I loved this game! It only took a couple of minutes per session, but the risqué factor made it so enjoyable. It was gonna be one of the things we did to keep our sex life hot and spicy once we tied the knot.

"You're so nasty," I teased as we used a few baby wipes from Casey's bag to clean up.

"Thank you," he commented, nodding proudly, which made me laugh.

"So what did they say when you went upstairs?" Sydney asked, settling back behind the steering wheel and looking out at the road.

"Their same old stuff. My mom really didn't say anything." I kinda lied, but really she hadn't. "And you know how Andra is with her nasty stuck-up self. She gets on my nerves."

"Forget her, baby." Sydney lifted his right arm and massaged my left shoulder. "She need to be worried about her own marriage."

"I know that's right. She don't have nothing to do with what goes on over here."

"We're gonna have to stick together and have each other's back in our marriage, baby, because if we let other people in our business, they will turn us against each other."

"I know, babe. Me and you against the world." I smiled.

"Me, you, and God against the world; and we gonna show 'em how it's done. As long as we keep God in the center of our marriage, we can't do nothing but be successful."

"See, that's why I love you."

"What? What's why?" he asked, glancing at me for half a second.

"Because I know you're a man who knows how to hold and keep his family together." I complimented him, rubbing his hand. "You are not ashamed to acknowledge God and make Him the head of our lives."

"Well, baby, I believe God really blessed me when He let me be a part of your life, and I'ma do everything in my power to take care of what He blessed me with." He squeezed, then patted my thigh as he continued. "I got a wonderful son who I love, and I'm about to have a beautiful, incredible, and sexy wife who I love. It don't matter to me what other people got to say about it. I'm just sorry that I can't give you the wedding of your dreams right now."

"Don't worry about that, Sydney. I'd rather have you as my husband than a wedding any day. A wedding is just one day that we can do anytime, but a marriage is a lifetime," I commented. "So what did your family say when you told them the news?"

"Nothing yet." He shook his head. "I haven't told them because they don't get excited about stuff like that."

"Oh." I thought his silence with his family was a bit strange. He seemed to have a great relationship with his parents and brother, so why wouldn't he have told them? "Suppose they want to come to the ceremony?"

"I just told you, we can't afford a real wedding right now."

"It won't be a big wedding, but we can do something small and just invite a few guests, like just our families."

Sydney moved his hand from my leg and rubbed his head. "I don't know about all that, baby."

"Just something small and intimate so we will have something to remember the day by."

"What do you mean by 'small'?"

"Like, maybe something at the house and we can serve dinner. We can have the guests bring a dish so it doesn't cost us anything."

"A house wedding? That's ghetto. You deserve more than that."

"I don't think it's ghetto," I rebutted, although I liked that he felt I deserved more.

"I want to give you what you worth, baby. I'd rather just wait till we can afford to do it right."

I paused pensively. On one hand, I could imagine sacrificing and just waiting for a bigger day, but on the other hand, I wanted at least a little bit of grandeur and celebration. "How long do you think it would be?"

He shrugged. "I don't know, babe. To do something nice, it's gonna be a couple thousand dollars; which we would have to save up for, but we got other things to do first before we think about that, 'cause like you said, it's just one day."

"I just want to do something, baby," I pleaded.

He sighed, implying that I was testing his patience. "Kareese, the most important thing to me is making you my wife. I don't need a bunch of extra stuff to do that."

Feeling like I was getting nowhere, I dropped it, but I'd made up my mind that I was gonna whip it on him later and make him agree to at least a little something.

When we pulled up to Sydney's mother's house, his mom was standing outside beneath her carport stirring something in a huge pot that looked like a witch's cauldron. Keith, his brother, was stooped down, poking at the fire beneath.

"Hey, Momma!" he greeted, cutting the car off, stepping out, and shutting the driver's door behind him. Knowing how he felt about not letting him get my door for me, I held my excitement to jump out and flash my mini diamond. Instead of coming around to my side of the car, Sydney walked over and greeted my soon-to-be mother-in-law.

"Hey, baby!" I could hear her say, although I was closed up in the car. Sydney hugged her tightly, slapped hands with his brother, then shoved his hands in his pockets and started up a conversation. Did he forget I was still sitting here? On top of that, I had to pee.

"What in the world," I mumbled, wanting to tap the horn, but I thought better of it not wanting to look like some kind of bourgeois princess. Instead, I counted to ten, then added ten more counts, growing impatient. Sydney didn't so much as look my way. This was crazy. I popped the door open and stepped out.

"Hey, Ms. Patricia." I waved before opening the back door and unbuckling Casey out of his seat. When I started toward Sydney, he stared, incredulously, with daggers in his eyes and flung them all my way. He said nothing, but his expression said, *What the hell you doing gettin' out the car?*

"What? I had to pee!" I stated, wondering why I felt the need to give an explanation in the first place. "Hey, Keith," I added, jumbling the baby in Sydney's arms before trekking for the door.

"Hey, Kareese," his brother answered. "How you doing?"

"Good! You mind if I use your bathroom," I asked, turning to Sydney's mom, already knowing I was welcome in Ms. Patricia's home.

"Help yourself, baby."

Once in the bathroom, I shuffled out of my clothes, sighed with relief, flushed, put myself back together again, and washed my hands— making a special effort to center my ring perfectly for my presentation to Ms. Patricia and Keith. If Sydney hadn't already told them our news, I was about to tell them for him. I headed back outside, ready to deliver our exciting news; but to my surprise, Sydney was standing at the car, holding my door open for me, looking like a chauffeur.

"Let's go," he stated as soon as I'd stepped both feet out the door. His jaw was tight with resentment, and Casey was already back in his car seat.

"What? We just got here." I hadn't even gotten any of her famous fried turkey and a slice of sweet potato pie yet. Ms. Patricia and Keith still stood at the pot, pretending not to notice us.

"Come on," Sydney firmly said, motioning with his head for me to get inside the car, unmoved and clearly not open to negotiating. A bit bewildered and discomfited, I took my seat. He slammed the door after me, jumped in the driver's seat, then spun his tires against the pavement, and screeched down the street.

"What is wrong with you?" His behavior didn't make any sense. Me getting out of the car on my own could not have been *that* serious.

"You know what you did." Sydney pulled his shades down over his face, then turned the stereo up sky-high, blasting reggae, which he knew I hated. Even if it had been music that I loved, it was way too loud to be enjoyable.

"I know you're not all bent out of shape because I got out the car," I said, adjusting the stereo's volume to a level that was barely audible.

Sydney ignored me, jacked the music back up and drove faster.

"What was I supposed to do, sit in the car until you decided to let me out?" I yelled, yanking at the knob, again silencing the music.

"You know that I open your car door."

"Well, you should have done that first before you started launching into a family discussion."

Sydney said nothing and kindly cranked the music back up sky-high.

"I'm not five years old. I can get out of the car if I want to," I yelled.

Sydney said nothing.

"I'm a full-grown woman! You can't hold me hostage in the car, like I need your permission to get out," I continued, feeling like I had to say *something*.

Sydney grunted and remained silent for the rest of the ride. When we got home, I didn't know whether to prove my adulthood by getting out of the car on my own, or offer some kind of apology by sitting there and waiting for him to do me the honors. I hesitated for just a second, trying to test the waters of how he was feeling. He got out, slammed the door, and went straight in the house. When we went to bed that night, I tried snuggling in his arms, but he turned his back to me. I couldn't believe he was *this* pissed off over a car door.

There was no way I could tell my mother about this.

Ms. Debi, Yalisa's mom, agreed to watch Casey for a couple of hours while Yalisa and I spent some much needed girlfriend time together.

"Don't worry about the baby; I got 'em." She bounced Casey in her arms and patted his back.

"Thank you, Ms. Debi. We won't be long."

"Take your time. He'll be fine."

It wasn't often that I got a break from mothering. I hugged Ms. Debi tightly, grateful for her babysitting generosity. It would have to be an emergency for my mom to consider keeping her one and only grandson, but almost every time I visited her, Andra's four- and five-year-old daughters seemed to be there running the place, with Andra nowhere around. Ms. Debi had pretty much become my second mom, letting me come over for dinner, talks, sleepovers, parties, and everything else since the time Yalisa and I were teens. I was one of the family, which was great, because I could use the additional family support. She had even agreed to let Sydney and me exchange our vows and have our dinner at her house. Her home was about 3,000 square feet and had plenty of space for the few spectators we'd have. I was thinking we'd become husband and wife in her den, right in front of the fireplace. The expansive counter space in the kitchen would allow for the covered dishes; the kitchen table would host the cake and small plates for serving; we could all eat and mingle in the dining room.

"Girl, I wish I had your mom." I sighed as Yalisa and I walked out to her car. Yalisa was an only child, and she and Ms. Debi had the best mother-daughter relationship I'd ever seen. They were like best friends.

"Don't say that." Yalisa ran a comb through her hair, then pulled on a tweed mod cap. "We have our issues."

"Not like me and my mom." We both got in the car and strapped ourselves in the seat belts. "Let's go to Target. I don't have mall money today."

"Okay." She shifted the car in gear and pulled off. "Ms. Adrienne is as sweet as pie."

"Maybe to you, but not so much to me."

"Girl, you need to cherish the relationship you have with your mom."

"Yalisa, there's nothing to cherish." I sighed.

"Yes, there is. She just wants the best for you."

"But does she have to be so nasty about it?" In my mind, I could see that awful grimace on her face when she'd looked at my engagement ring. "Well I wish me and my mom had a relationship like you and your mom. How about that?"

"I told you, we've had our issues."

"I can't tell it."

"She gets on my nerves sometimes. We don't always see eye to eye."

"What do you think the secret to your relationship is?"

"Communication. We talk about everything."

"Every time I try to talk to my mom about stuff, she starts fussin', screaming and yelling. I can barely get a word in edgewise most times."

"Well, what are you gonna do about it? Talking to me about it is not gonna fix it. You working on it is what will eventually make it better."

I fell silent and turned up the radio a bit, snapping my fingers to Michael Jackson's "Butterflies," but I thought about what I could do differently to improve my relationship with my mom. I was envious of Yalisa and Ms. Debi, but I wasn't sure if I had the emotional energy to work on my own child-parent relationship right now. I was slow to think that my mother didn't love me, but she definitely had a difficult time expressing it. It was the way she left me to fend for myself when I'd gotten pregnant, the way she didn't show up to my baby shower—politely declining Yalisa's invitation for a reason she never shared with me, nor had she bought a gift, and the way she always praised Andra for every little thing she did but seemed to find fault with anything I did. Feeling a headache coming on just at the thought of our strained relationship, I fished around in the bottom of my purse for some Tylenol. Target had a Starbucks just inside the main entrance; I stopped and grabbed a bottled Frappuccino, swallowed the two pills, and focused on happier thoughts.

"So I only have about four hundred dollars to pull something together for a wedding." We browsed along the party aisles trying to come up with a few creative and inexpensive ideas.

"That's doable, since you're not going to have to pay for a reception."

"Yeah, I'll just need to get the cake and a few decorations."

"And invitations," she added.

"Suppose I just did online invitations by e-mail?"

"That's tacky," Yalisa answered without hesitation. "Everybody doesn't have e-mail and everybody doesn't check it every day. Messages end up in junk folders and all that. I don't think that's a good idea." She reached down to a lower shelf and picked up a small box. "It's not like these are expensive." She held up a set of do-it-yourself invitations that could be run off on a home printer. "This is a box of twenty-five. Since there's only going to be a handful of people there, this should be all you need. And they are half off, you can't get any less expensive than this."

I took the box and looked over the blank stationery. The premade invites were sand-colored, with white trim, and featured a white ribbon that was to be strung through two holes at the top once the printed card had been placed in the included envelopes, which also had two holes to accommodate the ribbon. There were a few wording examples and layouts included to use as a guide, one of which was a monogram style. It would look pretty good with a large *C* at the top. I placed them in my cart, along with Jordan almonds, small netted bags, and a small package of tiny plastic mock wedding bands, which I'd picked to create my own favors.

"Oooh, look at this." Andra showed me a magazine page that featured turned-over paint cans, small boxes, and stacked phone books on a table, then covered with a gold tissue lamé to create a beautiful multileveled serving table. The gold made it look Christmassy, but if I used a simple white sheet or tablecloth and accented it with flower petals, it would look more fitting for a wedding. I added a couple of packages of silk flower petals to my basket.

Browsing through a few K-Ci & JoJo's CDs, I found the single for "All My Life," and added that to the basket for my walk song. Afterward, we swung by Sam's Club and nailed down the price on a few layer cakes and the Styrofoam stand to put them on, and voila! I'd pretty much had things worked out for a memorable day. With Ms. Debi's house and a few of these ideas, our day would hardly be able to be described as ghetto. Sydney would see.

I got home and unveiled to Sydney the plan for the day, showing him the invitations, the picture of the cake I selected, and the other things I'd bought. Instead of him being excited, or even indifferent, his face turned long and dejected.

"Kareese, why couldn't you have just waited like I asked you to?"

"What do you mean? I mean, it may not be the wedding of the rich and famous, but it's something that we can call ours."

"How do you think that makes me feel, baby, that I can't give you the kind of wedding you really want? And then I ask you to wait, and this is what you do?" He threw his hands up and let them fall in exasperation. "You go behind my back and ask people to give us this fake, imitation, bring-your-own-food wedding? How do you think that makes me feel as a man that I can't give my wife what she wants?" he asked a second time.

I hadn't thought about what Sydney would feel like. "I didn't know. . . ."

"I asked you to wait, Kareese. You couldn't do that for me?" His eyes dropped to my purchases on the table; then he shook his head. "I can't believe this," he mumbled under his breath, looking at the items like I'd dug them out of a filthy back-alley dumpster. Still shaking his head, he walked off to the bedroom.

I stood at the dining room table, dismayed and staring at the items myself. Now they didn't seem so acceptable. I could feel tears welling in my eyes and blurring my vision, and when my lids couldn't hold them back any longer, they fell onto the table and the box of invitations.

Before I went to bed, I called Ms. Debi and told her our plans had changed and we wouldn't be using her home, after all.

"Oh no! You're not calling off the wedding, are you?" She actually gasped.

"No, we're still getting married. We're just changing the plans a little bit." I felt myself choke, hoping she wouldn't ask for details. "I'll keep you posted."

"All right, sweetie. Let me know if you need anything."

It was an hour later before I crawled into bed, where Sydney lay channel surfing.

"I'm sorry, babe," I murmured.

He waited a few seconds. "You shouldn't have done that, baby," he spoke softly. "I'm the man; let me be the man. I want to give you everything you want. That's my wedding gift to you . . . to us. That's my job as a provider and as your husband. How do you think people will look at me if I'm not handling my business? If I can't handle something as simple as a wedding? People ain't gotta know why we not having a wedding right now, but we don't want to invite them in our business by having something shoddy. That don't make me look or feel good."

I thought Sydney had made some good points. "You're right. I didn't think about it like that. I'm sorry."

"I need to know that you're gonna have my back—not go behind my back."

"It won't happen again, Sydney." I leaned over and kissed his cheek.

He threw his arm around me and pulled me close. "Just let me be the man, baby. I got this. I got us."

Chapter Three

There were only seven days left before I would become Sydney's wife, and although I'd not been able to convince him to have something small, I was excited just as if we were going to have a celebrity-style wedding. All I needed was something special to wear; nothing too fancy or expensive, but something nice for a photo. I'd seen a couple of things that I liked; only thing was, I was a bit short on expendable cash, since I hadn't returned to work since having Casey. Sydney was the sole provider for the time being; which meant minus the money I had left in my savings, I had to go to and through him for every dime, then pinch pennies to make the money last as long as possible to keep from hearing his mouth about needing more. He was supertight with a dollar.

I had money on my mind as I pushed clothes back and forth in the closet, looking for something to wear for our day, when Sydney walked into our bedroom.

"Sydney, when are you going to add me to your bank account? I saw some checks that I think will be cute for us to have with both our names on it," I asked from the closet. I'd understood why we'd not joined our money before: A) I didn't really have any, and B) we weren't married yet.

"What do I need to do that for?" Sydney's brows were scrunched in what looked like sincere confusion.

"Because we're gonna be married, and sharing finances is a part of it."

"We don't need a joint account just because we're getting married. Who made up that rule?"

"I think we should get one, since we are going to be building a life together, and I don't want to have to come to you every time I need some money."

He folded his arms across his chest and puckered his lips for a few seconds as if to think. "I'm not really feeling that, Kareese."

"Why not? What about for paying bills?"

"I just don't think it's necessary. Just give me your paycheck when you start back at work and I will pay all the bills through my account."

"Give you my paycheck?"

Sydney shrugged. "Yeah. What's wrong with that if I'ma be paying the bills with the money?"

"What year is it, 1955?" I chuckled, thinking he was joking.

"I'm just saying. I'll manage the bills so you don't have to do it. Just give me the money and I'll take care of everything."

"Why can't you just give me the bill you need me to pay and let me pay it?"

"I don't have no problem with that. You can take the rent, then." He chortled at his remark.

"See, you're just trying to be funny!" I threw my hands on my hips, wincing.

"No, I'm not. You want to pay a bill, take the rent. Pay that." He walked out of the bedroom, but his voice escalated from the hallway, "You wanna call the shots and handle things? Be my guest."

"I'm not saying that I want to handle things, but what is wrong with us having a joint bank account? That's like Marriage 101," I retorted. "How many married couples do you know that don't have a bank account together?"

"I don't know nobody sharing their money with their wife. If you wanna mess your money up, give a woman access to it."

My mouth fell open momentarily. "What do you mean by that? How would I mess your money up, Sydney?"

"You might go out and see a new pair of shoes or something." Sydney was now in the kitchen, pulling at the refrigerator door.

"And? You don't think I'm disciplined enough to put bills before shoes?"

"How much money do you have in your savings account?"

"None now, I've not been working for months."

"How do you not have any money, when I been paying all the bills?" With a can of soda in his hand, he passed by me, went into the living room and collapsed on the sofa.

"I'm the one that buys Casey's formula and Pampers and other stuff!"

"So, are you saying that you wanna switch and let me buy that stuff and you pay all the bills?"

"No. I said we need a joint account. What's wrong with that, especially if you want me to hand you over my paycheck?"

"Okay, so how are we supposed to start this joint account? What kind of deposits are you gonna make?"

"What difference does it make! If we're married we're married! Why do I have to come up with some kind of agreement to make deposits for us to have a joint account? Suppose I need to pay for something and you're nowhere around?"

"So if you have your own account, and I have my own account, then there is no problem." He shrugged.

"That is not building a life together. That's just staying single. What is wrong with us having a joint account?"

"Nothing, if we're going to build it together. We both start putting in the same amount of money at the same time, and then it will be a joint account."

"So the only way you'll add me to your account is if I start matching the money you put in?"

"Don't you think that's fair?"

"Suppose I don't go back to work, and I just stay at home and raise our kids. Then what?"

"First of all, I don't plan on having any more kids, and secondly, you don't plan on going back to work?"

"Maybe, maybe not. If I go back to work, we are going to have to pay for day care, and for what that costs, I might as well stay home."

"Well, if you ain't going back to work, you for damn sure not getting on my account."

His words stung a bit, but I wasn't ready to quit yet. "But why? Are you scared I'm going to steal your money?"

"No."

"Well, what is it?"

"If I go to pay the bills and it ain't no money in the account, then what?"

"I just asked you if you thought I was going to steal your money and you said no, so why wouldn't there be money in the account?"

"Well, if we married, it wouldn't be considered stealing."

"So you are scared I will steal, take, borrow, embezzle—whatever—money from the account? So I'm supposed to come running to you every time I need to buy tampons and pads, then, huh?"

Sydney didn't respond as he flipped through channels and stopped on a basketball game.

"Well, you can at least give me an ATM card."

"I'ma ask you this again," he started without even looking my way. "How would we be building a *joint* account when I'm the only one contributing to it? What kind of *joint* account is that?" "You know what, Sydney? Just forget I asked. You wanna keep your stank money, then keep it!"

He shrugged again. "Fine with me."

Completely flustered, I grabbed my purse and keys. "I'll be back."

"You need to take Casey with you."

I heard him, but I didn't stop for a second. Slamming the door behind me, I stormed to my car, got inside, and headed straight to the bank. I told Sydney that I didn't have any money left, but I did have a few more dollars in my account and retail therapy was definitely in need. I'd be flat broke after this, but I didn't care; I'd just go back to work. And keep my own paycheck.

I called Andra to join me, thinking we could smooth things over from our Thanksgiving Day blowup and maybe she'd even be nice enough to buy me an outfit for a gift. When Andra and I were speaking, we got along fairly well. We both were kind of like the little girl in the nursery rhyme who had a little curl right in the middle of her forehead. When we were good, we were very, very good, but when we were bad, we were horrid.

"Andra, what are you doing?"

"Why, what's up?" Andra never allowed herself to be back-doored into saying that she was free until she knew what she was about to be asked to do.

"I'm headed to the mall and need some shopping help."

"What are you shopping for?"

"Something to get married in."

Andra let out a heavy sigh. "I don't even want to be a part of that mess you about to get yourself into."

"Andra, I'm asking you as my sister to come spend some time with me as I prepare to take the next big step in my life. I could really use some big-sister support right now, not opposition."

"Hmph. What you need is some sense talked into your head. What time are you going?" she asked before I could hang up on her.

"I'm headed there now."

"All right. Let me put my shoes on. I'll see you in a little bit."

"Bring your checkbook. I might need some backup."

"What?" she about shrieked.

"I'm just kidding." I quickly retracted my comment, not wanting to hear the tirade she would launch into. I didn't feel like hearing her opinion on what Sydney could be doing better.

As promised, Andra joined me at the mall, dressed in her usual diva style: tight jeans for her shapely figure, a baby-doll tee beneath a short-waisted leather jacket, stiletto boots, blingy jewelry, flawless makeup, and just from the salon hair. Beside her, I looked like a frumpy old hag. Maybe not a hag, but nowhere near as put together in my Danskin workout pants with a matching jacket layered over a plain T-shirt.

"What are you trying to buy?" she asked.

"Just a nice outfit."

"A nice outfit? What about a gown? That *is* what people usually get married in."

"We're just going to have something small and informal, so a gown would be too much."

The look on my sister's face let me know she was biting her tongue to keep her comments to herself. "What's your price range?"

"Like fifty bucks."

"What in the world do you think you can get for fifty dollars?"

"It's all I had."

"You should have got some money from your husband," she snidely commented, fingering imaginary quotation marks when she'd said "husband."

"I tried," I admitted. "But there was nothing extra in the budget." That sounded much better than—he probably wouldn't have given me ten cents.

We stopped at the pretzel stand and grabbed two pretzel-wrapped hot dogs and a couple of lemonades, which she paid for; then we took a seat on a nearby bench in one of the hallways.

"Do you and Coleman have a joint account? I'm trying to determine how Sydney and I are going to handle our finances," I threw out, hoping Sydney was wrong about his thoughts of men sharing their finances with their wives.

Andra looked at me like I'd asked the most ridiculous question in the world. "Yeah, why?"

"Just wondering. I was trying to decide if it's something Sydney and I should do."

"Why wouldn't you?"

"I don't know if I would want him to have access to my money." I chewed on my hot dog and waited for her thoughts, but then added, "I mean, once I go back to work."

"Then have your own private account and do a joint account for the bills."

While I shopped, I gave Andra's advice a lot of thought, wondering if keeping a secret account was something I should do. It seemed so dishonest and sneaky. On the other hand, we already had separate accounts, so really it probably wasn't a big deal. I just didn't like the fact that Sydney didn't want to add me to his account. It seemed backward to me and so—unmarried and still single.

"What do you think of this?" I held up a sleeveless beige bubble-hemmed dress trimmed in gold. It was stylishly loose-fitting and would easily hide my unshed baby weight.

Andra crinkled her nose. "Where are you trying to go with that on? To bed?" She pinched at the fabric as if fully touching it would contaminate her whole hand. "That's not going to look right on you," she added, observing my figure with disdain.

"Don't look at me like that."

"You need to start working out." She poked a finger in my side, causing me to smack her hand away. "I'm just saying."

"Some things are better left unsaid." I grimaced as I hung the garment back on the rack.

"You said you needed some help finding something. I'm gonna be honest." She shrugged as if my feelings didn't matter. "Unless you want to be standing in front of people saying 'I do' and looking a hot mess."

"Can you ever say anything nice to me, Andra?"

"I am being nice." She poked her lips forward and stretched her eyes wide, looking like a hoot owl before she rolled them away.

What had I been thinking when I asked her, of all people, to meet me? I would have done better just asking for opinions of random shoppers in the store. Strangers were too nice to be brutally honest, and Andra was too brutal to be honestly nice.

"You gonna need a good girdle for that," she said, cutting into my thoughts as I held up a white calf-length sweater wrap dress with a belted waist. I was thinking I could wear a pair of sexy fishnet hose and some short boots.

This time it was me who did the tongue biting for a few seconds. "Andra, it doesn't matter what I pick, I'm not going to have a Wonder Woman figure. I know that, you know that, and I'd appreciate it if you would stop trying to cut me down every chance you get."

"I'm not trying to cut you down, but you know what, I'll just be quiet. Get what you want to get." In the next two minutes, Andra drifted away to other racks that held garments in her size, instead of helping me. It was just as good. The last thing I needed right now was to be criticized for my weight or anything else. By the time I found something, Andra was nowhere to be found. I let her stay lost while I went to the dressing room, with an arm filled with clothes, and dug in my purse for my buzzing cell phone.

Where u at??

I threw the phone back in my purse, ignoring Sydney's text. Then I tried on four different garments, walking down the narrow aisleway that separated the right and left sides of the dressing stalls that led to a three-way mirror at the back wall. I hummed the bridal march every step of the way; then I sucked in my stomach each time I got to the mirror and turned to both sides.

Andra was right. I did have a few lumps and bumps that could stand quite a bit of trimming down, but the truth of the matter was, it wasn't going to fall off in the next seven days, so I may as well learn to love it for at least another week. I picked the best of the four outfits and headed to the register.

"Do you have a coupon, ma'am?" the cashier asked as she rang up my purchase. The store was famous for having coupons in the newspaper every week, worth fifteen-percent off, but I didn't think to get one.

"No, you can just ring it up."

"I have a coupon that I can use right here, and if you apply for a charge card, you can save an additional ten percent."

I crunched some numbers in my head, and reasoned that I could get a good deal on the dress, put it on a card and save my cash at the same time. "Do you have a pen I can use?" In a matter of minutes, I'd been approved for $1,000—by creating a fictitious income—which made me smile. Hugely. "I'm going to pick up a few more things."

I did bump into my sister while I circled the racks a second and third time and loaded my arms with more things.

"You haven't found anything yet?" she asked, her own arms filled with clothes.

"I'm still looking." I barely looked at her, absorbed in my own shopping world.

"Well, I gotta go. Coleman and I are going to catch a movie."

"All right. Thanks for coming."

"Mmm-hmm." As an afterthought, she glanced over her shoulder and said, "Let me know when the wedding is and I'll try to make it."

I didn't comment. I did create an a invitation using a basic template from my computer, printed two copies on colored cardstock, and cut the edges with scalloped scissors. Then I sent them to both my mom and Andra; but not so surprisingly, they hadn't responded. Per her comment, I suppose Andra hadn't opened, read, or paid much attention to hers at all.

I left the store two hours later with a new wardrobe for me and my baby, a watch to give to Sydney as a wedding gift, a nearly maxed-out credit card, and a bill that I was probably going to have to keep hidden from Sydney. I was in a much better mood by the time I got back in, but Sydney was fuming which immediately blew my shopping high.

"I thought you didn't have any money," he grunted, eyeing my shopping bag. I'd only brought one in the house; the others were hidden in the trunk of my car.

"Andra bought this for me," I lied in a mumble, not wanting him to know just how much shopping I'd really done, or that I'd gotten a new credit card.

He shifted his eyes, watching me move through the living room and toward the hallway. "You really expect me to believe that?"

"What's so hard to believe about that? She's my sister."

"You and Andra can hardly stand each other, and all of a sudden, y'all going out shopping like best friends? You must really think I'm stupid."

He had a point, and it didn't help matters that I was actually lying, but I stuck to my story. "Believe what you want to believe, then."

"So what'd you get?" he asked, following me to the bedroom, his eyes full of suspicion.

"I can't show you, because it's my dress for the wedding. You're not supposed to see it yet." Not that it was a gown or a wedding dress, but I guess it was my attempt at tradition.

Sydney wasn't buying a single word, signified by his narrowed eyes as I tossed the bag up on the top shelf.

"Why you ain't answer my text?"

"I was trying on stuff. My phone was in my bag and I didn't hear it," I lied.

"I know you had to go in your pocketbook for something," he argued. "And you ain't looked at your phone not one time?"

"Nope."

He crossed his arms and bobbed his head. "Mmm-hmm. I'ma tell you this. Next time you go walking out this house, go 'head and tell that dude you movin' in with him, 'cause you won't be coming back here."

"Who are you talking about?"

"Whoever you got to take you shopping."

"I told you, I was out with Andra."

"Right, Kareese."

"Call her if you don't believe me."

"Like y'all can't coordinate a lie. Please."

"What man in his right mind is going to buy a woman her wedding outfit? Doesn't that sound crazy to you?"

"The world is full of crazy people," he answered, blocking the entrance to the closet door.

"Well, like I said—believe what you want to believe." I pushed past him.

"And like I said, next time you ain't coming back up in here."

Chapter Four

Knowing my family wasn't really happy about the decision I'd made to marry Sydney, I didn't call to check to see if they would be joining me the morning I got up with the sole purpose of going down to the justice of the peace, which was all Sydney would agree to, for the time being, say my vows, and live the rest of my life as Mrs. Kareese Watson-Christopher.

"Mrs. Kareese Christopher. Mr. and Mrs. Sydney Christopher. Sydney and Kareese Christopher," I spoke out loud to the mirror. I loved the sound of my soon-to-be new name. "Sydney, Kareese, and Casey Christopher." Yeah, we'd be a real family at last.

"Hurry up, Kareese," Sydney called from outside the bathroom. "I'm heading on over there. Keith is pulling up now."

"Okay!" I hollered through the door. "Take the baby with you, please!"

"You bring him. He's still asleep."

"What?" Before I could retort further, I heard the slam of the apartment door. "Now, why would he leave him here," I huffed. How was I supposed to be a beautiful bride walking down the aisle if I had to carry Casey? Sometimes Sydney could be so selfish. It was bad enough that he'd hung out until three in the morning with his "boys," celebrating his last night of singleness. He swore to me before leaving that he wasn't going to do anything that would disrespect our relationship. I didn't exactly believe him, and when I said as much, he said: "If you can't trust me, then we don't need to be getting married tomorrow, or no other time."

That shut me up quick. I really wanted to get married.

"I'm not going to let this day be ruined," I said to the mirror, then hopped in the shower. I knew I was doing the right thing marrying Sydney because us continuing to "shack up" was just what the devil wanted. I'd learned all about how much he hated marriage and families when I attended a few women's conferences hosted by Yalisa's church. I'd even gotten Sydney to join me on couples' night. I had to coax and beg a little, but I was able to get him to come down to the altar for prayer when the pastor said he wanted to pray for all the couples that were contemplating marriage. I can still remember most of that prayer too:

Father, we lift these men and women up before you, Lord, as they seek your guidance in journeying into a sacred covenant and most holy union that you created and honor. I pray that you grant them wisdom, Lord, and understanding. We bind confusion and deceit and loose revelation and knowledge, O God, that their steps may be sure. We thank and praise you for healthy marriage relationships and stronger families. Give each of them a listening ear to hear what you would say to the hearts of these men and women, Lord, then give us the wisdom and strength to obey. These things we ask in your precious name, Lord. Amen.

I squeezed Sydney's hand all the way back to our seats, and knew we were making the right move when I saw him wipe away a tear. So forget Momma and them. I was tired of repenting for fornicating and I knew I wasn't gonna stop. I didn't want a long history of shacking up, and my baby needed his father. And if we weren't supposed to be together, he would have never run into me in the mall that day. There had to be some divine connection in that.

Three minutes was all the shower time Casey would allow me, which was enough. I'd learned over the past year that a quick shower was all a mother was ever allowed, unless it was after 9:00 p.m. and the baby was already sleep. Even then it could be risky.

"I'm coming, sweetie," I called, wrapping a towel around me as best I could, then rushed over to my baby. Casey's arms flew up in the air the second he saw me as he whined to be freed from his crib. I don't know why Sydney hadn't taken him; that would have been so much easier on me. "We're gonna be a family today," I cooed.

Carlos responded in his own language accompanied by sputters and spit bubbles and random arm flapping.

With Carlos in my arms, I padded to the kitchen where I ran a sink full of water to bathe Casey. While he splashed in a myriad of bubbles, I tried to feed him baby oatmeal with mashed apricots mixed in. I'm sure he ate some bubbles right along with it, and when I wasn't paying attention, Casey snatched the plastic cap off my head and splashed it in the water, getting the front of my hair wet. I felt like the Wicked Witch of the West when Dorothy unexpectedly doused her in the classic *The Wizard of Oz*.

"Boy! Don't you know I'm getting married today? You don't throw water on a woman's head on the day she's getting married." It must have sounded to Casey like I said, "Splash, baby, splash," because once he saw my reaction, he did it three more times, causing me to jump back.

"Casey, stop! Hello," I panted, picking up the ringing phone.

"You still getting married today?" Yalisa asked. I could hear a smile in her voice.

"Yes. Please say you are on your way over here, because I need help with this little boy."

"Where is Sydney?"

"He left already. He had to go pick up our bands or something. I don't know."

"Well, he wasn't supposed to see you before the wedding, anyway. You should have made him spend the night somewhere last night."

"I didn't have to make him do that. He did it on his own and came crawling back in here at three o'clock."

"Whaaaaat?" she drew out.

"Yep."

"And you went for that?"

"What else was I supposed to do? Block the door from him leaving?"

"No, tell him if he went out partying all night with some nasty booty-bouncin' heifers, shaking their behinds and boobs all in his face, you wouldn't marry him today, that's what!"

I didn't comment right away. I could only wish for that kind of strength and power. "Well, can you hurry up and come get your godson? I need to get dressed."

"I'm pulling up now. Open the door."

"Thank goodness!" I rushed to the door, wet baby in tow, turned back the deadbolt and peeked out, still wrapped in my towel.

In seconds Yalisa walked in. "Hey, Mrs. Christopher!" she squealed, throwing her arms around me. "Hey, little man." She reached out for Casey and thankfully he obliged her request.

"He just had his bath. Would you mind getting him dressed?"

"Of course not, but let's get you dressed first."

Yalisa had been more of a sister to me than Andra had ever been, despite the fact that Andra and I shared the same parents and were raised in the same household. I don't even know how it came to be that we grew so unpleasant toward each other. We were only a year apart, but somewhere in high school as she became more popular, and I became more obscure, as her figure developed into desirable curves, and mine rounded out quite a bit, as her hair grew long and silky, and I had a hard time managing my nappy locks, I think she became ashamed of me.

She never said it out of her mouth, but I saw
the looks she'd give me when we'd bump into
each other in the hallways. I noticed how she'd
move if I even came near her usual table at
lunchtime, and I never forgot the day I'd come
on my period unexpectedly and begged her
to give me a pad out of her locker, but she refused because her boyfriend was waiting for her
just down the hall. I'd already had my sweater
wrapped around my waist to cover my accident,
and told her so, but did she care? Not hardly. We
ain't been right ever since. Even the few months
I lived with her while I was pregnant, there had
been a few heated arguments and lots of eggshell
walking.

And now here it was on my wedding day, who
was it that was by my side? Yalisa. Even if Andra
and Momma had shown up for our "wedding,"
I felt pretty confident in saying neither one of
them would have come to help me or the baby
get dressed or support me in any way. It would
have been out of obligation, to criticize or just to
start some mess.

Within an hour, my skin was nicely scented,
I brushed a golden-toned bronzer on my face,
lined my eyes in soft sable, extended my lashes
with something by L'Oréal, colored my lips, put
on a beautiful light-blue-and-white lace bra,

panty and garter set, which Yalisa gave me as a gift, then slipped on the sweater dress that Andra had turned her nose up at, a pair of twelve-dollar Payless clearance shoes, and a simple necklace.

"You look amazing!" Yalisa gazed, covering her mouth with both hands as I twirled around. "Hold on, let me fix this." She reached toward some loose strands of hair and tucked them into my chignon. "Okay. No, wait—put these on." Yalisa pulled two diamond studs from her ears. "You need something borrowed. These are borrowed and old, so we're killing two birds with one stone."

I felt like a queen as I practically glided to Yalisa's Ford Explorer. It was the closest thing to an actual bridal march I would come to on this go-round.

"Hey, shug! You getting marr'ed today?" Miss Hazel, who made it her business to mind other people's business, came out her front door just in time to see me getting in the truck.

"Yes, ma'am."

"That's good. That's good. I'm glad to see that man is makin' uh honest woman outta you. You know a lot uh deez mens just putting babies and chi'ren all over town and don't think no more of they mommas than they do a rotten apple."

"Yes, ma'am."

"Is that his baby there? Or you get him from somewhere else?" she asked, bobbing her head at Casey.

"No, ma'am, it's our baby together."

"Dat's good. Y'all gone make a nice little family. God bless yuh, hear?"

"Yes, ma'am. Thank you," I answered with a smile as I watched her grab the pendant she wore faithfully around her neck. She always did that whenever she thought of her late husband. She'd shared with me that when he passed away several years before, she'd had his wedding band simply reshaped into a heart to preserve the integrity of the band, and hung it on a necklace he'd given her as a Christmas gift.

I wanted that kind of love. And today I was on my way to getting it.

Our first kiss as husband and wife was magical, but when we made love for the first time, I swear I felt our very souls connect. It was unlike any other lovemaking session we'd ever had before, and what made it even more special were the two little words that Sydney whispered lovingly, over and over, between kisses.

"My wife, my wife, my wife . . ."

Just hearing him utter those words brought tears to my eyes.

We lay, wet, messy, and spent; but completely satisfied, gazing into each other's eyes.

"I love you, husband," I whispered.

His lips turned upward into a slight smile. "Love you too, wife."

With a smile, I kissed his lips, then turned in Sydney's arms and nestled backward into his chest. His legs curled to meet mine, matching the curvature of my body, and draped his arm over my waist. I'd never felt as loved as I did in those few moments right before we drifted off to sleep. "Mmm," I moaned. "Promise me you will hold me like this forever."

"I promise," he murmured.

Chapter Five

Whoever said the first year was the hardest didn't actually tell the whole truth. The first year was actually like a slow ride into hell down a razor blade pole, and the second was the same ride all over again, only this time garbed in clothes soaked in gasoline. I did expect a little rain, but I had more of a *Sesame Street* kind of vision for my marriage: "Sunny day sweeping the clouds away." I found out quickly just how naïve my thoughts about marriage had been.

I'd enrolled myself back into school but hadn't been able to complete more than a semester. Within eight months of our union, I had conceived a second time, unplanned of course, and this baby was taking me through the wringer. I hadn't experienced one single day of trouble in my pregnancy with Casey, but this time I was constantly nauseated, highly uncomfortable, or just in pain. I spent most of my days in my pajamas lying down in an effort not to throw up, and seeing after the one baby I already had as best I could. When I didn't have the energy or strength to cook and clean, Sydney perceived me as lazy, rather than understanding the fact that there was a whole person taking up residence inside my body.

He had no compassion when it came to my complaints. He hardly had a kind word to say, and most days he ignored me, saying nothing at all. This wasn't how I envisioned my marriage or pregnancy going. The baby already made me overly sensitive and I'd cry at the drop of a hat. Any commercial that portrayed a mother-to-be flanked by an excited, caring, loving father, resting his head against her belly, listening for the baby's heartbeat, or feeling for movement, or kissing his child through the mother's flesh, made me bawl like a hungry newborn, wishing it were Sydney and I, instead. I didn't know what I'd done or said to make Sydney despise me the way he did. I knew he wasn't overjoyed about us having another baby, but I expected him to become more accepting that a new addition to our family was just around the corner as I was headed into my final trimester.

As if some magical knob was turned from high to low on a disagreement control, we argued less frequently, which was just a trade-off for not speaking at all in most cases. Even so, I made the best of the peace, and avoided subjects that were sure to get us into a wrangle of any sort, and these days just about anything would. One thing that made both of us smile was we'd recently filed our tax return and expected a few thousand dollars back. We needed the financial relief and we both had plans for our share of the money, which we'd split in half. Sydney talked about putting some accessories on his car; while, like any other woman, I planned to shop. I did have my eye on an in-home bath spa gadget that I'd caught sight of in the mall. It would be my gift to myself, since presents at Christmas had been pretty scarce. The little money we did have, we spent buying Casey stuff he didn't need, and surely wouldn't remember. I'd gotten Sydney a bottle of cheap cologne and some dress socks, and his gift to me was a coffee mug and some slippers. It wasn't much, but we weren't disappointed. The tub spa looked like the very thing I needed in my current state of perpetual back-and-belly pangs. Oh, what a luxury it would be to nestle down in a tub full of bubbles on top of a pulsating, vibrating mat that offered a varying array of water massages. What I wouldn't give to be the woman on the box, eyes covered with a satin blindfold, and holding a glass of wine. I'd skip the wine for now, but the rest of it I'd take in a second. Priced at less than a hundred dollars, it would leave me plenty of money to pick up postpregnancy clothes and other luxuries. My mouth watered every time I checked the mailbox in anticipation.

"Did the check come today?" Sydney would ask every day when he came in from work before he said anything else. He was just as anxious as I was.

"Not yet."

He'd grunt and go on with what he was doing, or what he planned to do. The day the check did come, he could see it on my face. The check would require both our signatures and both our presence at the bank. When he came in from work, both Casey and I were dressed, my hair was combed and my purse was under my arm.

"Let's go to the bank!" I sang, waving the check in front of him with a smile.

"Oh, it came?" he asked to confirm.

"Yep! Let's go!" I felt like a child on Christmas Day, with visions of shopping carts and new purchases dancing in my head, but my dreams were put on temporary hold when the teller at Sydney's bank informed us that she was required to put a three-day business hold on the check. Both our feelings were hurt, but what could we do? She offered us a hundred dollars from the deposit, but outside of that, we'd have to wait. We took her best offer in the form of two $50 bills, each of us taking one from the bank cash envelope once we got to the car.

"I can't wait to get my bathtub thingy," I prattled. "That's gonna feel so good to this pregnant body." My feet fluttered as I drew my shoulders up to my ears, hardly able to wait for my sumptuous soak.

Sydney said nothing in return; he just bobbed his head a bit, but I thought nothing of it. I was too busy spending money in my head. Three days later, I figured out what his silence was about.

"Did the check clear?" I asked, in desperate need of some retail therapy and still imagining my long-awaited bath.

"Yeah." He sat on the couch and pulled off his shoes. "You cook today?"

"No, I was planning on going out to dinner, since the money would be in the account today."

"Why you just can't cook? I get tired of eating out all the time."

"We don't eat out all the time, Sydney. I'm talking about a sit-down dinner at a real restaurant."

"I don't feel like it tonight."

"Okay, well, just give me my half of the money, and Casey and I will go."

"I didn't bring any money home," he announced, turning on the television with a press of the remote.

My brows crinkled. "Why not?"

"I was just thinking . . ." He paused to act like he was captivated by a commercial. When it ended, he started flipping channels.

"You were thinking what?"

"You ain't work none last year. All that money that got held came out of my check, so really . . . it's my refund."

What? What did he just say? "What?" my mouth repeated. "What do you mean?"

"I mean just what I said. You didn't work none last year, so they ain't hold no tax money back off your check. The only person they took money from was me, so I'm the only one who should be getting some back."

"That part might be true, but did you claim me as a dependent? Yes!" I barked before he could answer. "Did you claim our son? Yes!" I answered again. "You got extra money for us being on that tax return, and you know it."

"All I know is you didn't work last year. You didn't pay taxes last year because you didn't have a job. So how they gonna refund you something that was never yours."

Lord, I didn't feel like crying today. I really didn't. I willed back the water that threatened to spill from my eyes while I stared hard at Sydney, who focused again on the TV.

"Are you serious?" I planted my hands on my hips and furrowed my brows. Sydney didn't answer, so I did the only thing that made logical sense. I went and stood in front of the TV.

"Move, Kareese," he ordered.

"I'm not moving until you give me some answers."

"I already told you, you ain't work, so you don't deserve no refund."

"How you gonna sit there and say that!" I screamed, completely infuriated. "I didn't work outside this house, but I did plenty of work inside of it. I'm your wife, Sydney!"

"Yeah, a wife who don't do nothing."

I picked up the closest thing I could put my hands on, which happened to be one of Casey's shoes, and hurled it at Sydney. "You make me sick!" I screamed. Sydney's hands flew up as his body quickly leaned to the side, dodging the shoe; then he sprang to his feet, charging toward me.

"I know you didn't just throw something at me!" he growled, grabbing me by my forearms.

"Get off me!" I yanked and wiggled to get out of his grasp, but his grip was too tight. "Get your hands off me!"

"You gonna throw something at me?" he asked incredulously. "You done lost your damn mind!" he said, shaking me, then tossing me almost effortlessly toward the couch. "Over *my* damn money? You must be crazy!" He stormed to the bedroom "I wish I *would* give your ass another dime!" he yelled sarcastically before slamming the door behind him.

I'd lost my fight against my own tears, which were now out of control. I didn't care that snot ran out of my nostrils and over my lips; hurt, confused, humiliated, and feeling like a fool, I was completely immobilized.

Casey had come peeking out of his room. Seeing my tears, he came over and leaned onto my lap.

"You're sad, Mommy?" he asked, tilting his head and peering into my face. I couldn't even form words or motions to answer my baby. "Stay wight here." He motioned with his fat little three-year-old hands. "I be wight back, okay?" He waited for my answer, and when I didn't confirm, he checked again. "Okay, Mommy?"

A nod was all I could do.

Casey ran off but returned moments later with enough tissue for an elephant to clear his trunk. "Here, Mommy," he offered. "Blow your nose." Casey placed a hand on top of my head and pressed the tissue in my face, making it hard for me to breathe, but easy for me to chuckle, despite my tears.

"Thank you, baby."

"Feel better?" he asked.

"Yeah. Thank you."

"You not gonna cry no more?" he asked, shaking his head.

Man, how I wanted to say I wouldn't cry anymore.

"I think I will be okay." I nodded, taking the tissue and cleaning up my face.

Casey climbed up on the couch with me, reached for my head, then cradled it against his own, patting my face with his hands.

"Don't cry no more. Okay, Mommy? Don't be sad no more."

"Okay, Casey."

Sydney never did give me any more than the fifty dollars he'd handed me at the bank that day. I guess that was the extent of his generosity. He got a paint job for his car, along with some seat covers, and bought Casey a few things. The least he could have done was bought me the bathtub thing I wanted. It wouldn't have sufficed for the more than $1,000 that in my mind was rightfully mine, but it would have been the least he could have done. Especially since two weeks later, Mother's Day came and went. He sent his mother a large bouquet of mixed flowers, a card with a hundred dollars stuffed inside, and a gift card for Red Lobster.

Like a fool, I expected him to surprise me with the one thing I wanted in the whole wide world, and when I asked him about a gift for me, his reply was "You ain't my momma."

If I had the resources, I probably would have left Sydney right then. But I was broke and jobless, so I couldn't. On top of that, I knew I would be reacting purely out of emotion. I felt miserably trapped in my marriage to a man who had no emotional regard for me. What had happened in less than two years to make what I thought was a great relationship so wretched and depressing? What made Sydney marry me in the first place? He could have stayed single and let me stay single instead of making me think that he loved me and ruining my life.

Sydney completely blew me away when he came home with an announcement that turned my world upside down. He walked in the door, coming in from who knew where, slammed his keys on the table, and eyed me directly.

With an angry snarl, he said, "I don't believe that's my baby."

"What?" I looked up from the magazine I'd been reading and focused my attention on him. I couldn't have heard him correctly.

"You heard me. I don't believe that baby is mine," he repeated, virtually stabbing me a second time. "I know you 'bout to have it and everything, and you can stay here until then, but after that, you gettin' out my house."

"Your house?" I shifted Casey to the side and rocked myself up to my feet. "What do you mean your house?" That should have come second in line to the whole paternity-denial issue, but I guess survival instincts of keeping a roof over my head kicked in first.

"I pay the rent here. I pay the bills here. You don't do a damn thing but sit on your ass, run up the light bill and eat up all the food. This is *my* house and I want you out." His words were firm and non-negotiable, while my thoughts barely formed to make any logical sense in my mind.

"Sydney, I don't know how you missed this alert, but we're married. That means your house is my house. It ain't no such thing as *your* house and puttin' me out."

"Wanna bet? You just wait till you have that baby. I don't know where you're gonna go, but you getting up outta here."

By now, rivers of running water streamed from my eyes. Again. "Why would you say this is not your baby?"

"I just don't believe it," he said flatly, hunching his shoulders.

"Why, Sydney?" I shouted, becoming angry. "I haven't done anything but sit up in this house and try to be a good wife to you, and you gonna stand there and tell me this baby isn't yours?"

"How do I know that all those days you were supposed to be in class if that was where you really were? Every time I turned around, you talking 'bout they canceled the class for the day or you just ain't going. Yeah right! Now I'm supposed to be stupid. I be texting you, and you don't answer half the time. And how do you call yourself being a good wife when it ain't no dinner cooked." He began counting on his fingers. "The laundry ain't done, and the house looking like a hurricane done been through here!" He motioned his hand to a pile of Casey's toys in the middle of the living-room floor.

"I'm pregnant! Or did you forget that? You got hands that can clean up just like I do!"

"I know plenty of people that been pregnant and they keep up with all their responsibilities. Their houses don't look like this. They keep themselves up, still look sexy and comb their hair. They still cook for their family, so I don't know what you trippin' off of, but I know how to fix it." His next sentence had the impact of bullets exploding from a sawed-off shotgun. "I don't love you no more. I want you outta here, and I want a blood test." He snatched his keys back up and left, not sharing with me where he was going. He left me beyond stunned, speechless and most of all heartbroken. His words reminded me of a passage of scripture I'd read. They were quick, powerful, and sharper than a two-edged sword, separating the soul from the spirit and the joint from the marrow. The only thing was, it wasn't the word of God that cut me so deep, it was Sydney's word—the accusations from a husband who was supposed to love me like he loved himself.

As if the baby had understood every word, he began tumbling inside me, pressing against my organs and sending shooting pains into my pelvic area, forcing me to take a seat at the kitchen table. I rubbed a hand gently across my belly, hoping it would calm him down, but he tumbled on for the next five minutes. With my head dropped into my palm, I thought about everything that had just taken place.

Not his baby? A blood test? Was he serious? That was not a slap in the face but rather a punch that brought on a headache that I didn't need. I regretted, in retrospect, having lied to him about where I'd gotten a completely new wardrobe, and ignoring his "where are you" texts, which were overwhelming when I was in school. I could barely make it through a class without him blowing up my phone. And he'd been right about the sporadic canceling of classes, and then me being too sick to go other times. I guess a lot of times, he couldn't tell if I was at class or not. But even with all that said, it still didn't mean or indicate in any way that I'd cheated on him.

He was fifty ways wrong even to let those words escape his lips, but it said a whole lot for why he'd been so cold, uncaring, and evasive. Is that what Sydney really thought of me? I had a hard time wrapping my head around the thought that those were his true feelings and beliefs. At any rate, paternity could be proven. So in the whole scope of things, it wasn't that big a deal, but the fact that he thought that I'd cheated and gotten myself pregnant by another man sure was.

And an even bigger concern to me was his wanting to put me out. The whole "not my baby" bit just might be an insecure little phase that he was going through, but suppose he was serious about me getting out of "his" house? Where was it that I was supposed to go with an almost three-year-old and a newborn who was going to be here in four short weeks? I had no job, no money, may as well as had no family. What in the world was I going to do? Not that he could *make* me leave. I was on the lease, just like he was. But it was agonizing to know that he didn't want me there, and nobody stays long in a place where they are not wanted.

Over the next month, I did my best to fight for my marriage and try to show Sydney that I was a good wife. Regardless of how much pain I was in, I managed to prepare meals, even if it was just a couple of hot dogs and frozen French fries. I put more effort into keeping up with the laundry, although the smell of detergent literally made me gag. I had to hold my breath just to load the washer, then quickly wobble away until I made it to the next room. I didn't have much in the way of maternity clothes, but the few I did have, I started putting them on every day and taking my hair down from the scarf I would usually keep on twenty-four–seven. It made no sense to fuss with my hair, just to sit up in the house being miserable, but I felt I had everything riding on this and just had to do what I had to do.

Sydney was unfazed, often reminding me that he still wanted me to leave. He hardly ever ate the meals I cooked, turning up his nose at what I left in pots on the stove. I never knew what time to expect him in. Or he'd announce that he'd already eaten. He showed no appreciation of having clean clothes without having to wash them by himself, nor did he seem to appreciate that the house was just a tad bit tidier than it had been in months. To him, none of it mattered.

It was in the wee hours of the morning that Carlos sought to be free of my womb. The familiar pressing pain of contractions woke me from my sleep, but I ignored them. As Carlos had kept me in so much pain this past month, I didn't recognize it as labor. As the contractions came more often and intensified, I finally woke Sydney, shaking his shoulder.

"I need to go to the hospital." I prayed he wouldn't say something hurtful like, "You need to call the dude who got you pregnant and tell him to come get you."

"You in labor?" he asked, grunting, barely moving.

"I think so."

He lay still for a few more minutes until I shook him a second time. "Sydney."

"I'm coming." With a heavy sigh, he sat up, dragged his legs off the bed and rested his head in his palms for two minutes. In the meantime, I brushed my teeth and pulled on a pair of sweats and a T-shirt. By the time I got a still-sleeping Casey dressed, Sydney was ready.

He sat by my side through a few hours of labor, watching me struggle and groan with each excruciating contraction, then stood by my side while I pushed forth another beautiful baby boy, anxious to see if the baby would carry any of his physical features. I had hoped that the baby would emerge with Sydney's rich dark skin, large eyes, slanted brows, and toe nails that nestled deep into his toes like a picture in the frame.

Carlos was nothing short of beautiful, but he looked exactly like me. His skin was fair, and there was no darkness at the tips of his ears or around his fingernails to give indication that he would grow into more color. There were no easily recognizable features of Sydney anywhere, and when Sydney saw that, he held to his suspicion that I'd birthed another man's child. He didn't say it at the moment, but I saw it in his eyes, and in the way he held Carlos. His arms were stiff and his eyes inspecting, very different than the way I saw him cuddle and adore Casey.

I waited for Sydney to mention the blood test, but when he didn't, I made myself believe that he had accepted the fact that Carlos was indeed his. It wasn't until a few days later, after I'd gotten home, that he reaffirmed his uncertainty.

"You still gotta go," he said with no feeling. "I'ma give you about a week to heal a little bit, but after that, that's it." As usual, he blurted out his words and left. And as usual, I cried for an hour, wondering what I was going to do, where I was going to go, and why didn't my husband love me anymore? Well, I did know why—he thought I'd cheated on him, but he had no real reason to think that. Still sniveling, I called Yalisa.

"Can the kids and I come stay with you for a little while?"

"Of course," she answered right away. I had told her weeks ago of my dilemma, so she knew what it was about and had opened her doors to me right then. I didn't think at the time I was going to have to take her up on it, but there I was. "Where is Sydney?"

"He just left, I don't know where he's going. Don't care at this point."

"When do you want to come? Nobody's using that guest room but my shoes and some clothes on the bed."

"As soon as possible, I guess." I sniffed as I used the back of my hand to wipe my nose and shook my head in defeat, disappointed that I'd actually depended on a man for my well-being instead of seeing after myself. I decided right then that I would never be pregnant or unemployed again. This would be the one and only time I traveled down this road. "I'm sorry for asking you to do this. I don't have any money or nothing to offer you."

"Don't even worry about it. Your husband ought to be ashamed of himself. How is he gonna put his wife out on the damn streets right after she had a baby? Asshole!"

As right as she was, something inside me still cringed when someone said anything bad about Sydney. He was being an asshole, but only I was allowed to say that. I wanted always to be able to stick up for him and have his back, like we'd said we'd do way before we got married, but Sydney had made it hard. Not just hard—impossible. There was nothing I could say in his defense, but I loved him.

"I'ma start packing our things now. I can't be here when he gets back, Yalisa. I just can't."

"Do you need help?" she offered.

I knew that I did, but I declined, anyway. "Nah, I'll just grab the essentials."

"Well, I'll be here."

"Thank you, Yalisa," I mumbled shamefully. I was embarrassed for both Sydney and myself. Here I was begging for a place to stay, when my husband and I had an apartment. He was putting me out over some stone-cold idiocy. He knew that Carlos was his; he was just using it as an escape hatch from our marriage. If he wanted out, he should be man enough just to say that.

Chapter Six

I loaded a box of Pampers, cans of milk, all my WIC-provided food, and two baskets of clothes into the trunk and front seat of my car, then loaded the backseat with both children's car seats. Toting my newborn and holding my toddler by the hand, we treaded to the car. I strapped them in and I unwillingly, yet willingly, left my husband.

It hurt. I didn't want my marriage to be over. I wanted to prove my family wrong, but more than that, I was committed to my wedding vows. For richer or poorer, till death we parted. Only a fool would expect every day of a marriage to be sunny and bright. There were bound to be some dark moments, and I knew that going into my marriage. Granted, I didn't expect pitch black darkness to come upon us so suddenly or heavily, but I wasn't ready to just call it quits.

The first few nights at Yalisa's I spent isolated behind the closed door of the guest bedroom, curled up on the bed with my babies, and cried, but only in a way that Casey wouldn't recognize. I had to wait until he drifted off to sleep to weep. During the day, I'd open the bedroom door, but I still kept confined to the room, not wanting to mess up anything in Yalisa's home. She'd made me feel welcome; yet I was overcautious, as not to wear my welcome out too soon, since I wasn't sure how long I would need to be there. It was bad enough that I couldn't offer her a single dollar.

I tried to make heads or tails of my life, wondering what my next move was, but I couldn't even think straight. For starters I had to find a way to get money, and right now welfare seemed like my best option. I got up early the next day, dressed my boys, and went down to social services to apply for benefits. I felt so stupid and worthless telling the caseworker that I had two kids, no job, and no money. I had judged and terribly talked about other women who were in this same situation, without knowing the circumstances that got them there. I'd looked down my nose and thought of those women as lazy, ghetto, trifling, unmotivated, uneducated, and every other disparaging word. Now here I was—Kareese Christopher—trying to get government assistance. A couple hours later, I left with a plastic card loaded with a few hundred dollars in food stamps and shame that consumed me to the point that I could barely hold up my head. Shame that I'd looked down my nose at other people who needed help, and shame that I'd become one of them. Judge not, that ye be not judged, right?

I'd been gone from my own home for twelve days before I heard from Sydney, and only after I texted him telling him that the baby needed diapers. He'd texted back:

K—be by there afta 5

Knowing he was coming, I fixed myself up, dressing in a pair of white leggings and a fuchsia-and-white handkerchief-hemline minidress. It fit loosely around my middle to hide the leftover Jell-O jiggle from carrying Carlos, and with my breasts still filled with nourishment, they were large and round, giving the illusion of a stunning figure. I flat ironed my hair and let it fall around my face and shoulders. A brush of bronzer over my face gave my complexion a healthy glow, which I enhanced with eye shadow, mascara, eyeliner, and lip gloss. It may have been a bit much, but so what? The last thing I needed was for Sydney to see me looking a mess, not that he'd not seen me at my worst before.

I dressed my boys in something decent to give the appearance that we were either going somewhere, or had just gotten back from somewhere. Then I sat and waited in the living room until he arrived. My heart skipped a beat when the doorbell rang and I made myself count to ten before I stood to answer the door. Right before I did, I pulled off my engagement and wedding rings and pushed them down in my bra.

"Here you go." Sydney thrust the package toward me. "Where Casey at?" He glanced at me for a split second, looked at his watch, then away at his car, as if afraid to allow our eyes to meet.

"Casey, your daddy's here," I called over my shoulder. Casey was only one little boy, but his feet made the sound of ten hungry children all running toward food.

"Daddy!" he shrieked.

"What's up, man?" He scooped Casey into his arms and hugged him. "You doin' all right?"

"Yes. You wanna see my bwudder? Him seep."

"He's asleep?" Sydney clarified.

"Yeah!" Casey bobbed his head excitedly. "Him seep onna coush. Go dat way." He turned in Sydney's arms to point behind him.

"Naw, that's all right. We gonna let him stay sleep, okay?"

"Okay," Casey easily agreed.

"We'll be back," Sydney said, finally looking me in the eye and beginning to walk off.

"Where are y'all going?"

"I'm taking my son to the store," he answered over his shoulder without breaking a stride.

For only a second, I thought that Sydney might be trying to run away with my baby, but then I remembered how selfish he was, and how much time he spent out of the house instead of inside it. Sydney was not about to strap himself down with a baby if he could help it. He would be back. "Bye." Fifteen minutes later, Casey returned holding a small Slurpee cup and a package of M&M's. Thirty minutes after that, Sydney texted.

Where ur rings at

The nerve of him. What did he care?

IDK
Whatchu mean u don't no
What diff does it make
Oh so u aint married no mo
Your call

Right away I wished I could recall that last message. It gave him too much power. It wasn't his call; he'd made his call when he told me to leave. Whether I stayed married or not was actually my call—not his.

I no we goin thru sum stuff rite now but you still look good

I rolled my eyes and, at the same time, gleamed inside that he'd noticed. I mean, what woman doesn't want attention from the man she loves? Saying "thank you" didn't seem appropriate, nor did any other response that came to mind, so I didn't respond.

He texted, Can we start dating again. I cracked a smile. I couldn't say what had taken place in the past two weeks that made him have a change of heart. All I know is I was desperate for him to love me. And my desperation made it so easy to find sincerity in his request, even if it was only in my head.

Dating?

I didn't want to seem too anxious.

Yeah, u no, I come get u, take u out, we get to no each other all over again

It did sound like fun, but were we beyond this?

IDK
Y not. How else r we gonna bring r family back 2gether

Our family? Did that include Carlos? I was too scared to ask.

We'll see
What kinda answer is dat?
That's the best answer I can give right now

He was silent for more than an hour but finally returned the text with:

If I gotta fight 4 my family Im willing 2 do dat.

I was apprehensive at the notion that he wanted us to reconcile so quickly; what had changed over the past eight days that had him rethinking our breakup? Then again, maybe I was looking a gift horse in the mouth. I had been praying about our marriage, and regardless of what a great friend Yalisa had been, this wasn't the best place for me to be with two babies—cramped up in a single bedroom with all of our belongings stuffed into a couple of laundry baskets. My mind flew back to the night before when I'd been randomly thumbing through my little pocket Bible and read about Saul being converted to Paul. God had completely changed his life in a matter of minutes, so it was possible that Sydney had changed.

Yalisa wasn't a bit impressed when I'd shared with her that Sydney and I were going to start dating again.

"I think it's a romantic way to start over," I said with a half smile, imagining being in love all over again.

"I think he's just horny."

"It can't be just that because he could sleep with any old body. Why would he come back to me?"

"Because he doesn't have to put in any work to have you," she said flatly, lifting Carlos to her shoulder and patting his back.

I drew back at the sting of her words. She made me sound like some kind of cheap, no-standards floozy.

"What do you mean by that?"

"He knows you. He doesn't have to be impressive, or do anything special. He can be selfish, say a few words to get you going and you'll give him what he wants—some tail. I hate to say this, but you need to do a self-esteem check. If it were me, I wouldn't give Sydney the time of day right now." She rolled her eyes, not so much at me, but at the thought of Sydney, I assumed. "You should have told him no."

"I wish you wouldn't be so cynical when it comes to Sydney."

"I'm just being real." She shrugged. "I don't like how he treats you."

"Yeah, but when you talk about him, it hurts me. I know he's not perfect, but he is my husband and I do love him." She pressed her lips together tightly like she was trying to hold words inside. "And sometimes I just need for you to listen."

"Mmph," she huffed.

"And I don't have self-esteem issues. I have marriage issues, and every marriage has them."

Yalisa raised her brows, twisted her lips and nodded. "You're right." She was unconvincingly patronizing. "It's great that your husband suddenly wants to date you, even if he did kick you *and* his kids out of your own home." We stared at each other in silence for a few seconds. "I don't have anything else to say."

I took Carlos from her and headed to my room. All that she did say made me feel guilty about seeing my own husband. Low self-esteem? Please. I felt fine about myself, except the fact that I hated the permanent stripes on my stomach. Plenty of marriages went through a little break period and then came back together again to be better and stronger. And sometimes a break is what's needed when there're more bills than money, and more arguments than passionate moments. What did Yalisa know about any of that? She wasn't married, she didn't have kids. She didn't even have a boyfriend! So how was she the expert?

Two nights later, she didn't say much as she watched me jump, tug and grunt my way into a pair of pre-pregnancy jeans, which gave me a serious muffin top, and pulled on a black halter top.

"Do I look okay?" I turned in front of the mirror on the dresser while I sucked in my gut.

She shrugged. "You look cute."

I cut my eyes at her while I pushed a pair of cubic zirconia studs through my lobes, realizing that confiding so much in Yalisa had been a mistake. She knew almost every nasty detail of my marriage, which was way too much. I should have kept my business to myself. Now she was standing here looking at me like I was some kind of fool for wanting my marriage to work. I would need to learn how to be more discreet. I'd already cut my real family off because whenever I tried to talk with them about my life and marriage, they always had something bad to say about my husband.

"You didn't think enough of us to invite us to the wedding, so don't come over here crying about your problems," Momma had said shortly after our nuptials, when Sydney and I had gotten into our first big argument. I couldn't believe she was being so mean and unwelcoming.

"I told you we ended up not having a wedding, and I did invite you to the ceremony."

"When? You didn't tell me about nothing," she argued.

"Yes, I did. I sent you and Gene an invite and you never responded, but you know what? I'm glad you didn't show up!"

Her eyes widened in shock. "I'm your mother," she reminded me. "How can you say that!"

"You know what, Ma, sometimes I can't tell if you're my mother or not! How could I have felt good about you being there, knowing you didn't want to be, and you didn't want me to be?" I'd answered. "Look at the way you and Andra acted when I announced our engagement."

"I didn't do anything but shrug my shoulders."

"Yeah, Ma, that's what most mothers do when their daughters say they're getting married. They just act like it's nothing. They do exactly what you did; they don't do anything."

"You didn't give anyone a chance to do anything," she wriggled verbally, trying to find an out. "I would have come to the wedding."

"For what, Ma? To criticize me? To find fault with it? To tell me how much you didn't want to be there?"

"Well, I—"

"You know what, Ma? You sure weren't going to give us your blessing."

"You don't know what I would have done."

"What were you gonna do, Ma?"

"I was g—gonna . . ." she stammered. "I was gonna be the mother of the bride and be whatever you needed. Just because I wasn't doing cartwheels about the marriage doesn't mean I wasn't going to support you."

I didn't want to hear that crap. She could say anything at this point, since it was too late, but we both knew how she felt about my husband. Just like Andra, she talked bad about him every chance she got, and there's only so much of that a woman's going to take if she plans to honor her marriage. And I was committed to doing that. Sydney and I swore not to let family members come between us, and that included unsupportive mothers, snotty sisters, and opinionated best friends.

And speaking of my sister, I hate to admit this, but Andra had been right about the whole money situation: part-time money couldn't cover full-time bills.

I wanted Sydney to do more with his life than wash dishes at the pizza parlor or cook and serve fried chicken. He made just enough to cover our rent each month, bouncing back and forth between the two eating establishments, depending on which one was currently working his nerves harder, or offering more hours. If he'd worked them both at the same time, that would do a little more to cover our monthly expenses. The rest of his time was spent trying to be a network marketer. In my opinion, that equated to him clicking around on Myspace, Facebook and YouTube all day. It wouldn't have been so bad if he was actually making money from it.

But anyway, hopefully, we were now at a new place in our marriage. A new beginning.

We needed that.

When Sydney pulled up to Yalisa's house and blew the horn, picking me up for our first date, I thanked Yalisa again for agreeing to babysit.

"Hey," he spoke as I took a seat on the passenger side.

"Hey."

"You look nice."

"Thanks." I blushed, sucking my stomach in as best I could. "Where are we going?"

"Just to the apartment."

Just like that, my hopes were deflated as I remembered Yalisa's words that Sydney didn't have to try to impress me. I was sure if he was taking someone else out, he would be driving to a restaurant somewhere. Who takes somebody to his house for a first date? Maybe he just didn't have the money, but he wanted to start working on our relationship, which made sense. No, it didn't. I'm sure he still had tax money that he hadn't spent. He could have taken me out, if he wanted. I wasn't going to accept this from him.

"Why are we going there? That's not a date."

"Because I got something special set up for you there."

Hmm. We'd see.

"Let me see that rock," he requested, licking his bottom lip.

I did have my rings on, but I wasn't playing the rock game on this ride. I looked at Sydney like he was crazy. "There's some things you're gonna have to do first before you see my rock again." Like move me back in our home. I couldn't just give up no booty like it was a regular, ordinary day.

When we arrived at our home, Sydney opened the front door and led me into our dimly lit living room, where he'd set a couple of wine-filled glasses and a tray of strawberries and cubed cheese on the coffee table, and the aroma of cooked food filled my nostrils. I was unable to determine specifically what he'd prepared.

"You can sit down," he offered as he went to the kitchen, but instead I followed him past the dining-room table set for two, into the kitchen and looked over his shoulder at a pot of spaghetti and a few pieces of garlic toast.

"Mmm! Looks good." I turned back toward the living room to enjoy a glass of wine. Sydney joined me a few minutes later and fed me strawberries. It was hard to smile and bite a strawberry at the same time, but I managed.

"Wanna dance?" He stood and pulled gently on my arm, coaxing me to stand with him. He pushed on the stereo remote with his other hand. A jazz rendition of "That's the Way Love Goes" ushered us into a two-step. It was initially awkward, but we fell into an easy groove before midway into the song. The next track was something slow by Kemistry. Sydney pulled me close to him and started a slow drag that barely required us to lift our feet from the floor. Our bodies simply swayed together seductively. He felt good.

The song ended and we pulled away from each other for dinner, taking our wineglasses with us. Then after the meal, Sydney had me sit on the couch again with my ears covered by a pair of headphones, while he disappeared down the hallway. I nibbled on more cheese and fruit, sipped more wine, crossed my leg and closed my eyes. This was nice. Sydney was probably preparing our bed with rose petals or something, but I didn't plan on having sex tonight. After all, it was our first date. I'd let him give me a massage or something, though. I'd just begun to drift off when Sydney came and got me, placed a blindfold over my eyes and led me down the hallway. Then he spun me around three times so I wouldn't know which direction I was facing. When he uncovered my eyes, I saw the bathroom illuminated with candles, a bathtub overflowing with bubbles, and sitting beside it was the motor part of the bathtub spa I wanted.

"Thank you, Sydney!" I gasped, throwing my arms around his neck. He did care!

"You're welcome, baby." He hugged me for a full minute, rubbing my back, then started helping me out of my clothes. At this point, I didn't mind it a single bit. I couldn't wait to get in that water.

It was everything I imagined it to be; I only wished for a few extra inches in the length of the tub so that my whole body could be immersed at the same time. Sydney left me alone in the bathroom for several minutes; then he returned with the remaining strawberries.

"I want you to come back home, Kareese," he said, pushing a piece of fruit to my lips. "I was wrong and I'm sorry." He bit his bottom lip as he looked into my eyes, trying to read them for an answer. When I said nothing, he bent forward and kissed my forehead. "You don't have to say anything right now. I know you need to think about it."

I let out an inaudible sigh of relief when he'd added that last part. I wasn't ready to answer; although I knew what my answer would be . . . Undoubtedly, yes.

Thirty minutes later, he helped me out of the tub, patted me dry, lotioned me down, and started making slow sweet love to me. He started with a mixture of wet kisses, warm suckling, and soft tongue circles, which began at my neck and teasingly made a gradual decline to below my navel and between my thighs. Sydney straight took my breath away, enveloping my flesh with his lips. I arched my back and lost myself in the moment. The more he responded to me, I responded to him; grabbing, moaning and crying out in passion.

"I'm not on anything," I said, panting, when he kissed his way upward and positioned himself to massage my inner walls. I was not yet six weeks postpartum and had no need for any type of birth control since we'd not been together.

"I know, baby," he whispered. He leaned over me to the nightstand, opened the top drawer, and pulled out an unopened box of condoms. "I picked these up today," he offered before I could jump to any conclusion about why he had condoms in his possession. He rolled on his back to ease the thin sheath down his manhood; then he pulled me on top of him. "Show me that rock, baby."

And that I did. We rocked, rolled, turned, and twisted, and it was all good. Sydney left no stone unturned and gave it to me right, until I'd had enough. I couldn't do anything but fall asleep, and Sydney, pulling me close to him just like he'd done the day I married him, fell asleep right with me.

The next day while Yalisa was at work, my two babies and I moved back home.

Chapter Seven

I thanked God every night for bringing Sydney and me back together. I did everything I could to keep things going well. Sydney wasn't nearly as mean as he'd been while I was pregnant, and he hadn't said another word about Carlos—who was quickly approaching his first birthday—not being his baby. Every day that he didn't bring it up, I took it as acceptance, scared that broaching the subject would cause more of a ruckus than I was willing to deal with emotionally. I made sure to keep up with my domestic responsibilities; I made it my business to tell him that I loved him every day; I did my best to keep our sex life hot. The only thing was, love—home-cooked meals and buck-wild sex on demand—didn't pay the bills. There was no other way to look at things; Sydney needed to stop messing around and get a real full-time job. Even with me working a part-time job, we were still struggling to meet our financial obligations on time every month.

It seemed like all we could do was pay on a bill instead of pay off a bill.

Instead of nagging, I tried to be strategic in my approach to encourage him, reading somewhere that the best time to convince your man to do something was right after sex when you're spoonin' because that was when he was in his most euphoric and agreeable mood.

"Baby," I whispered one night after an intense and gratifying lovemaking session.

"Hmm?" he moaned in my ear and planted kisses on my shoulders, snuggling up to my back. I smiled because he was in perfect position.

"Yalisa told me that her brother said they are hiring and they need people bad."

He sighed. "Where he work at?"

"Gutter Glove."

"Doing what? Climbing on ladders and putting gutters up on houses? I ain't doing that mess," he uttered.

"But it pays almost three times what you're making right now, and we could really get on our feet and get ahead."

"Yeah, we'd be getting ahead, but at what cost? I'll never get to see my own family, and suppose I fall off of a ladder or something like that. I heard about dudes doing that kind of work and something happens to them and the job don't even want to cover their medical expenses hardly. You know how they do, baby."

He came up with more excuses when I told him about jobs at the bank, construction companies, car dealerships, waste management, and even Kellogg's. Who wouldn't want to work for them? But if the job wasn't too hard, the location was too far, or the people were too stuck-up, or the workload was too demanding, or it didn't pay enough—although all of them paid considerably more than his current jobs combined *and* included benefits—the hours weren't right or it just simply wasn't the job that he wanted.

"Naw, baby. I'ma just keep on working on my business; all I gotta do is meet the right people. Do you know how much them cats on the gold level make per month?" he'd explain. "Man, they getting paid! They be making like five figures a month."

I thought carefully for a minute before I came back with my negation. "It's just a little stressful, Sydney, wondering how we're gonna take care of the kids and pay bills every month, and I don't feel like we are using all of our resources."

"Can't you work some extra hours or something?" He snuggled up closer to me and yawned midsentence.

I was working as a cashier at Wal-mart for minimum wage and minimum hours to go with it. I didn't really mind working more hours, but I didn't make the schedule. "If I do that, the day care bill is going to go through the roof, you know that. It's already sky-high."

"Get your sister or your momma or somebody to babysit."

"What? You know we don't get along like that."

"I'm just saying. I'm sure one of them won't mind keeping the boys."

"Are you gonna mind them talking about you and how you won't keep your own kids when you hardly work?" I asked, becoming irritated.

"Stop telling people that I don't work. You know that ain't true. Just 'cause I don't answer to the Man don't mean I don't work. I refuse to be a slave."

Yeah, whatever. He wanted me to pay extra money in babysitting when most days he was as free as a bird and could keep the kids. I couldn't even respond. I stared straight ahead, studying as much of the pattern on the drapes that I could make it out in the darkness. I'd been initially excited for him and impressed by what I thought was ambition when he shared with me that he was starting his own business, but all it pretty much equaled up to was that he didn't want to get a real job. I saw no signs of the millions of dollars he swore he was going to make with every opportunity. He would catch wind of some new product, legal services, energy drink, girdles, coffee, skin cream or whatever; and he would swear that it was the one that was going to work. This was the one business that we were going to make twenty grand a month. This was the one product that people couldn't live without. This was the one opportunity that we were going to make the "small" financial investment up front, but be super-rich in ninety days. He was supposed to go out and meet people to gain new prospects or sell products, but did he do it? No.

In the meantime, day care expenses were costing me an arm and a leg. And so were half the utilities and food, since the food stamps were cut off months ago. There was only so much free pizza and chicken I wanted to eat. What I really wanted was for the bills to be paid. On time. And I wanted a man who took pride in working, not one who constantly made excuses not to work.

What kind of man would make his wife take on more hours if he wasn't trying or even willing to do so himself? I understood the whole entrepreneurial-spirit thing, but if it wasn't working, it just wasn't working. Sydney was just being lazy. I wanted more for us and didn't understand why he didn't. There was so much I wanted right now and didn't have. Why did everything seem so out of reach? Every check was predestined to go to a bill, and every bill was a struggle to pay. There was nothing wrong with having meager beginnings. However, if it was in our power to do better, I felt like we should at least try.

"I'm not going to complain," I coached myself. "Complaining gets you nowhere, but prayer changes things." I'd bought myself a plain hardcover journal to keep track of my thoughts, but, more important, my prayers. I cracked the binding, dated the page, and began writing:

Lord, I know you know my heart and mind, so you know how confused I feel right now. I want to be a good wife to my husband, and I want him to be a good husband to me. Isn't he supposed to work? I mean more than he does so that he can take care of our family? Please help him to grow spiritually and help him to be more accountable with his time and finances. And help me to see you in him. Help us to grow closer to you.

I wrote a lot more stuff that day, not just focusing on Sydney, but I also journaled about what things I felt I needed to do better as a wife so that my husband would be more responsive to me. I couldn't deny that there were two sides to every coin, and I knew that I was far from perfect. Maybe I could put in a few more hours or look for ways that I could support Sydney's business ventures. I could probably organize a few meetings or files or something, or create a blogging site for him if that would help. Maybe I could reach out to some of my friends or coworkers. How many times had I heard you reap what you sow, and give and it will be given to you? This could work—I just needed a paradigm shift.

I started reading the thirty-first chapter of Proverbs every morning, focusing on what the woman described there did for her family. She did all kinds of stuff—work being one of them. She wove tapestries and went to the marketplace to sell them, was accountable with her money, and made her husband proud of her. It made me wonder if Sydney was or had ever been proud of me. He had never said as much, but now that I thought about it, I wasn't sure if I'd given him a reason to be. I couldn't think of any special accomplishment I'd achieved that would make him look me in the eyes and say, "I'm so proud of you, Kareese." Sometimes people say it after they watch a woman go through labor, but I think Sydney had been too overwhelmed and nervous about the whole thing to have even thought that when we had Casey, and too suspicious with the whole "I don't believe that's my baby" ordeal when we had Carlos. I had yet to finish my degree and graduate, which could have been a moment for him to have said he was proud of me, if I had gotten that diploma. I hadn't even dropped my baby weight and gotten my figure back, but on the contrary, I'd blown up like a balloon, weighing more now than I did when I was full-term pregnant.

I couldn't judge Sydney; I could do better. The next time we spooned, I offered him an apology about being too demanding and critical, and not fully recognizing or appreciating how much he did for our family.

With a new mentality, I found fewer reasons to complain, and I focused on more things for which to offer praise. And as far as our money situation, at least the ends did meet, even if it wasn't until the middle of the month sometimes, or thirty days after the date, but they did eventually meet. After four years, though, I was ready to stop living from paycheck to paycheck and start living in abundance. It didn't even have to be abundance, but more than what we were doing. So I tried to do more, since Sydney wasn't going to do it.

"If anybody doesn't want to work their shift, let me know. I need some extra hours," I'd announce, walking into the employee break room at work. A few people asked me to work for them and I was happy to take their hours, although the increase in day care didn't make it worth it. Then Sydney had the nerve to be watching my paycheck like a hawk.

"How many hours you got this week?" he asked, approaching me as I prepared dinner.

"About thirty."

"Oh good, so that's gonna be like what? About a hundred fifty or a hundred sixty dollars after taxes, right? Let me see your check stub."

"For what? It's just a few extra dollars."

"'Cause I'm tryna keep the bills paid around here and I need to know what's coming in."

"Just tell me what bill you need me to pay," I countered. I just didn't see the need in practically handing Sydney my paycheck. It's not like he didn't know what I made.

"Why can't you just let me be the man and take care of stuff?" He reached for my purse and peered inside, looking for the envelope that held my pay stub.

"Why can't you let me be a grown woman and handle my own check?" I shot back, snatching my purse away from him. "You don't need to see it. You don't come in here flashing your pay stubs to me."

"But I take care of the bills."

"Some of them."

"Have you ever had to pay the rent?" he argued.

"Nope and I shouldn't have to."

"So why you just can't tell me how much money we dealing with?"

"Why can't you, as the man, make more money? Then you wouldn't need to be concerned with mine!" I stabbed at pieces of frying chicken to turn them over in spattering grease.

"You supposed to be my wife and help me out. We supposed to have each other's back."

"I do have your back, but that doesn't mean you can have my check."

"So you not gonna let me do my part," he stated more than asked. "You wanna be the man, huh? Move. I'll cook, since you wanna be the man."

"So to you, the man supposed to take all the money?" I folded my arms and moved away from the stove and handed him a set of pot holders.

"The man suppose to make sure the money is being spent in the right places."

"Well, the man should bring in more income, then. Where have you ever read in the Bible where a man tracked down his wife's money? I bet you can't find it nowhere. Don't let the macaroni burn," I added sarcastically.

"So what you gonna do, just put the money in your own secret account?" He placed the pot holders on the counter and put his hands on his hips.

"Sydney, I told you, if you need me to pay a bill, then let me know. I'm not giving you my paycheck and letting you know every dime I get, though."

"Well, we ain't gonna never get ahead, then," he ended, walking off.

"'Cause you won't get a job!" I yelled behind him.

Sydney and I went to bed angry and frustrated with each other that night, but I didn't care. It wasn't the first time we'd argued about my money. For the way I had to beg Sydney for every dollar he ever handed me, when I wasn't working, he wasn't going to start squeezing me for every penny that I brought home now.

If I needed or just wanted some extra cash before, it would have been easier for me to go to a bank and get approved for a loan. Didn't matter what I needed it for. It could have been for a loaf of bread, a can of formula or a pair of panties. Sydney wanted a full explanation of what I needed money for, and then he wanted to see receipts afterward. I had gotten sick of it fast, but since I wasn't working, I had no choice. It did push me, though, to hurry up and get a job. That, along with how helpless I'd felt when he put me out. No matter how I tried to forget about that, it was very much in the forefront of my mind. I never wanted to forget it so I wouldn't make a mistake and find myself in that same predicament again.

I'd started at Wal-mart right away when we'd reconciled, and had been there for two years now, and had gotten a couple of raises and small promotions, if they could be called that. I went from cashier to becoming a lead cashier, which paid a dime more an hour. Then lead cashier, to cashier supervisor, which took me up twenty-five cents more. I was grateful, but I wanted more.

I couldn't do a whole lot without my finished degree, but I learned how to maximize my experiences and improve my vocabulary to have a stronger résumé. I turned "ringing up customers" to "cash-handling and reconciliation experience." I turned "waiting on people fast" to "personalized and efficient customer service." I turned "price checking" into "discrepancy resolution." I turned "checking IDs for buying cigarettes and alcohol" to "confirming information to uphold and support company and legal policies." Before I knew it, Yalisa had helped me land a job as a teller for Freedom Federal Credit Union, where she worked.

That's when I found out Sydney didn't want me doing better than he was.

We both were excited when I came home from the interview, finding him in his usual spot at the computer, reading people's Myspace and Facebook statuses.

"I got the job! I—I—I got the job," I sang while doing the tootsie roll and snapping my fingers. "Come dance with me," I requested, keeping the rhythm of the song I made up about my accomplishment. "I got the job."

Sydney jumped up and joined me, bumping, gyrating, and waving his arms in the air as if we were at the club. "Hey, hey, hey, heeeeey!" he sang with me. We laughed at our celebratory antics, wrapping our arms around each other and ending the dance with a quick kiss.

"So how much you make?" he asked next. I shared with him my new hourly pay rate, which was almost twice as much as I made at Wal-mart, and twice as many hours. "That's good, babe," he said, hugging me, but his facial expression read something different. "I'm proud of you."

"You know this is a full-time job, so you are going to have to start keeping the boys here so that we don't waste money on the additional day care expense for Carlos going for more hours."

"What do you mean? You just got a super raise! You make enough now to let him go all day."

No, he wasn't trying to spend up my money! He was the king of hoarding his little paychecks. "Sydney, we can use the money for other stuff."

"I'ma still need to be free to work my businesses."

"What about stuff I want?"

"Like what? We got somewhere to live, we got food, and you got clothes."

"There's more to life than just that."

"Like what, Kareese? What is it that you're trying to buy?"

"A house maybe, or get a better car." I paused for a few seconds. "I'd like to have a wedding."

"For what? We're already married."

"Because I want a wedding. A day set aside for me. Well, for us, but the whole special day of me primping and being pampered and being a queen for a day."

"That don't even make sense, we been married almost five years now. You talking about us not using our resources? Now *that* is just a waste of money," he said. "And time."

"Confessing your love for me in front of our family and friends is a waste of money and time?"

"Yeah, it is. What do we need to do that for? I don't have to confess nothing to nobody."

"What about doing it for me? Because it's important to me and it's what I want."

"It always can't be about what you want."

"So, can it be about what I want at least one time?"

"I don't know about this one time. We got other financial things to think about first, like keeping the boys in day care."

"I'll pay for it, Sydney."

"No, Kareese."

"Why not—if it's not coming out of your pocket?"

"We don't need to waste our money on something we already got. That's just stupid."

"If it's my money and that's what I want to do with it, then what's the problem?"

"How is it just gonna be *your* money? It ain't no 'your'—it's 'our,' or did you forget that we married? You was supposed to trade 'me' for 'we' four years ago."

"And you were supposed to do the same thing. You don't come home on Fridays handing me your paycheck. You won't even put me on your bank account, and then you want to tell me what I can't do with my money?"

"You can pay for a wedding if you want to, but I bet you I won't show up!" He guffawed.

My mouth dropped as I stood speechless. No, he did not just say that to me.

"You mean to tell me that you are that dead set against remarrying me that you would actually not show up to your own wedding, knowing how much it means to me?"

"It wouldn't be *my* wedding, it would be *your* wedding. I already told you how I feel about it." Sydney went back to clicking around on the computer. I bit into my bottom lip as my eyes randomly scanned the room and my mind ran in circles for what I could or should say next, but I couldn't think of anything.

"I'm going to get the boys." I grabbed the keys off the table and stomped to the door, not bothering to change out of my interview clothes or the pumps, which were squeezing my feet.

"Take my car and put some gas in it for me, please," Sydney uttered behind me.

I wish I would put gas in his car for him to run all over town with, when he didn't even want to keep his own kids on his days off! Nor was I going to up the kids' day care expense just so Sydney could sit at home. My job started in two weeks and I was just going to get up in the morning and go to work. Sydney would have to deal with the boys on his own. Casey was already in school, so it would just be a couple of hours in the morning and a few in the evening before I got home for him; but as for Carlos, Sydney was going to start having him all day, or else *he* was gonna find a babysitter.

Instead of going straight home, I took the boys to Chuck E. Cheese's, one of my least favorite places to go. It was just too noisy and there were too many kids running around for my liking, but it would be better than going home and having to look at or deal with Sydney.

Facing the play area, I sat at a table by myself and thought about Sydney's views on money and renewing our vows, while the kids ran rampant laughing and chasing each other. Did Sydney really mean what he'd said? He wouldn't show up if I planned a wedding?

I poked at the cold pizza on my plate, thinking about my new salary and what I wanted to buy for myself, when I remembered a piece of mail I'd stashed in the car. Sydney had always been secretive about his money. Every month when his bank statements came, he'd snatch them out of the mail as soon as they arrived and hide them somewhere, never leaving them open or out around the house. Wondering what he was hiding, I confiscated his statement one day when I beat him to the mailbox. Instead of bringing the statement into the house with the rest of the mail, I put the envelope in the trunk of the car underneath the spare tire so I could inspect it later. I'd forgotten about it until just now.

"Casey," I called into a plastic tunnel full of hollering kids.

"Yes?" he answered, crawling toward me.

"I'm going out to the car real quick. I'll be right back."

"Okay," he said in a rush, before crawling away, then waving at me through colored port-holes. I retrieved the envelope from the trunk, returned to the booth, slid an ink pen through the glued seal and got quite a surprise. I found that as much as we scrambled every month for bill money, Sydney had been saving a hundred dollars out of each paycheck, having it direct deposited into a savings account and had a siz-able amount stored up. I stared at the figures on the paper until my vision blurred the printed ink.

All this time, Sydney had money. All that talk about how we didn't have the money for this or that—he had the money. "Can't you work extra hours, babe?" and he had the money. "We can't afford a wedding," and he had the money. "I'ma need you to pay the phone bill this month," and he had the money. "You're supposed to be my helpmeet," and he had the money. "You were supposed to trade 'me' for 'we,' and 'yours' for 'ours,'" and he had the money. I was outraged and outdone.

Here I was, thinking we were dead broke and trying to make an effort on my part to do better for our family, and he was stashing money all along! Then he had the nerve to be concerned about how much money I was making? I guess he was going to increase his direct deposit amount, while I paid more of the bills. I couldn't even confront Sydney about it without confessing that I'd stolen and opened his mail. I would have to keep this secret to myself and work around it. Crushing the paper in my hands, I threw it in the trash right there in the restaurant so it couldn't come back to haunt me around the house. Sydney could get another copy from the bank if he needed.

I now regretted sharing with him my new salary. If I had only remembered to look at his bank statement earlier, I probably would have lied about what I'd be making at the credit union. But one thing was for sure: I was going to have to put some plans in place to better secure myself financially. If he could put away money out of every paycheck, then I could do it too. It wasn't in my nature to hide stuff, but I was going to have to learn how to do it quick.

Maybe Sydney actually had been saving all this time to buy us a house or pay for a wedding and a honeymoon. Maybe he was going to surprise me and let me do it big, then whisk us away to somewhere like Greece or Rome or Paris. Then we'd come back to the States and he'd pull up in front of a house that I didn't recognize. He'd open my car door and just say:

"Come on, baby, I got some friends I want you to meet."

"What? I look a mess, Sydney, plus I have jet lag from the flight."

"We're not going to be here that long, I promise."

I'd sigh, but I'd get out of the car and he'd lead me up a long driveway to a two-car garage.

"Who is it, Sydney?" I'd ask, sighing.

"A coupla friends."

"Why we gotta come visit them now?"

"I just been promising them that I'd swing by and I wanted to get it over with."

He would open the door and I'd walk into an immaculate four-bedroom home, with pictures of our family already hung on the walls.

"Welcome home, baby," he'd say. "It was so hard keeping this from you because I had to

save up for a long, long time to pull this off. I had to give the key to Keith so the movers could put all our stuff in while we were away."

I'd gasp and walk around the house in awe and surprise, grinning the whole while; then we'd go upstairs and make love in our new bedroom.

It was a great fantasy but highly unlikely, given the conversation and borderline argument we'd just had that drove me to sitting in this indoor theme park and casino for kids being run by an oversize rat.

Only because I made them, the boys sat down just long enough to munch on a few bites of pizza; then they ran off again. Any other day, I would have long been ready to leave, but with this newfound information, I blocked the kids and noise out, and turned over a tray liner to the back side. I started calculating how much money I could save out of each paycheck and keep hidden from Sydney, and what was the quickest way to get my savings account to match and surpass his. I could lie and tell him that the recruiter messed up on my salary offer and stated the wrong amount; then I could save the difference. I listed our monthly expenses, and strategized on which ones I would have to pay so that Sydney's suspicions wouldn't be raised.

By the time I called the boys to leave, I had everything pretty much figured out. A sista was gonna have to do it for herself.

Chapter Eight

Sydney came home from work, took a shower, and came to bed ready to have sex, as usual. It was hard for me to open up my legs to him, knowing that he'd been lying to me all this time, but I made myself do it, like I had done for the past six months since I'd found out about how much money he was hiding. Even when I hinted around for things that we needed in the house, or how a bill was about to go unpaid, and said things like, "We're going to have to come up with the money somchow," he never gave any indication that he had it in the bank. Nor did he produce any cash.

Not wanting him in my face, I let him in from behind and falsified my moaning and groaning, encouraging Sydney to finish his poking faster. When he was done, he collapsed and pulled me to him. "I'll be ready for round two in about an hour," he remarked, chuckling.

I lay there silently in random thought about how challenging marriage really was. When I heard Sydney begin to snore softly, I scooted forward out of the spoon.

"Where you going?" he mumbled, putting forth a little effort to keep me in place.

"I need some water," I lied. I wasn't thirsty; I just couldn't lie there one more second in the arms of a man who refused to exert any more effort, no matter how slight, to better his own life, and then could be so selfish on top of that. It was a turnoff, no matter how good the sex could be.

"Bring me something to drink when you come back," he mumbled. "Please."

"Okay."

With no specific purpose other than to get out of Sydney's presence, I walked to the kitchen and leaned against the counter, folding my arms across my chest. There was complete silence other than the ticking of a wall clock. The sound drew my eyes to it and reminded me that there were only three sleeping hours left before I would have to get up, get the kids ready, and go to work. Sydney was working from four to midnight, so it only seemed logically right that he would get Casey off to school, and keep Carlos during the daytime, but he still refused, forcing me to pay the extra day care money, anyway.

I was so disgusted with my lying, lazy husband. Which made me think about Quinton LaRowe.

I'd met Quinton about three months before when I first started at the credit union. Quinton was single, business-minded, and as fine as they come. He worked for corporate finance, based in Maryland, which kept him safely out of my immediate surroundings, but it allowed him to run around all day in my imagination.

The credit union had flown me out to Vegas for a week of training, when Quinton and I crossed paths. He'd flown into Raleigh from Maryland and was on a connecting flight to the same training. We shared the same seat row assignment.

"Hello," he'd said casually as he placed his carry-on in the overhead compartment and then took his seat next to me.

"Hello." I was only being cordial with my response, until I noticed the small Freedom pin on his lapel. "You work for FFCU?" I asked, pointing at his sport coat, but it was by far the least notice-able thing about him. What struck me more than the company pin was first his scent; subtle, sexy and alluring. Next was his smooth mocha-colored skin, an expertly groomed goatee framing his mouth, and a head full of short, wavy hair, tapered on the sides and faded in the back—not the messy cornrows that Sydney wore like he was trying to hold on to his youth. He wore no wedding band—not that I was looking to date him, but I couldn't help but glance curiously. He was casually dressed in a crisply starched white shirt, black khakis, gray-black-and-white argyle socks and black leather loafers. A Movado watch circled his wrist, which matched his belt and shoes. And he had a job. A real job. A real good job.

"Yeah, I do," he answered, glancing at me for just a second.

"So do I, at the Raleigh site."

"I just came from there. What department do you work in?"

"Front line."

"Hmm. I've never seen you there before."

"I just started about three months ago."

"Oh, okay, yeah." He nodded. "You like it?"

"I appreciate being employed. I think it's a great company to work for. Ultimately, I'd like to do something else with my life than just being a teller."

"Like what?"

I smiled pensively. There wasn't a time that I could remember that Sydney had asked about my interests. My shoulders rose and fell in a silly schoolgirl kind of way. I hadn't made much time for dreaming as I tried to keep marital drama at a minimum. I found myself embarrassed when I realized I didn't really know what I wanted to do, but I had to make up something, or else look foolish.

"I'd, uh, like to work with young ladies in the community. You know, impacting their lives in a positive way and helping to prevent"—I shrugged again, searching for words—"teen pregnancy, and just letting them know that someone is in their corner." I assumed I came off as halfway believable because Quinton smiled at me.

"That's fantastic," he commented. "Our African-American communities need that kind of support," he added. "Are you a part of any women's organizations that support that type of cause?"

"A few." I nodded, hoping he wouldn't ask for names.

"Where'd you go to school?"

"Wake Forest."

"What field of study?"

"Social science," I answered, leaning on Andra's credibility and suddenly wishing I'd taken the many opportunities to re-enroll myself into school.

"But you ended up at Freedom, huh?"

"A dream deferred, but only until I get my master's."

"Oh, okay!" His raised brows and nodded suggesting he was impressed. "I like that. A woman with some goals and a plan. You married?"

"Yep," I answered. My hands were covered with a pair of black knit gloves, which I probably wouldn't need once I got in Nevada, but the temperature was in the low forties on my side of the nation.

"Lucky man. He has an intelligent, beautiful, and purpose-driven wife."

I blushed. By the time we landed, we were talking and laughing like old college friends.

"You wanna grab something to eat," he suggested once the plane touched down. "Just lunch," he added, taking note of my hesitancy. "No drinks, no tricks, no games."

"Umm, sure." It was just lunch, and I was going to keep it like that. Not to mention he was a legitimate co-worker. It wasn't like I picked him up off the streets. "Do you mind if it's in the terminal?" That felt safer to me.

"The terminal? You've got to be kidding me! This is Vegas, baby! And you know what they say, 'What happens in Vegas stays in Vegas,'" he teased. "Not that anything is gonna happen," he quickly added.

He was right. This was Vegas, and considering the hell I was going through at home, enjoying lunch with a co-worker was a small and completely innocent pleasure.

We ended up at Jimmy Buffett's Margaritaville, where I enjoyed mixed greens tossed with mangoes, sugared pecans, tomatoes, cucumbers, and habanero mango ranch dressing, topped with chilled grilled chicken, and a Pink Cadillac margarita just to be grown; because I really wasn't a drinker. Quinton chose grilled sirloin steak served with Hawaiian butter, mashed potatoes, and fresh vegetables. He ordered some kind of specialty beer to accompany his meal.

"You plan on seeing the city while you're here?"

"I guess I should make the most of the trip." I shrugged. "I've never been out here before, but I have always heard about it."

"I've been here a time or three. You oughta let me show you around."

"If I didn't know any better, I would think you were trying to date me," I teased.

He chewed through a mouthful of steak. "Can you blame me?" He grinned.

My self-esteem inflated, I smiled. "I guess I can't."

I only saw Quinton in passing during the day, since we were in separate training sessions, but each time we passed each other, he would wink or smile, or do something to give me just a tiny bit of attention. Drawn in by his humor, wit, and charm; I agreed to have dinner with him before the week was out. I looked forward to it.

I dressed in a pair of black slacks, a black sleeveless mock turtleneck, and four-inch pumps. My ensemble was accented with silver jewelry, I wanted to look and feel alluring and sexy, even if I had to suck in my stomach. Turning before the mirror, and satisfied with what was reflected, I headed toward the elevators to meet Quinton in the hotel lobby. On the way down, Sydney called me.

"Hey, babe," I answered casually. I knew there was no way Sydney had taken a flight out to Vegas, but I looked both ways when I stepped out of the elevator, paranoid that he was around some corner keeping a close watch on me.

"Kareese, why you ain't get no babysitter for the week? I'm sitting up here tryna get some stuff done this week and these kids 'bout to worry me to death."

"Because we didn't need a babysitter. You're the daddy, be a parent for a change," I snapped. "I ain't never seen a man who tries to duck taking care of his own children as much as you do, Sydney."

"Well, if I gotta sit up here and watch him, I can't go to work this week."

"You say that like that's really going to impact the finances."

"What do you mean by that?"

"You know exactly what I mean. So what, you work twenty-five hours a week, making minimum wage. Do you really think somebody is depending on that money?"

"You need to watch your mouth!"

"And you need to get a real job, Sydney. Grow up! Be a man."

"How the hell you gonna disrespect me like that?" he fired back. "I am a real man."

"No, boo-boo. Real men work full-time jobs."

"Boo-boo! I got your damn boo-boo!"

"I'll talk to you later. We have a dinner tonight." I snapped my cell phone closed just as Quinton walked up, sporting a pair of loose-fitting jeans cuffed at the hem and a simple black V-necked tee, showing off toned biceps, and suggesting equally toned pecs and midsection. Looking like an Aéropostale model, he grinned as he walked up.

"You dressed it up for me, huh?"

"Excuse me? This is how I always dress, and if it wasn't, I sure wouldn't be doing it for you. I got a man." Right away I regretted not just throwing on a pair of jeans and comfy sweater. Was I that transparent that he knew I'd put forth a little extra effort on his account?

He threw his hands up in surrender. "I'm sorry, my mistake."

"I'm just saying, don't get it twisted, 'cause I don't even know you like that."

"All right, calm down. Sheesh!" We took a couple of steps in silence. "Is it okay if I get the door for you, or is your man gonna do it?"

I winced. "Very funny. I'll get my own door, thank you very much."

"You're so cute when you're mad."

"Whatever. Where are you taking me?" My eyes absorbed the glamour of the strip with its flashing lights, limo-filled streets and pedestrians strolling leisurely on both sides.

"What do you have a taste for?"

"Something that I can't get in North Carolina."

"Oh, well, that's easy. Just pick a spot." He raised his arms as if offering me the sky. "You ever been to the Eiffel Tower?"

"The one in Paris, or is there one here? I've been to the one in the Kings Dominion amusement park in Virginia." I giggled.

"There's a restaurant here that looks out over the city, replicated from the Paris landmark. We can go there."

"Sounds good."

While we dined, Sydney texted me what seemed like a thousand angry messages, which only fueled my fantasy of lying in Quinton's arms—sleeping, but fully clothed—like Bernadine had done with James in *Waiting to Exhale*. I wasn't in the middle of a divorce like she had been, but I definitely had my share of marital woes.

"So, are you enjoying the married life?" Quinton asked as if he could see straight into my soul.

"It has its perks, it has its drawbacks."

"If you could do it all over again, would you be married right now?"

That was a good question. Luckily, I had lifted my glass of blackberry sangria to my lips and had time to think while I swallowed. I wanted to be married, and I loved my husband, but I wished things were different between us. Marriage wasn't exactly living up to what I had imagined. I wasn't supposed to be carrying my husband; he was supposed to be carrying me. He wasn't supposed to be hiding money. We weren't supposed to have separate finances. I cleared my throat and pasted a smile on my face. "Yeah." His eyes seemed to search my face for the truth. I hoped my eyes gave off some kind of romantic and reminiscent twinkle, although I didn't half believe it myself.

"To the same man?" Quinton added.

Prepared this time, I answered more quickly and with lifted brows. "Yes," I dragged out.

"Liar," he challenged after a few seconds of quiet studying. "I saw disappointment all in your eyes when I asked you that."

Caught off guard and uncomfortable, I looked away for just a second.

"You're not happy and it shows. You can't hide that behind a Halloween mask."

"Yes, I am." Quinton only stared at me. "What're you looking at?" I grimaced with irritation.

"Nothing," he answered, shaking his head. "If you're happy and you know it, clap your hands." He snickered before taking a swig from his glass of wine.

"Hardy har har," I said, not cracking a smile. "I don't appreciate you trying to stick your nose in my business. If I'm happy or not, that's between me and my husband. You need to shut up talking about what you don't know about."

"You want to know how I know you're un-happy?"

"You mean how you *think* you know?"

"Oh, I know." He nodded with assurance. "Because if you were happy, you wouldn't be out having a quiet romantic dinner with another man. It's all right to lie to me, but don't lie to yourself."

I was speechlessly taken aback, but I didn't have time to be. "I only came out here because you were worrying me to death. Ain't nobody that interested in having dinner with you; I'm perfectly fine having dinner by myself in my hotel room," I shot back, pushing away from the table, grabbing my clutch, and standing. I would have put a little extra "pop" in my booty as I walked away, but I was too mad. He had his nerve! "You ain't all that!" I added over my shoulder, swerving my neck and not caring about who was looking. Thinking he would try to run after me, I dashed into the ladies' room, pulled out my phone, and dialed Yalisa's number, bypassing the five missed-calls indicator, all from Sydney.

"You having a good time out there in Sin City," Yalisa chirped. "I've got your sons over here, by the way."

"What? What are they doing over there?"

"Sydney called me and asked if I could keep them because he picked up some extra hours tonight at work."

"Extra hours? As allergic as Sydney is to work? Girl, you know that's a lie. He told me he wasn't working at all this week. You need to go straight over to his job and see if he's back there in that kitchen."

"He had on his uniform when he dropped off the kids," she said.

"Mmm-hmm, but anyway, girl, you know Quinton LaRowe?"

"From corporate finance?"

"Yep."

"What about him?"

Just when I was about to spill the whole story, I thought better of it, just in case somewhere along the way Yalisa found a reason to blackmail me. "Why he gonna ask me out to dinner, like somebody want him?" I puffed. But truth be told, as the words left my mouth, I felt a pulse of excitement and flattery.

"Are you going?"

"No, I'm married, remember?"

"So what? He didn't say have sex with him, he said have dinner with him. There is a difference, you know. You can use that time to pick his brain a little bit about going to the next level at work."

"You know how guys do. It just all starts with dinner, when all they really want is something else."

"And you act like you scared you won't be able to say no; like you won't be able to put him in his place. So what he wants something else? That doesn't mean you have to give it to him. Go and make a good impression, but keep him guessing. Dogs don't chase if you don't run."

"I don't want him chasing after me."

"So don't run—go to dinner. We all like a little bit of attention, so stop acting like you don't."

"You know what? You make me sick." I giggled, admitting to what she'd said last. "I still ain't going, though."

"Hmph! Let him mess around and ask me to go somewhere with him. I don't care if it's to the doggone Burger King, I'll walk right up in that place just like we're a couple."

"Yeah, because you're still single." I laughed. "Lucky you! But listen, I'll call you later. I'm about to go to the gym and get on this treadmill," I lied.

"All right, girl. Behave yourself."

"Of course. That's all I know how to do."

"And rub corporate elbows, not booties!" She chortled at her quip.

"Whatever. Bye!" I tossed the phone back into my purse, freshened up my lip gloss, then peeked out the bathroom door to avoid seeing Quinton before heading for the elevator. As I stood waiting for its arrival, I counted the cash in my purse to ensure I had enough to catch a taxi back to my room.

"I thought you were gone." Quinton strode up behind me, with a foolish grin on his face. I didn't even bother to comment, but instead my eyes did a cut and roll away from him. "You can at least let me get you back to your room safely," he offered.

"No, thank you." My lips were puckered out so far I could have kissed the moon.

"Come on, Kareese. I didn't mean any harm, and I'm sorry if I offended you."

"Apology accepted," I said without delay but in an icy tone.

"I can get a little beside myself sometimes, and other times I don't know when to shut up."

"You sure don't." The elevator chimed, and its doors slid open, inviting us into its intimate interior.

"Let me make it up to you," Quinton offered, holding his arm against the sliding door to prevent it from shutting prematurely while I passed in front of him.

"It ain't nothing to make up. You don't owe me anything."

"Yes, I do. I offended you, and I didn't mean to."

"Don't even worry about it."

Although we were several floors aboveground, the elevator moved at almost thrill ride speed to bring us to the first level. The closed-in atmosphere was uncomfortable, even though we were boxed in for less than a minute. Sounds of ringing and singing slot machines filled my ears as the doors reopened and I wasted no time clicking my heels away from Quinton. He chased a few steps behind me and gently grabbed my arm.

"Wait."

I came to a dead stop, cut my eyes over my shoulder, but I couldn't see Quinton fully, only his silhouette in my peripheral. "I bet you better get your hands off of me."

Immediately he drew back, but I kept my stance for a full three seconds before I walked toward the doors of the casino.

"Kareese, please. Look, let's just play a few slot machines and end the night on a good note. I promise I won't say another word about your personal life," he said from behind me.

I kept walking.

"Come on. It'll be fun." He waited for my response, which I didn't give. "I'll pay for your first hundred dollars," he sang, jumping dead in front of me, and waving a bill in front of my face. "You could play the right machine and win a million dollars . . ." he continued with line two of his song.

I didn't mean to, but I cracked a smile.

"You can go home rich . . ." he added, lifting his eyebrows and taking his voice up an octave, still waving the money.

Lord knows, I could use the money. I looked at him with a smirk, then snatched the bill out of his hand. "Let's go."

"Cool!"

All of a sudden, I thought about how I looked, dressed in four-inch heels, standing on the Vegas strip, and snatching money out of a man's hand before following him inside a hotel and casino. This man had me out here looking like a two-bit hooker.

Chapter Nine

I'd had so much fun hanging out with Quinton, I dreaded going back home to the drama Sydney and I shared, which now seemed ten times magnified. After spending about a week with someone who was actually doing something with his life, had money to spend on luxuries, had a great sense of humor, was intelligent, and I'd be remiss if I left out sexy—Sydney seemed lazier and less ambitious than ever. On top of that, he had become increasingly insecure. Every little thing I did, he scrutinized and questioned. Every day after work, he wanted to know who I'd talked to and who came in the bank and who did I wait on and who tried to flirt with me. It was sickening. And, yeah, I did pretty much spend a week in Vegas with a man who was not my husband, but I did exhibit enough self-control to keep on my clothes. We did kiss a little bit, though, but the way it happened was completely innocent.

***

Quinton was standing behind me as we took turns placing varied bets on the Triple Sevens slots.

"You can't always bet the max," Quinton coached, playing just twenty-five cents and winning back fifteen. "You have to trick the machine by betting low sometimes."

"Low risk, low return," I chimed just before smacking my hand on the max-bet button, sending the reels into a spinning frenzy. Then, like magic, three triple red sevens backed by pictures of flames stopped on the screen, one at a time. The machine started blasting music and repeatedly clanked a mechanical sound of coins falling onto metal, which kept going for what seemed like forever. "That's how you do it, baby!" I shrieked, slapping Quinton a high five.

"Yeah!" he hollered in excitement. "Make that paper, girl!"

We jumped, screamed, and slapped hands until the machine stopped at a whopping $43,000. And in the middle of our celebration, somehow our lips met. As if a slow-motion button had been pushed, we came together, his arms circling my waist, and our eyes focused on each other. There definitely was a spark that instantly ignited flames inside my panties. In reality, I'm sure, all of a quarter of a second had passed. I acted as if it had no effect on me whatsoever, turning back to the machine and hitting the "cash out" button. Seconds later, I held a slip of paper that was worth more than my annual salary.

"You know you have to split that with me, right?" he quipped, flashing a grin.

"Split it? Who won it?"

"Who paid for it?" Quinton asked, reminding me that it was his money that led to the win.

"You *gave* me the money, remember? So technically, I did," I answered, cabbage patching my way to the cash cage.

"Well, I guess I'll just have to blackmail you to get my half."

"And just how are you gonna do that?"

"Call your husband and tell him you were out with me all night long."

"Whatever. You can't blackmail me if I tell on myself." I stuck my tongue out at him and kept dancing.

"Yeah right!" He chuckled.

"But you're lucky I like you, 'cause I don't believe in giving money to grown men." The last thing I needed was to have him telling Sydney on me.

Quinton and I filled out the appropriate paperwork to split and receive the winnings, and I left the casino happier than I'd been in a very long time.

We took a cab back to our hotel. Quinton walked me to the door of my suite, then asked if he could come inside for just a few minutes. Now, as many times as I've seen this very thing happen in the movies, where the guy asks to come in, he and the girl always end up having sex. Then he leaves her before the sun comes up; so knowing that, you would think I would have said, *Quinton, I don't think that's a good idea*. And maybe I would have said that, but I felt obliged to entertain his company for a few minutes because we had just won all this money together.

Every response other than no, which I thought to say, sounded just like what every other woman had ever said, and ultimately ended up with her panties off and her legs in the air. At any rate, I let Quinton in and we sat on opposite ends of a small sofa watching back-to-back episodes of *The Family Guy*.

"Why are you way over there?" Quinton tossed a pillow at me, which I grabbed and placed behind my head.

"Because it's safe, and you're not slick."

"Slick? What do you mean by that?"

"You know what I mean." I drew my feet up onto the couch. Quinton stared at me for a few seconds, then he grabbed one of them, and began to tickle me.

"Stop it!" I giggled and kicked at him with my free foot, which led to him diving on top of me and digging into my sides. All the wiggling, squirming, and laughing transitioned into bumping, grinding, and lustful panting. He studied my eyes for as long as I could keep them open, then my guilt caused me to close them. That wasn't exactly the best thing I could have done; it only encouraged Quinton to press both his lips and his pelvis into mine. Feeling the softness of his lips and the hardness of his manhood, I all but melted beneath him. The warmth of his kiss resonated from my lips, down my body to my toes, then back up again, stopping at my hot spot, and heated things up in that area. I flexed my womanly muscles a few times as my body became alive and hungry.

When our kiss broke, I found the strength from somewhere to whisper, "You shouldn't be here." He was silent. "And I shouldn't be here," I added, motioning with my eyes that I meant lying on a sofa underneath him.

Quinton stayed put for a few more seconds, his eyes bouncing from my left eye to my right, then back to my left again. "You're beautiful."

I bit my bottom lip. Sydney never said stuff like that to me anymore. Our lips met again; then Quinton moved his lips to my jaw, then to my neck as one of his hands began to cup my breast, while his thumb grazed my nipple. Slowly he lowered his kisses to meet his thumb and took my flesh in his mouth, causing me to arch my back to meet him.

He let out a sexy moan and I felt his manhood throb, knocking on the door of my panties. I was about to be caught up and I couldn't let that happen. Regardless of Sydney's faults, he was my husband, and I owed it to him to be faithful. After a few more minutes of working ourselves up, I found the strength to push Quinton away. With little resistance, he lifted his weight, stood, and slowly walked himself to the door.

"Good night." He didn't wait for me to answer, but the door shut immediately behind his voice. My flesh was disappointed, but my soul was relieved that I hadn't cheated on my husband. Not exactly. But I did find myself thinking and fantasizing about Quinton, secretly wishing he were back on top of me. Thirty minutes later, he texted me:

Thanks for a great evening.

I texted back a smiley face, immediately deleted the thread, then smiled myself to sleep.

Quinton and I did go out one more time before I headed back to the East Coast. We again had dinner, and then thought we'd try our luck once more at the slot machines. This time we played at separate machines, sitting side by side, and moving every fifteen minutes to different machines.

"So, have you enjoyed your trip out here?" he asked, racking up $1.25 in winnings, causing me to jerk my head toward him, thinking he had hit it big again.

"Yeah. I needed the break," I offered, turning back to my own machine.

"You ready to go back?"

"Not really. I miss my sons, but other than that, if I could stay longer, I would."

"What makes you say that?"

"Being married is no joke."

"Did you get married thinking that it would be a walk in the park?"

"No, but I did have some expectations that have gone unmet." I hit for $5.45. "And I've had a few things happen that I didn't expect at all."

"Like what?"

I would never tell him that Sydney had put me out on the streets just a few years ago. "Like him taking care of the bills, and really being the head of the household," I continued, spilling my guts about how disappointed I was in my husband. "Sydney just doesn't have any drive, no passion, no desire," I complained. "He's just unmotivated."

"Sydney, huh?"

"Yeah," I confirmed without looking up.

"What made you marry Sydney? Sydney put that smack down on you?" he scoffed referring to sex, to which I rolled my eyes.

"Love." I shrugged. "We had a son. Let's change machines, this one is robbing me blind." While we cashed out and moved, I gave more thought to why I'd married Sydney. As we walked, I added a few more answers. "Didn't want to keep living in sin. Got tired of my family looking at me sideways. Wanted a complete and authentic family."

"So you settled," Quinton more stated than asked, inserting his cash slip into a machine fashioned after the *Wheel of Fortune* game.

I didn't like the way that sounded. Had I settled? "Maybe," I answered, sincerely unsure of what my reply should have been.

"Sounds like you did. Sounds like you didn't know what you were getting yourself into."

"I just wanted to have someone that was really mine. Someone to come home to and would hold me at night. Someone to share my life with. Especially having a baby and all. I mean, you get tired of just being out there by yourself, having to deal with the world by yourself, deal with bills by yourself, coming home to yourself. Don't you get tired of that?"

"Sometimes, but not really. I have too much going on in my life to think about stuff like that."

"You never think about how nice it would be to come home to a cooked meal, and someone who has already done the laundry, or waiting for you dressed in something sexy, and has a hot bath waiting for you?"

"The 'something sexy' part, hell yeah!" He chuckled. "I think the rest of it is overrated, though. I know how to cook, so I don't need a cook. I've been doing my own laundry since I was ten, and what I don't wash myself goes to the cleaners, so I don't need that either."

"Not that you need it, but wouldn't it be nice?"

"I've gotten along this far without it."

I stared at Quinton for a few seconds, trying to figure out if he was serious or not.

"What about love, though?"

"What about it?" He didn't even look over at me.

"Don't you want that someone special just to share your life with? To come home to at the end of the day and just wrap your arms around her? Or to spoon with at night and dream the impossible dream together, in the comfort and safety of the arms of someone who really, really cares about you?"

"I bet you read a lot of romance books, don't you?"

What was that supposed to mean? "Not really, but I believe in romance."

"I don't," he shot back.

I didn't say another word. I don't know why, but I felt rejected, even though Quinton was nowhere close to being my man. I guess a part of me had imagined he could have been falling for me a little bit when he'd asked me out to dinner and was in my room doing the humpty-hump. It put things back in perspective that all men wanted some free tail.

Let me get this man out of my mind, I coached myself, which I hadn't been able to do since my trip. Every time I closed my eyes, I remembered what it felt like to have him lying on top of me and how our lips met. And what his lips felt like when he suckled on my breast.

And when Sydney and I made love, I imagined it was Quinton, until my fingers touched those ugly cornrows Sydney wears. I didn't have any business daydreaming about another man, and I twirled my wedding ring around my finger as a reminder.

Even if Quinton did have a genuine interest in me, what was I going to be able to do about it?

Chapter Ten

I don't care what people say, money does change people, because I had a new attitude. The day I set my feet back on North Carolina soil, I plopped my casino winnings into a new bank account without Sydney's knowledge, making an initial deposit of more than $18,000—more money than I'd ever had in my whole life at one time. It felt good to have money at my fingertips for once. It felt even better that the money could't be touched, wasted, or plotted on by Sydney. When tax time came around, I was prepared to tell Sydney that we'd make out better filing our taxes separately with me claiming Head of Household for the kids to maximize our refund, to make sure my winnings stayed hidden.

I paid up most of our bills, which Sydney never gave much attention to, anyway, and I did a little bit of shopping, but I had to be careful not to overdo it so that he wouldn't suspect anything. I did tell him that I'd won a few dollars when he asked me if I'd done any gambling. All I would admit to was $200; to which he responded, "Good, 'cause I'ma need you to pay the light bill with that, since they cut my hours this month." I didn't even comment. I did look at him sideways, though. "What you looking at me like that for? It's halfway your fault that they won't put me on the schedule."

"And how is that my fault, Sydney?" It was only because I now had a secret-stash account that I was able to maintain my composure.

"'Cause you ain't get no babysitter for the kids while you was gone outta town." He spoke bitingly. "I had to call in that whole week, to sit up in the house with him; then they talkin' 'bout, 'If you don't wanna come to work, we gonna give your shift to somebody who do.'"

"Well, they should have done that a long time ago," I mumbled under my breath, but loud enough for Sydney to hear.

"What?"

"What, what?" I shrugged. "You know it's true. You don't want to work for real."

He furrowed his brows. "You wrong for that."

"Am I?"

"See, that's your problem. You don't know how to support a man. I'm out here trying to do something good for us, and all you want to see is what I don't do."

"What is it that you think you do so much of, Sydney?"

"I need to be asking you that!" his tone escalated. "Why you always expect me to do everything? This is supposed to be a partnership; this is supposed to be about us and we, not just me. I be tryna get you to help me with my businesses, and you always acting like you got something to do."

"I do have something to do—it's called work! And it takes both of us working full-time jobs to run this household, but part of us doesn't want to do that. Part of us wants to chase a pipe dream that is not leading to anywhere but down the drain."

Sydney stood silent, at a loss for words for a moment, just glaring at me, as he tried to think of something to say.

"I don't know who you been hanging around lately, but they 'bout to make you mess up a good thing."

"What good thing is that?"

Sydney shook his head, looking at me like I was some sort of alien. "You ain't gone miss your water till your well run dry."

"Did I ever have water in my well?" I asked, with crinkled brows. "I've been parched for so long, I don't remember what water even tastes like." Mocking him, I patted my throat and coughed. "Can you refresh my memory of what water even is and get me something to drink . . . please?"

Clearly offended by my ridicule, Sydney marched to the kitchen, opened, then slammed the cabinet after he pulled out a glass. Turning to the sink, he filled it with water. He returned to the living room a few seconds later. "Here you go." He handed me the glass and placed his hands on his hips, waiting for me to drink.

"Thank you," I sarcastically remarked, taking the glass and then lifting it to my lips. As soon as I began to sip, Sydney hit the bottom of the glass upward, knocking it into my face and drenching me with water before it fell to the floor and rolled on the carpet. "You still parched? You thirsty now, damn it?" My hand flew to my mouth, covering sudden pain that shot through my gums and jaw, while I choked and spit for a few seconds, trying to recover. "You want some more to drink, or you ain't thirsty no more?"

My tongue chased the pain around the insides of my mouth, doing a nonvisual assessment, then steadied on my front two teeth. Oh, my God! My tooth was chipped. I made a dash for the bathroom mirror and parted my lips to view the damage. At first, all I saw was blood, which scared me. I quickly rinsed it away; then I saw that a huge chunk of my front right tooth was gone. It made my stomach drop and brought immediate tears to my eyes. Suddenly, I looked like a whole different person.

"You wanted some damn water! Well, there you go," Sydney continued, stomping his way to where I was. He started to say something else, but then he stopped when he saw my reflection in the mirror, with tears streaking my face and bloody teeth. His eyes widened and he put a hand on my shoulder. "What happened?" he asked, peering around my head. "Get off me!" I jerked away, still gaping at my mouth.

"Kareese, I'm sorry." He looked nervous and a bit scared, his eyes showing that he couldn't believe what he'd done. "I'm sorry. I didn't mean to do that." Sydney didn't say another word for two minutes, while I stood there and wiggled my teeth, inspecting intently. "Let me see," he coaxed softly, nudging me to turn my head toward him. I resisted first, but then I slowly turned to him, as if taking a look at it could magically fix it. "I'm sorry," he said again. "We need to go to the emergency room," he said just above a whisper. I pulled away from him and turned back to the mirror. I could hear him sigh heavily, with what I thought was remorse, as he walked off, leaving me there in the bathroom, feeling all kinds of emotion.

How was I going to go to work tomorrow, looking like this? And what was I going to say to people when they asked what happened? I was too ashamed to say that my husband hit me in the mouth with a glass. Maybe I could just say he bumped into it by mistake. I was embarrassed—thoroughly. I felt ugly, deformed, and decrepit.

"Come on, let me take you to the doctor," Sydney offered, returning to the bathroom, his hand slightly cupped, holding the piece of my tooth that had been knocked away. This sight disgusted and angered me even more. "I'm sorry, Kareese," he repeated, but I didn't want to hear that bull. I had absolutely nothing to say. I rolled my eyes and tried to squeeze past him without our bodies touching. I yanked away when he reached out for me.

For more than an hour, Sydney, Casey, Carlos, and I waited in the emergency room for a non-Emergency visit. When they finally did call my name, got my vital signs, sat me in a curtained "room," and had a doctor come in, she did a five-second glance and simply told me to go see a dentist.

For the two weeks it took me to get an appointment, I barely spoke a word to Sydney, and I lost more and more respect for him whenever I looked in the mirror. It didn't matter to me that he was suddenly able to get more hours at work, helped out a little more around the house, and even cooked dinner a few times and gave the kids a bath. I came to bed late every night and refused him sex, since I could barely look at him, let alone let him crawl on top of me. I couldn't even dream about Quinton with my mouth all messed up. Sydney had me looking like a snaggletoothed witch, and how would Quinton find that attractive?

Luckily, the dentist was able to repair my tooth, so my smile and self-esteem were restored, but I hadn't forgotten or forgiven. What Sydney did was deplorable, mistake or not. I still had a hard time speaking to him, even after the dental work was done. I didn't know how I felt about things, about us. I had mixed feelings about whether I should love Sydney enough to stay with him, or would I be foolish for staying with a man who put his hands on me? Except that is not exactly what had happened. But suppose Sydney really intended to chip my tooth but had figured out a way to make it look like a mistake?

That's what my mother would say.

Why was he trying to throw water on you in the first place? she would question. It wouldn't matter that water, in and of itself, is pretty harmless when thrown on a person.

Plus, no matter how much I would try to explain what I thought his intent was, I knew it wouldn't come out right. It didn't sound right when I tried to justify it to myself.

What is he gonna try to do next time? Hold your head down in a tub full of water and call it washing your hair? She would take it over the top like that.

Sydney would never try to hurt me purposely. Would he?

Every single day for about a month, I thought about leaving him. I figured I could make it on my own, now that I had a bit of a financial cushion. The only thing was, I wasn't sure that Sydney meant to do it, and if I should be trying to forgive him. I felt a huge wave of guilt even thinking about reneging on my wedding vows. Not to mention the fact that I'd be snatching the boys away from their daddy.

Chapter Eleven

FFCU_QLaRowe: When are you coming up here to see me

FFCU_KChristopher: I could use a trip right now, especially if you giving more money away.

FFCU_QLaRowe: So what did you buy yourself with the money I gave you.

FFCU_KChristopher: Don't even try it. I won that money fair and square. Be glad I shared with you. Anyway, I just picked up a few things. Nothing to write home about.

FFCU_QLaRowe: You should have let me take you shopping. I would have bought you anything you wanted. You deserve to be spoiled, you know. You're a beautiful woman.

FFCU_KChristopher: Thanks.

FFCU_QLaRowe: I don't know why you were all uptight and shy while we were there.

FFCU_KChristopher: Maybe because I'm married.

FFCU_QLaRowe: But you're not happy.

FFCU_KChristopher: Déjà vu. I thought we agreed not to discuss my personal life.

FFCU_QLaRowe: I'm just saying—it's obvious that you're unhappy.

FFCU_KChristopher: And you feel like it's your job to cheer me up?

FFCU_QLaRowe: Somebody's gotta do it. I don't know why it couldn't be me. I think we were vibing pretty well.

FFCU_KChristopher: Even so, I have morals. I'm not sure what kind of morals you have.

FFCU_QLaRowe: I have morals too. Maybe they are not always perfectly aligned, but I do have them. I guess I get a little thrown off when I see a beautiful and sexy woman such as yourself.

FFCU_KChristopher: So I guess you try to sleep with every beautiful and sexy woman you see then, huh? Whether she's married or not.

FFCU_QLaRowe: Oh, that's so low!

FFCU_KChristopher: You're the one that said you get thrown off.

FFCU_QLaRowe: Believe it or not, I'm not attracted to a lot of people. Skin-deep beauty is so superficial. I've tried that and learned quick that a woman has to have more than looks. That is what caught my attention about you.

FFCU_KChristopher: Thanks for saying so.

FFCU_QLaRowe: I'm serious. I don't know what all is going on in your personal life, but

I do know that if your husband is not treating you like a queen, you shouldn't be with him, taking his crap.

FFCU_KChristopher: Every marriage has its ups and downs. If you quit during the downtimes, you didn't have much of a marriage to begin with.

FFCU_QLaRowe: That's true, but you are going through more downs because, from what you told me, you got married for all the wrong reasons in the first place. You got married hoping that your husband would fall in love with you. Do you know that he loves you?

FFCU_KChristopher: Of course he loves me! What kind of question is that?

FFCU_QLaRowe: He might care about you a whole lot, but there's no way he loves you. If he did, you wouldn't be so miserably married. You are only fooling yourself if you think he does. All I know, if you were my wife, you wouldn't have been walking around Vegas looking like you just lost your best friend.

FFCU_KChristopher: I have to go.

FFCU_QLaRowe: Really? I think you're just running from the truth.

FFCU_KChristopher: And I think you're just trying to get a piece of booty.

FFCU_QLaRowe: How am I trying to do that, and I'm a thousand miles away from you? If that was all I was after, I would have pushed the envelope when we were out in Vegas. I'm just telling you what I see. Like I told you before, you can lie to me, but don't lie to yourself.

FFCU_KChristopher: I'm not lying to myself. I told you, I know we have problems.

FFCU_QLaRowe: What do you love about your husband?

I thought for a few seconds and nothing rushed forward to my mind.

FFCU_KChristopher: Since when does someone need a reason to love somebody? My love is unconditional.

FFCU_QLaRowe: Sounds like you can't think of anything.

I hated that Quinton could see right through what I tried to keep hidden.

FFCU_KChristopher: How about he's the father of my kids?

FFCU_QLaRowe: What kind of provider is he? You told me he had no ambition and drive.

FFCU_KChristopher: Our bills are paid.

FFCU_QLaRowe: See, you're scared to answer the question. Why do you keep covering for him?

FFCU_KChristopher: Why are you so concerned about my marriage, Quinton?

FFCU_QLaRowe: Because I think you need someone to talk to and I'm a good listener and I like you, Kareese.

FFCU_KChristopher: ok

FFCU_QLaRowe: Tell me you don't think about me every day.

FFCU_KChristopher: Not really. I'm too busy to not be focused on my work.

FFCU_QLaRowe: Yeah right. You miss me, don't you?

I could never admit to him that I dreamed about playing "show me the rock" with him.

FFCU_KChristopher: I had a great time and I appreciate your friendship, but I can't say that I miss you.

FFCU_QLaRowe: Yes, you do. You are wishing you were with me right now.

FFCU_KChristopher: I gotta go, Quinton.

FFCU_QLaRowe: No, you don't.

FFCU_KChristopher: Really, I do.

FFCU_QLaRowe: I know a runaway when I see one, but I bet you this . . .

FFCU_KChristopher: What's that?

FFCU_QLaRowe: Ain't nothing smoking in your bedroom like it used to be because you're too unhappy.

I couldn't deny it. Sydney could keep his pipe to himself.

FFCU_KChristopher: Bye, Quinton.

As more and more customers filled the lobby, I logged out of IM to focus on my job, but couldn't help but think about what Quinton had said. I did consider the fact that he would have said anything to get whatever I would have put out, but, truthfully, I was pretty unhappy in my marriage. "Unhappy" sounded like too strong a word, though. I wasn't jumping up and down about my current marital situation, but I wasn't ready to admit to unhappiness. Stagnantly married, maybe—definitely not unhappily.

Chapter Twelve

"Keith finally getting married, they set a date." Sydney shook his head and guffawed as he came in the house after being gone all day on a Saturday. He tossed a picture of Keith and his wife-to-be, Stephanie, on the bed for me to see.

"That's great! Good for them," I commented, picking up the photo. It was a beautiful shot of the two of them on the beach; their love for each other was apparent. Standing behind her, Keith hovered over Stephanie, his arms crossing over her stomach. Stephanie's arms reached up and around Keith's neck, pulling his head down to meet hers. The both wore genuine smiles, like they had just heard the funniest joke in the world, except their eyes were fixated on each other instead of an onstage comic. Sydney and I didn't have a single picture that came close to looking like that. "When is the wedding?"

"Couple of months from now. They wanna give everybody enough time to get money for tuxes and dresses and stuff."

"They look so nice," I commented, wishing it were Sydney and me. "Don't you ever wish we had a wedding, Sydney?"

"Not really. People don't need all that just to get married."

"Suppose we were renewing our vows," I tested.

"That's stupid. If you're married, you're married. What do you need to redo or renew your vows for?"

"Some people do it because they didn't get to have a wedding," I planted. "Some just want to remind their spouse of how much they love them by experiencing the commitment that they made all over again. And they are so romantic, and sometimes they rekindle the love that a husband and wife initially had for each other, but maybe it fizzled out over the years."

"I wouldn't do that mess," he dismissed. I sighed.

"Some people want to show each other that in spite of everything they've been through, their love for each other is as strong as the first time they married."

"That's some people; that ain't me." Sydney knew how badly I wanted to have a wedding. I'd only mentioned it like ten other times. I just needed to change the subject before he made me upset.

"Are you in the wedding?"

"Yeah. As his older brother, I'm the best man, you know. He wants Casey and Carlos to be ushers or something too. All three of us will need a tux."

"Oh, that will be nice to get some pictures of the three of you all dressed up." Too bad I wouldn't be in the photos in a sparkly or lacy white gown as the bride. I'd just wear a really nice dress that day and get some pictures of the four of us together. My dress wouldn't be as nice as the bride's gown, but I'd find something that would do the tuxedos justice. Maybe something off-white and tea length so that I wouldn't look like I was trying to upstage the bride, but elegant enough for a nice photo.

"I tried to tell him, he don't know what he's getting himself into."

"What do you mean? I think marriage is a beautiful thing."

"Yeah, if you're married to the right person."

I paused at the thought of what he could have been implying and decided to take the low road. "Do you think Stephanie is not the right woman for him?"

"I don't know. I don't know that much about her."

"So why would you try to talk him out of getting married?" I studied Keith and Stephanie's poses and expressions more intently, envious of their moment of happiness captured by the photographer's flash. "I didn't say I tried to talk him out of it. I'm just saying, it's a whole lot more to it than people think."

"What did you think it was going to be when you married me?"

"I thought you was gonna be cooking a lot more, I'll tell you that much."

"What else?" I asked, offense setting in.

"A whole lot of stuff." He spoke frankly while he undressed. "Cookin', cleanin', sexin', paying bills, letting me be the man of the house."

"The man of the house takes care of his house," I stabbed back, sick of having this conversation.

"And the woman of the house supposed take care of her man, clean up the house and cook on a regular basis. You ain't doing all of that like you need to be."

"I always cook," I defended.

"Please. I ain't talking about that out-the-box Hamburger Helper mess that you call cooking. That ain't cooking. I'm talking about cooking real food. You wanna cook, boil some potatoes, chop up some onions, fry some chicken, make some biscuits, fix some gravy, cook a roast, bake some real macaroni and cheese. *That's* cooking! You need to go take some lessons from my momma," he snapped thoughtlessly. "Ever since you been working at that bank you don't never cook no more."

"If you want your momma's cooking, then you shoulda married your momma, or at least stayed at her house, where she probably ain't mind you sitting on your behind all day instead of working a for-real job!"

"See that's your problem. You don't know how to respect your husband."

"And you call what you're doing respecting me?" I narrowed my eyes and shot invisible daggers his way. "Where you been all day?"

"Out working. Then me and Keith went to get something to eat."

"Working where? Running your mouth to women?"

"If it's keeping a roof over our heads, I don't know why you got a problem with it."

A couple months back, I'd convinced Sydney to move us from the small apartment we were living in when I initially met him into a beautiful three-bedroom brick home I'd found for rent. It was almost $100 more a month than what the apartment complex charged for rent, but Sydney agreed to pay it once I promised to pay all the utility bills. It seemed like a fair compromise since I had a nice salary, and wanted the luxury of living in an actual house with a yard for the boys to play in, an extra bedroom, a dining room and a den, not to mention two full bathrooms. And it made us look like home owners. As much as he complained each month about the extra rent money, Sydney was pleased to live there just as much as I and the boys were.

"So if I start hooking on the streets to keep the bills paid, that's all right with you?" My voice began to escalate, the more I talked. Sydney didn't answer, but I barely gave him a chance. "Why are you allergic to a real job?"

"This right here is what I'm talking about. That's the BS that Keith don't know about—all this mouthin' off and naggin' and fussin' and whatnot. And don't even mention tryna get some after you say 'I do.' He can forget about that! If I woulda known I was gonna be givin' up sex instead of having more sex, I woulda never gotten married in the first place."

"So you married me just for sex?"

"That was a big part of it!" he yelled. "You gonna act like your legs stuck together with damn superglue; then you wonder why I stay gone all the time. What I supposed to do, sit up in the house and beg you for a hot meal and some ass? You must be outta your mind."

Did Sydney just confess in a roundabout way to cheating on me? And now that I thought about it, Sydney had recently purchased new under-wear—one of the number one signs. I didn't think anything of it, because the few pairs he did own were quite raggedy. What I didn't think about was he'd been perfectly content wearing those same tattered drawers for years. Even so, I wasn't ready to accept even the mere thought that Sydney was cheating on me. What was wrong with a man getting new drawers if the ones he had looked like he'd been wearing them since he was fifteen?

It was ridiculous for me to think that Sydney would just come out and straightforwardly admit infidelity, but the words tumbled from my lips just the same. "Are you cheating on me?" I asked incredulously.

"Ain't nobody got time for this mess. I'm 'bout to go," he dodged.

"Go where?" Out of habit, my arms folded across my chest.

"Out."

"Out where?" I countered.

"Don't worry about it." He changed into a pair of jeans and a casual shirt. "I'm going out with my brother," he quickly added.

"You just came from being out with Keith and you're gonna go right back?" I stated, letting him know I didn't believe that for a second, especially after he just pretty much told me he'd started going elsewhere for sex. "Yeah right! Sydney, I promise you, if you leave this house, I will throw all of your clothes in the front yard, spray them with the water hose, stomp them in the ground, and then pour bleach on them, so you better go shopping while you're out."

"You better not touch my clothes," he warned continuing to dress.

"You better not leave this house, then." I planted my hands on my hips, adamant about where I stood.

"I'll be back," he responded, paying me no mind. "Late!"

"Suit yourself."

Sydney grabbed his keys and walked out the door; seconds later, I heard him start the car and back it out of the driveway. I stood in place, fuming and thinking through what just happened and all that he'd said. Throwing all his stuff in the yard would be out of my usual passive character, but I was going to have to show Sydney that I wasn't playing. A part of me was scared to be that bold, but too much of me was motivated to get started and show him that I was a woman of my word and he wasn't just going to walk all over me. Well, he wasn't going to continue to walk all over me, especially after he just pretty much admitted to screwing some other woman.

Before I started pulling his clothes out, I grabbed a bottle of ibuprofen, shook two pills into my hand and walked to the kitchen to get a swig of water. I swallowed the pills, then padded to the laundry room for the bleach. As I pulled the gallon-sized jug from the shelf over the washing machine, I heard Sydney's key in the door. He came in, threw his keys on the couch and stomped to the bedroom. I'm not sure what it was that made him change his mind, but, I swear, had he not come back, he would have been a naked somebody because I was set on destroying every shred of his clothes.

"Back so soon," I mocked.

Sydney looked at me and rolled his eyes as he pulled off his clothes and jumped in the shower. While he was in the bathroom, I lay in bed and admired Keith and Stephanie's picture again. Never had I felt the way Keith and Stephanie looked. It brought tears to my eyes because it fiercely poked at the huge void that I felt Sydney and I had in our marriage. It seemed like every time I turned around, I was crying about something in this raggedy charade of a marriage. I didn't remember there ever being a time when I felt truly happy for more than a day or two. Like any woman getting married, I was happy on the day we exchanged vows, but I don't think I could look back at any specific point in our union and say that we'd happily married. Maybe I'd been happily married, or at least thought I was. Had I been so desperate for a ring and a husband that I'd just accepted any old thing?

No one was around to see my tears or to judge, but I felt embarrassed and disgraced. I felt stupid for not listening to my momma, and not seeing what had been right in front of me all along. I should have never married Sydney, even if we did have a baby together. And now I was stuck in a mess that I'd vowed before God to stay in, until one of us gave up the ghost.

Without a word, Sydney emerged from the bathroom, pulled on a pair of boxers and a T-shirt, turned the light out—although I was using it, and got in bed, turning his back to me.

"Sydney, do you love me?" I asked, laying the picture on my nightstand and settling under the covers.

"I don't feel like talking," he mumbled.

"You don't have to talk. I'm just asking for a yes or no answer."

"I said, I don't feel like talking."

"With all those words you just said, you could have just answered the question." I started counting the words of his last sentence. "That was seven words right there. You could have just as easy said 'yes' or 'no.'"

"You getting on my nerves."

"I just asked you a simple question," I pressed.

"And I told you, I don't feel like talking!" he spat. "You gonna mess around and get your feelings hurt."

I wanted to hear my husband say that he did love me, but now that he'd threatened to hurt my feelings, I somewhat changed my mind. Maybe if he told me "no," I could find the strength within myself, or the excuse I needed, to justify leaving him. I'd be crushed to hear it, but a tiny sliver of my being wanted to hear him say "no" and then we could move forward. Apart.

"You mean to tell me you can't tell your wife that you love her?"

"You didn't want me to go out and I didn't. I came right back home, and now you 'bout to worry me to death. If I didn't love you, I wouldna come back."

"Because you love me, or because you love your clothes?"

"So you just gonna make me talk, huh? I said, I didn't feel like talking, but you gonna twist my arm and just make me talk to you."

"Just tell me you love me, Sydney." I really needed to hear my husband tell me that he loved me. I needed him to turn over and cup my face in his hands and concentrate on my eyes and say, *Kareese, you are my wife, and you are the love of my life. I love you and I'm in love with you. I don't always get it right, and I know I get on your nerves sometimes, but it is not indicative of the love I have in my heart for you. Yes, I love you. I love you, and I love you some more.* Then he would kiss me tenderly, igniting a fire that would have us making gentle, passionate and intimate love, where he'd look in my eyes between our chorus of moaning and repeat to me, again and again, *Yes, I love you, baby, yes.*

Instead, he said, "I wish you would just shut up and let me go to sleep."

This time I turned my back to him, pressed my lips together to keep tearful gasps from reaching his ears. Fresh tears stung in my eyes and I fought back the urge to sniff, not wanting him to know I'd started crying. He was right, my feelings were hurt. The fact that he refused to tell me "yes," pointed more to what his answer was. He just hadn't been bold enough to say it.

Not just hurt, I lay there also feeling incredibly guilty. I felt like a hypocrite. There I was about to throw my husband's stuff out on the street for cheating, when I had no solid proof, when I'd been gyrating with Quinton. Had Sydney been caught in the same situation? There was no way that I would excuse it as not cheating. Even as much as I tried to minimize my behavior, Quinton and I had gotten to the place where we chatted almost every day on instant messenger. Quinton always brought a smile to my face when his chat box popped up. He was one of the reasons why I looked forward to going to work each day. The conversations did get a bit racy, but since he was not even in my same state, I shrugged it off as harmless.

FFCU_QLaRowe: Hey, sweetheart. How's it going this morning?

FFCU_KChristopher: Great—how are you?

FFCU_QLaRowe: Cool. What you got on today?

FFCU_KChristopher: You know me, I'm keeping it hot. A skirt, boots. Something simple, but sexy.

FFCU_QLaRowe: Send me a pic.

FFCU_KChristopher: Nope.

FFCU_QLaRowe: Why are you so scared to do stuff? What harm is a picture gonna do? Geez.

FFCU_KChristopher: I got work to do, don't you?

FFCU_QLaRowe: You need to let me work on you. That's all right. I know where to get pictures from. I look at your picture on Facebook every day.

FFCU_KChristopher: You need to quit it.

FFCU_QLaRowe: You should post some new ones up there. That way you don't have to be a chicken about sending it to me.

He had a point.

FFCU_KChristopher: I might do that later.

FFCU_QLaRowe: Post a back shot.

FFCU_KChristopher: See now you trippin'!

FFCU_QLaRowe: I still remember what you looked like when you were trying to run out of the casino. I purposely stayed a few steps behind you just so I could enjoy the view.

FFCU_KChristopher: What?!

I blushed.

FFCU_QLaRowe: I was like dayyyyyum! I don't mean any disrespect to your husband, but you make a brother wanna leave the one he with and start a new relationship with you. (In my Usher voice)

FFCU_KChristopher: Oh, so you're seeing somebody?

FFCU_QLaRowe: Kinda. But it ain't nothing.

Quinton wasn't my husband or boyfriend, so why did I feel slighted?

FFCU_KChristopher: Mmm-hmm. Were you seeing her when we met?

FFCU_QLaRowe: Not really. We got a hit-or-miss, on-again, off-again thing going. It ain't nothing. Convenience.

FFCU_KChristopher: Just something to do, huh?

FFCU_QLaRowe: Yeah, pretty much.

FFCU_KChristopher: That's probably all you want with me—just something to do.

FFCU_QLaRowe: Not at all. If I had you, I'd be set. You're the real deal.

FFCU_KChristopher: Whatever. You probably say that to every girl you meet.

FFCU_QLaRowe: Not these crazy women in this city. Every other girl you meet dances at some nightclub for a few bucks. Nobody wants something everybody has got a piece of. That's like the whole family taking turns eating with the same fork. It's just nasty.

FFCU_KChristopher: So she dances? I mean strips? LOL

FFCU_QLaRowe: No. She doesn't live here. Besides, she ain't the one, anyway.

FFCU_KChristopher: What makes you say that?

FFCU_QLaRowe: She's not a full package. She got a nice body, but other than that, ain't a whole lot going on.

FFCU_KChristopher: What's a full package to you?

FFCU_QLaRowe: A woman like you. Smart, beautiful, intelligent, busines-minded, sexy body, delicious ta-tas, super soft lips, knows how to work them hips, and can arch that back to meet the stroke. I know you're (unhappily) married and everything, but I get excited just thinking about you.

I swallowed a lump of guilt while I crossed my legs and thought about the sinful pleasure of Quinton, but I was glad I didn't indulge. I couldn't help but think about what he would have felt like, thrusting inside me and loving me down. I bet Quinton was some kinda good too, just judging from the little bit he did give me that night. He knew what to do with his hands; he'd worked them nice and slow, caressing my curves, squeezing slightly at my waist, cupping my chin in his hand, stroking my hair. He did at one point slide his hand inside my pants too, but when his fingers just lightly touched the button and did a tiny flicker, making me catch my breath, I pulled back while I had a chance. It was so quick, it didn't even count. But I did remember what it felt like.

He took up more time in my thoughts than Sydney did, and why shouldn't he? Sydney was a joke compared to Quinton. Sydney didn't take the time to love me right. He'd become more and more sexually selfish, rushing through, thrusting madly, and grabbing; instead of skillfully stroking and embracing me. Methodical instead of lovingly spontaneous, unless, of course, something was in it for him. He always got his, regardless.

FFCU_QLaRowe: I wish I could have held you all night, but I was forced to just suck on my fingers, instead.

And just like that, I was on fire.

FFCU_KChristopher: There're lots of people that have that same wish—join the club.

FFCU_QLaRowe: You are so desirable.

FFCU_KChristopher: And you're very charming, but magic charms don't work here.

FFCU_QLaRowe: You should come up here and see me.

FFCU_KChristopher: No! But thanks, Quinton.

FFCU_QLaRowe: Why not? Just come for a few days—tell your husband it's for business. You know you want to see me.

He couldn't have been more right. I would have loved to go up to Maryland and just spend a few days. Not having sex with him but just out and away from home and having a good time. It would be stupid of me to think that Quinton wouldn't have sexual expectations, though. And, honestly, I did want to have sex with Quinton.

FFCU_KChristopher: I just can't drop what I'm doing and get away like that!

FFCU_QLaRowe: Okay, but you know you missing something good, though, right?

FFCU_KChristopher: Can't miss what you never had.

FFCU_QLaRowe: You've had enough to know that it's good.

FFCU_KChristopher: Yeah, but all that's good ain't good for you.

FFCU_QLaRowe: Girl, I'm like a glass of milk—I do a body good.

FFCU_KChristopher: I'm lactose intoler-
ant. LOL!

FFCU_QLaRowe: If you bounce up and
down on this pogo stick, I promise you,
you'd be making a trip up here twice a
month to get some more. You'd be on a
biweekly subscription.

The more Quinton teased and flirted, the
hotter and wetter I got.

FFCU_KChristopher: I'm not coming up
there, Quinton.

FFCU_QLaRowe: Don't cheat yourself,
treat yourself, baby girl. Tell me you don't at
least wanna try it out.

FFCU_KChristopher: I don't wanna try it
out.

FFCU_QLaRowe: Liar. I bet your panties are soaking wet right now—tell me the
truth—they are, aren't they?

My womanhood contracted and released like
crazy, but I wasn't going to admit it.

FFCU_KChristopher: Just because you
let your imagination run like the wind and
control your body parts doesn't mean I can't
control mine.

FFCU_QLaRowe: You know you want
me. You're just scared to say it.

FFCU_KChristopher: Suppose I did say it. What are you gonna do about it?

FFCU_QLaRowe: Come up here and find out.

FFCU_KChristopher: I'm not coming all the way up there and you're playing around!

FFCU_QLaRowe: I'd make it so good to you, you'd be trying to bottle me up and sell me like crack.

FFCU_KChristopher: LOL! LOL!

FFCU_QLaRowe: Stop being scared and come on up here. I'll make it worth your drive and have you calling my name and doing yourself all the way home.

FFCU_KChristopher: I don't have to drive all the way up there for that. I can do that right here in NC on my way home.

FFCU_QLaRowe: Promise that you'll call me when you do, so I can listen in!

I wanted Quinton bad, and had he been anywhere near the Raleigh/Durham area, I would have been somewhere finding out if he was a man of his word. I was so hot and horny that when I got off work, I rushed to Wal-mart and picked up some chicken tenders and potato salad so the boys could feed themselves. I took a quick shower and just lay spread-eagled on the bed waiting for Sydney to come home from wherever he was and work me over. I made sure I was butt naked, turned over and tooted up.

Judging from the moan that immediately escaped his lips when he came into the bedroom, I could tell Sydney was pleasantly surprised. It was well after nine o'clock, although he now worked strictly day hours now.

"Come and get some of this," I cooed, bouncing my butt up and down.

"What done got into you?" Sydney asked, stripping off his clothes.

"I want some of what you got."

"Well, let me give you some of what you want then."

Sydney wasted no time jumping on the bed and pulling up behind me. With one hand, he grabbed firmly at my hinged waist, while the other hand guided his manhood to my honeypot. He worked his way inside and started a smooth, even rhythm.

"Yeah, baby. Like that," I coached, imagining it was Quinton. "Lay that pipe."

"Mmph!" Sydney grunted. "You like that."

"I love it, baby. Put it on me," I purred, winding my hips back to meet his thrusts.

Sydney sped his stroke up, slamming himself against me while I filled his ears with every nasty thing I could think of to heighten the experience.

"Yeah, I like that!" he huffed. "Talk dirty, baby; you gonna make me unload this gun!"

"Not yet," I panted. I drew away from him long enough to turn over on my back. Sydney dived between my legs, slurping and working his tongue like a greedy madman. He was on his A-game, and my thoughts and fantasies of Quinton intensified my sensitivity and reaction. I held Sydney firmly in place, and at the same time, I grinded, bucked and jerked into a full no-holds-barred orgasm, biting my bottom lip to keep from crying out Quinton's name. Heaving and panting for every breath as if it were my last, and unable to take another circling of his tongue, I grabbed desperately for Sydney to come up for air and reenter my body. He complied, locking my legs around his arms and giving me every inch of what I'd asked for.

"Damn, Kareese!" he exclaimed in pleasure, sliding back into my walls. "Unngghh," he grunted, over and over, with every plunge, as he built momentum. "You gone make me . . ." Before he could squeeze out his last high-octave word, he pushed forward a final time, releasing inside me with a groan. He was frozen in place for a solid six seconds before he began to relax in a slow collapse, completely out of breath. It was undoubtedly the best sex we'd had in a long time.

Inside of two minutes, we both had drifted off to sleep, Sydney just seconds before me. We stayed locked into each other until I began to squirm under his weight in discomfort more than an hour later. Feeling me move beneath him, Sydney shifted his weight, withdrew himself, cupping his manhood in his hand, and lifted himself from the bed and headed for the bathroom. He stood at the sink, running water and soaping up for the next few minutes, while I watched in lust, thinking about a second round.

"So what got into you tonight?" he asked, padding back from the bathroom with a washcloth and handing it to me.

"It had been a while since we really got down to business like a husband and wife." I grinned.

He stood looking at me, waiting for me to finish my quick cleanup. "You sure that was it?"

"Why? You didn't enjoy it?"

"I'm not saying I didn't. I'm just wondering what made you all"—he circled his hand in the air, looking for words—"freaky and whatnot."

"I don't know. I just needed some bad."

"Mmm-hmm," he said in an unbelieving tone. "I think it's more to it than that." He walked back to the bathroom, dropped the washcloth in the sink and returned to bed.

There was, but I wasn't fool enough to say it. "Like what?"

"It's something. You just don't come home one day all of a sudden being a freak in the sheets when you ain't been wantin' to do it at all in the past damn year."

"Maybe I realized I needed to start doing better in the sex department and keep my man satisfied at home."

"Yeah, but what made you all of a sudden realize that. I been telling you that for a while now."

"Nothing in particular," I lied, wishing he would just drop it.

"Something done happened," he said suspiciously.

"Nothing happened, Sydney. I see I can't come home and make love to my husband without it being some uncalled-for drama."

"I just want to know who you made love to first before you got home," he accused.

"Why would you think I'm cheating on you, Sydney?"

"'Cause you coming all out the blue with some new mess that you ain't been doing. I been tryna revive that freak in you for I don't know how long."

"So why can't I just be trying something new?"

"Yeah, that's exactly what you doing, but where did you get it from? That's what I want to know. You ain't never just been laying wide open before with your ass all in the air, waiting for me to come home. You ain't been asking for me to put it on you, you ain't been winding it up and throwing it back—but I'm just supposed to believe you just all of a sudden started feeling a little spontaneous and came up with that? You must think you married to a fool."

"I tell you what, then. We will just go back to what we've been doing and that's hardly having sex at all, since you don't appreciate some new spice," I said, attempting to throw him off. "I swear, you can't be happy about nothing. If I don't wanna have sex, you complaining. If I wanna have sex, you complaining about that too."

"I don't know who you done started screwin' at that bank, but when I find out, I'ma deal with it."

Chapter Thirteen

Quinton wasn't logged on yet, so I started my chat session with Yalisa, instead.

FFCU_KChristopher: Sydney thinks I'm cheating on him.

FFCU_YKnight: When has Sydney not thought that? He's been thinking that ever since you married him.

FFCU_KChristopher: I know, right?

FFCU_YKnight: What is making him think that this time?

FFCU_KChristopher: 'Cause he stupid

FFCU_YKnight: Well, that ain't nothing new, no offense, but something had to happen for him to all of a sudden start thinking that.

FFCU_KChristopher: It's really kinda crazy. I decided to spice it up in the bedroom, but then he talking 'bout, where I get that from.

FFCU_YKnight: Oh, you tried some new tricks on him?

FFCU_KChristopher: It wasn't even tricks. It was just a little bit hotter than normal.

FFCU_YKnight: Sydney need to stop trippin' and go with the flow.

FFCU_KChristopher: Girl, I get tired of having to fight with him at every turn.

FFCU_YKnight: That's why I'm glad I'm not married.

FFCU_KChristopher: From what I've shared with you, do you think I'm unhappily married?

FFCU_YKnight: What makes you ask that?

FFCU_KChristopher: I'm just curious about what you think.

FFCU_YKnight: I think you and Sydney have some issues that need to be worked through.

FFCU_KChristopher: Like what?

FFCU_YKnight: Like him not doing his best to take care of his family.

FFCU_YKnight: Like how he doesn't treat you the way you want to be treated.

FFCU_YKnight: Like how he almost makes you beg for stuff when he's sitting on a ton of money that he thinks you don't know about.

FFCU_KChristopher: Ouch!

FFCU_YKnight: I'm just saying. You asked.

FFCU_KChristopher: I know.

FFCU_YKnight: Why? What's going on?

FFCU_KChristopher: I'm just thinking about our marriage and what I'm getting out of it.

FFCU_YKnight: You're a better woman than I am.

FFCU_KChristopher: What makes you say that?

FFCU_YKnight: Because I wouldn't be putting up with that mess you be going through. Uh-uh, that couldn't be me.

FFCU_KChristopher: Well, he is my husband and I did make vows to stick with him for better or for worse.

FFCU_YKnight: Then it doesn't matter what I think, whatever is important to you is what matters.

FFCU_KChristopher: I talked to Quinton today.

FFCU_YKnight: About what?

FFCU_KChristopher: Nothing, really. We've just kinda kept in contact ever since we hung out in Vegas.

FFCU_YKnight: YOU WENT OUT WITH HIM??? WHY DIDN'T YOU CALL AND TELL ME???

FFCU_KChristopher: Not went out—hung out. There's a difference. I don't go out with other people.

FFCU_YKnight: Hung out—went out—same thing.

FFCU_KChristopher: No, it isn't.
FFCU_YKnight: Were y'all at work, or did you go to lunch during work hours or dinner after hours?

I hesitated. Dinner sounded like a date, and a date was definitely "go out," not "hang out."

FFCU_YKnight: Well? Which one?
FFCU_KChristopher: Hold on a minute, I got a customer.

It was a lie, but I couldn't tell Yalisa that I, as a married woman, had gone out on a date with another man. Especially the way things escalated, and his lips ended up inside my bra, and his hand inside my panties. If I admitted to dinner, I'd end up oversharing, and I didn't need to let that cat out of the bag. And if it did get out, it would be stupid to put it in a form that could be printed or forwarded. If I did tell her, which I wasn't, it would have to be face-to-face.

Ignoring my computer was easier than saying anything further. I changed my chat availability to "busy" and then processed some credit apps that were pending. I had no business leisurely chatting at work anyway. I hoped that by the time Yalisa and I talked again, the conversation would be long forgotten.

Why did I feel so guilty? Really, nothing happened between me and Quinton. It was just dinner . . . and let's not forget I stormed out. It was just the casino; there were a million other people there. And it was . . . it was . . . Well, let me scratch off what it wasn't. It wasn't sex. If it wasn't sex, then it wasn't cheating, and if it wasn't cheating, then I was okay. As long as I kept it to myself.

I was going to go home and make love to Sydney real good again tonight. Maybe if I got buck wild like I did before, he would be less suspecting about me cheating on him. And I wasn't cheating. Chatting wasn't cheating. It was just empty words that Quinton didn't even mean. If Quinton came to town right now and I met him down at the Holiday Inn, pulled my panties off, and rode him like a rodeo bull; he would forget all about me before morning. He would have accomplished his mission of getting a dip in my pool.

Sydney did have a point, though. Had I not been thinking about Quinton, I probably wouldn't have been even remotely interested in sex. I was tired of having that regular stuff that was over in ten minutes just so Sydney could get a good night's sleep. After about a year or so of that, I just didn't want to do it as much anymore. It was a chore. I think over the years, it just got kinda boring and I lost interest, along with his lack of affection and my chipped tooth.

Sometimes Sydney made me be interested, fondling me whether I wanted him to or not. Even if I pretended to be too sleepy or just plain asleep, he would fondle incessantly until I finally rolled over onto my back to allow him entry. I can't say that I didn't enjoy it; it was just the "getting there" that became more and more of a challenge for me. There were even times when my mind wanted to do it, but before my mind could convince my body, my mind had changed itself. Then there was the time he did something so mean and cruel, that I swore I would never have sex with him again.

One night just as I begin to drift off to sleep, Sydney wanted to talk about our sex life.

"Why don't you want to have sex with me?"

I pushed a sigh into my pillow and mumbled a confused "What?"

"Why don't you want to have sex with me?" he said again.

"I don't know what you're talking about, Sydney," I uttered, keeping my back to him. "I'm just tired."

There was silence for a couple of minutes before he called out my name.

"Kareese." When I didn't answer, he tapped me hard on the shoulder four times. "Kareese!"

"What!" I snapped. "Can't you see I'm asleep?"

"I wanna know why you don't want to have sex with your husband," he said more aggressively than he had before.

"I told you, I'm tired!" My tone was full of irritation. "What do you want to do—make love to a rag doll?"

"Why you tired every single night?"

"Because there's stuff to do every single night!" I barked, flipping over onto my back. "You act like you don't know how to work the damn stove, when you get off work, or run the vacuum cleaner! You expect me to run around this house like Alice, the Brady Bunch's maid, and just open up my legs for you whenever you get hard. You ain't married to a robot."

"It don't seem like I'm married at all, since I can't get no sex from my wife," he spat out.

"Maybe *you're* the reason why you can't get no sex! Did you ever think of that? When is the last time you tried to set a mood around here instead of just hopping in the bed like a gorilla wanting to mate? You think you can just talk to me any kind of way and do whatever you wanna do and I'm just supposed to be okay with you just having your way with my body? Are you crazy?" By now, I was fully awake. "You come up in here all hours of the night, from who knows where, half pay the bills, don't wanna do jack-smack in the house besides sit up and watch TV, but then you want me to be doing backbends and cartwheels over some sex? You didn't even get me nothing for my birthday!"

"I'm not obligated to get you something for your birthday, but you damn sure are obligated to give me some ass when I want it! If I gotta start buying ass, then I might as well get me a ho who ain't too tired to do the damn job, and do it right!"

"And when you find her, bring her home to cook your dinner, keep your house clean, and raise your kids!" I screamed in anger. "And maybe I can get some sleep around here so I can get up in the morning, go to work and pay the bills, 'cause you sure as hell ain't doing a good job of it! And *maybe* that's why you can't get none! Maybe *that's* the answer to your question!"

We both stared at each other through the darkness for several seconds. My eyebrows were knitted tightly together and Sydney looking a bit shocked and hurt. Not saying another word, he slowly turned his back, lay against his pillow, and pulled the covers up over his shoulder.

I lay awake for probably twenty more minutes, replaying the two-minute verbal exchange in my head. What did he think I was, a 7-Eleven store? Just come in anytime, get what you want and go on about your business? Please!

The next evening when I came in from work, I smelled food as soon as I cracked the door, which not only made my eyebrows shoot up, but it also brought a smile to my face. Kem's twangy voice filled the house from the stereo system, and the living room had been tidied and vacuumed. I walked in the kitchen to find my husband pulling a meat loaf out of the oven; there was also a bowl of mashed potatoes centered on the stove and a dish filled with green bean casserole. Carlos and Casey were collectively mixing some instant ice tea, one did the pouring and the other did the stirring.

"Hey, Ma!" the boys chimed with smiles.

"Hey," I answered, completely surprised and impressed. "Wow!"

"Hey, babe," Sydney said, glancing over his shoulder, then back at his dinner. "Dinner will be ready in a few more minutes." Pulling the oven mitt from his hand, he approached me and swept his lips across mine. "Go 'head in the dining room. We'll be in there in a minute."

Carlos and Casey set plates, forks, napkins, and glasses filled with ice on the table, while Sydney brought in the food, setting each dish on trivets. It was the first time in a while that we all sat down and ate together as a family. We held hands; Sydney led the grace, then fixed my plate.

"How was your workday?" he asked.

I gave a half smile and shrugged. "Work was work, that's why they call it work."

"Nothing exciting happened?"

"Not really, same stuff, different day." The meat loaf was delectable. I'd never had green bean casserole before, so I looked at it with a single lifted brow, but surprisingly, it was delicious, as were the potatoes and buttered rolls. "So what brought all this on?" I waved my fork over my plate.

"I heard what you had to say." He bobbed his head a little as he took in a mouthful of food. "Thought I'd try listening."

Shucks. This meant he was going to expect sex. I had to start psyching my mind up so I would be in the mood later on, but then Sydney did something that completely caught me off guard and had me all caught up.

After dinner, while the boys washed the dishes, he took me by my hand to the den, where he'd placed a single red rose and a long velvet black box on the coffee table. It had been so long since I'd gotten a romantic gesture from him, I gasped.

"I'm sorry I didn't acknowledge your birthday," he whispered, pulling me into his arms and beginning a slow drag dance, subtly grinding his hips into mine. His hands slipped below my waistline and cupped my behind, while he nuzzled his face into my neck, making me giggle. He danced me over to the table, then handed me the box, which held a gleaming tennis bracelet in sterling silver.

"Thank you, Sydney!" I gushed as he fastened it around my wrist.

"You're welcome." He landed his lips on mine and slowly circled his tongue, continuing his buildup with more pronounced gyrations. I melted like butter to his touch and my body prepared itself for a long, sultry night of love-making.

We danced a while longer, if it could be called dancing, then began our trek to our bedroom. Fully engaged, energized and ready, there wasn't a tired bone in my body, and Sydney did not disappoint. I'd truly forgotten just how wonderful good lovemaking could be. I mean, I was tugging the sheets, squeezing the pillows and reaching for things that weren't even there. Sydney was turning me inside out! By the time we were done, I was completely exhausted but very exhilarated at the same time.

Sydney held me tightly from behind, letting me rest my head on his forearm rather than on the pillow. And there we lay, spooning until morning.

I was still giddy when the sun came up, although Sydney had long left for work. As I lathered up in the shower, my skin tingled, reminding me of what my husband had put on me just a few hours before.

"Mmph, mmph, mmph!" I reminiscently moaned. "I think my mojo is back!"

Feeling sexy, I put on the sexiest panties and push-up bra set I owned, which I had to dig out of the very back of my drawer. I pulled on my panty hose and a gray sweater dress, which flirtatiously hugged my every curve. I pushed silver hoops through my ears, draped my neck with a long silver necklace, then searched the sheets and the bedside for my new bracelet, but couldn't find it. I didn't have time to do a full shake-the-sheets-out search. It was okay, though; it wasn't enough to wreck the mood. I was feeling so good, I even put on makeup, and sprung for a pair of pumps instead of the flats I usually wore to work.

All day long, I sang Jill Scott's "The Way" and "Whatever." I sent him all kinds of nasty, freaky, sexual text messages all day, feeling my body pulse, flinch and flex beneath my dress.

I couldn't drive home fast enough to start an encore performance, even if no one had thought enough to start dinner. I'd get my groove on, then fix something quick and easy for the kids. This time when I walked in, I found Sydney sitting in the den watching ESPN. With one hand on my hip and the other crossed over my head, and my freshly glossed lips puckered out seductively, I paraded around the room, vying for his attention. When he didn't budge or even look my way, I sauntered over to him and slowly sat in his lap.

"Watch out now! The game is on," he said, nudging me away.

"Can't you watch it later?" I whined, slipping my hand inside his pants.

"Stop." He pulled my hand from his manhood and tossed it aside.

"Come on, baby," I purred. "I've been wanting you all day."

"Whatever. I see what I gotta do to get a piece 'round here. Somebody gotta trick your ass."

His words had the impact of a swift kick to my stomach and knocked the wind straight out of me, stopping me dead in my tracks. I studied his face for any sign of teasing, but there was none. Instantly tears began to burn in my eyes. Sydney had used me. What I thought was love and passion was all a manipulative game.

"And by the way, I took that bracelet back to the store."

I'd been completely humiliated, manipulated and played. I'd actually thought that we'd had a beautiful and passionate night of lovemaking, but it had all been some game? Every time I thought about it, I couldn't help but break out in tears, regardless of where I was—work, driving, home, wherever. And not just at the sex part, but the whole setup of the evening. The dinner, the music, the gifts, even involving Casey and Carlos. The whole thing just hurt so bad. And then he had the nerve to tell me about it? He could have at least kept his tricks to himself, but the fact that he didn't just showed me what little regard he had for my feelings.

I made up my mind, right then and there, that my marriage was not going to make it. I just had to find a way out. I now loathed and despised Sydney. Needless to say, there was no way I could make myself sexually vulnerable to him again. As sexy as I'd felt the day before, I woke up the next morning feeling like my self-esteem had been thoroughly shattered. It didn't help that I was already battling my weight and was extremely self-conscious about my figure. I stood before a full-length mirror just after my shower and took a look at the damage to my body from carrying a pair of ten-pound babies, not exactly eating right and simple age and gravity. There were bulges and dimples everywhere, although I was only a size twelve. Not only were my breasts no longer firm and bouncy, but now flat and elongated from breast-feeding both boys, and severe stretch marks were along my belly, upper thighs, sides and behind. My body looked a total mess. How was it that these celebrities were able to pop out babies and look like nothing ever happened? I know they had money for boob jobs and liposuction, but none of them ever got a stretch mark? What about noncelebrities? Just everyday people, like my coworker Darhice, who had twice as many kids as I did but still had a body of a nineteen-year-old model. It just wasn't fair. Even if I worked out, what was I gonna do with all this loose skin just above my pubic hairline. That wasn't going anywhere.

The more I looked at myself, the more depressed I became, and the angrier I got with every *Essence* magazine I owned that showcased beautiful, unblemished black women in provocative poses. Even if the article was about something like weight, or diabetes, or fibroids, or child bearing, the woman always had a near-perfect body. A size-four perfect body, a size-eight perfect body, a size-sixteen perfect body. Was I the only person life had happened to?

I shamefully pulled away from the mirror, unable to stand the sight of myself anymore; then I dragged myself to my dresser, pulled on a plain pair of underwear and a bra that didn't match, threw on a loose-fitting sweater twinset and a pair of plain black slacks. Taking the scarf from around my head, I brushed my hair into a simple style and pushed it out of my face with a headband, smeared on some regular lip balm and headed for the door.

Sydney and I had only had sex one other time since then, but it was very obligatory on my part. None of my body was turned on, and all I could do was wish that Sydney would hurry up. While he did kiss my neck and shoulders a few times, there was nothing passionate about his actions. He was rough and jerky, almost robotic, only seeking a release. He couldn't come quick enough; and when he did, he rolled off me and fell sound asleep. I, on the other hand, lay awake, feeling emptier than I'd ever had in my entire life.

So I could completely understand how my coming home wet and ready took him by surprise. He better be glad that Quinton kept my mental fire lit, else he wouldn't get that. As long as I could think about Quinton, while I had sex with Sydney, I could keep the spice going.

Before I went home, I struck up a conversation with Quinton to get my juices flowing.

FFCU_KChristoper: Hey.
FFCU_QLaRowe: Hey.
FFCU_KChristoper: You busy?
FFCU_QLaRowe: A little. What's up?
FFCU_KChristoper: Nothing. I was just going to say bye before I left.
FFCU_QLaRowe: Done so soon?
FFCU_KChristoper: Yep.

FFCU_QLaRowe: Must be nice.

FFCU_KChristoper: Yep.

FFCU_QLaRowe: I will be here for at least two more hours.

FFCU_KChristoper: That's too bad. What are you working on?

FFCU_QLaRowe: Some end-of-the-month reports.

This was going a little slower than I wanted. I had to think of a way to turn up the heat.

FFCU_KChristoper: I'm going home to take a nice long soak in the tub.

FFCU_QLaRowe: See, now why you had to say all that?

FFCU_KChristoper: What? I'm just sharing.

FFCU_QLaRowe: You tryna be funny.

FFCU_KChristoper: No, not at all. Just had a long day and I'm looking forward to some me time in the tub.

FFCU_QLaRowe: Want me to come wash your back?

I smiled.

FFCU_KChristoper: Would you come if I asked you to?

FFCU_QLaRowe: I'd leave work right now and hop the next plane!

FFCU_KChristoper: Yeah right.

FFCU_QLaRowe: I'm serious—I'd be down there in a heartbeat if you didn't play so much.

FFCU_KChristoper: What do you mean?

FFCU_QLaRowe: You know what I mean. Last time I saw you, you got me all excited for no good reason.

FFCU_KChristoper: No—YOU got you all excited for no good reason!

FFCU_QLaRowe: Tell me you weren't turned on—never mind, you don't even have to say it.

FFCU_KChristoper: Ain't nothing to be said.

FFCU_QLaRowe: I bet I could get you to say a whole lot if I was there right now.

FFCU_KChristoper: Oh yeah? Like what?

FFCU_QLaRowe: Girl, I'd have you screaming my name so loud, you wouldn't be able to talk the next day.

FFCU_KChristoper: And just how would you do that?

FFCU_QLaRowe: I'd give you a few inches of this soul pole.

FFCU_KChristoper: LOL! What is that?

FFCU_QLaRowe: I can show you better than I can tell you.

FFCU_KChristoper: Yeah, you would definitely have to show me that one. That's something I ain't never heard of before.

FFCU_QLaRowe: It will change your life and have you begging for more.

FFCU_KChristoper: Every man thinks that.

FFCU_QLaRowe: Like I said, I can show you better than I can tell you.

FFCU_KChristoper: Well, come on down here, then. You got about an hour before I get naked and get in the tub.

FFCU_QLaRowe: Mmm! Don't tease me like that, girl. If I come all the way down there, what you gonna give me?

FFCU_KChristoper: Depends on what you want. I'll take you to get something to eat.

FFCU_QLaRowe: Oh, I definitely want something to eat, but it ain't gonna be at no restaurant.

FFCU_KChristoper: What you got in mind, then?

FFCU_QLaRowe: You know how to feed a man?

FFCU_KChristoper: It depends on what you want to eat.

FFCU_QLaRowe: You ever had a Cadbury chocolate egg? It's like smooth brown chocolate on the outside, but the inside is this thick, supersweet and gooey stuff inside. You got anything like that?

FFCU_KChristoper: I sure do.

FFCU_QLaRowe: Can I get some of it if I come down there?

FFCU_KChristoper: I don't know. What am I gonna get in return?

FFCU_QLaRowe: You can get anything you want, sweetheart. I'll take you on a ride you will never forget.

FFCU_KChristoper: Is that right?

FFCU_QLaRowe: I got a 100% satisfaction rating.

FFCU_KChristoper: By how many reviewers?

FFCU_QLaRowe: Don't worry about all that, just find out what all the hype is about.

Quinton was boring me. He wasn't getting down and dirty, like I needed. I needed him to say a few magic words to get my hotbox hot and my wet spot wet. He was talking too slow.

FFCU_KChristoper: Well, I'll talk to you later. Have a good night.

I deleted the conversation and clicked off chat before leaving. I was just going to have to drum a hot fantasy up in my head before I got home, or read a Zane book or something. I did have a couple stashed somewhere in the house, but they couldn't be that lost.

I cooked dinner, checked homework, and read a few chapters; entertaining myself until Sydney dragged his hips home. Again we made love like wild animals, with me thinking about Quinton giving me the ride of my life. It was amazing how much my sex life changed just by mentally changing men.

When we were done, I had to silently repent for mentally cheating on my husband: *Lord, I know you are not pleased with me flirting around with Quinton. I know if you cheat in your mind, it's the same as cheating for real and I ask your forgiveness for cheating on Sydney.*

I wanted to tag on that Sydney halfway deserved it, but I had to remember that I was talking to God and not to Yalisa or just any old body. I did kinda feel that Sydney drove me to my flirting and carrying on, though.

Help me to stop, Lord. I know I can't expect my marriage to get better if I'm engaging in sin. But suppose Sydney doesn't really love me at all? You've heard some of the things he's said to me. I know that doesn't make my behavior right, but it sure opened the door.

I just need your help, Lord, because I don't want to be a cheater. If I keep playing around with Quinton, I can already see that I'm going to end up somewhere in the act, and I really don't want that. Help us to rekindle our love for each other, Lord. Amen.

Chapter Fourteen

The next couple of months were silent and unbearable for me, but I couldn't find a good angle to walk out on, especially because I'd been using Sydney to fulfill my Quinton fantasies. I had avoided chatting with Quinton to try to stop my mental adultery. But if Sydney and I weren't making the bed squeak, we had nothing to say to each other. Sydney had started spending a ton of time with some woman named Suzetta. He claimed she was the woman who had enrolled him in his latest and greatest business venture, so it was necessary that he kept in close contact with her to make sure he was successful.

Whatever.

Every time I turned around, he was on the phone with Suzetta; he was e-mailing Suzetta; he had to go set up some business meeting for new prospects with Suzetta. I did go to one of the so-called business meetings just to check this Suzetta chick out.

It was a Friday night, and as soon as I got in from work, Sydney was trying to head out the door.

"Where're you going?" I asked, watching him straightening his collar. He was dressed in tan slacks and a black polo shirt. He slipped his arms into a brown-and-black houndstooth sport jacket; his camel-colored loafers had been shined. Sydney had always carried himself well, but he looked a little extra groomed tonight.

"To a business mixer," he answered, brushing past me and picking up the leather Kenneth Cole laptop bag I'd purchased for him a few Christmases back when I was trying to be more supportive of his ventures.

"What kind of business mixer?" His hair cut was fresh and his cologne was enthralling. Like he was going somewhere else, for something else.

"Kareese, you know what I'm tryna do, so don't start trippin'." He placed a mint in his mouth and dug in his pocket for his car keys.

"Where is it going to be?" I asked, folding my arms across my chest.

"The Marriott."

"Well, I'm going with you," I asserted.

"I'm 'bout to leave right now and the kids ain't ate yet." He stopped to face me with an expression that let me know that he wasn't trying to be escorted by his wife.

"That's fine. They won't die if they miss a meal." I turned toward the dining-room table, where the boys were still working on homework. "Carlos, Casey—let's go."

"Where you gonna take them?" he asked.

"They're coming with us."

"That ain't gonna work. Y'all 'bout to mess me up, and this is my money." Sydney had a scowl on his face as he stepped quickly toward the door.

"I've been to these things before and I've seen kids there." He wasn't going anywhere without me tonight. Especially to spend the evening with some heifer named Suzetta.

"I don't need them to be there. I'm tryna get some business done, and kids and business don't mix. You need to stay here with them," he ordered. "They not even finished with their homework."

"They can bring their homework with them. It ain't like they're gonna be wild and running around the place. They know how to sit still and be quiet." Casey and Carlos joined us at the door.

"Y'all gone back in there and finish your homework," Sydney said, looking at them both. Without questioning, the boys turned around and headed back to the table.

"Why we can't go, Sydney?" I asked suspiciously.

"I told you. They ain't ate, and their home-work ain't done. Stay home and be a mother for a change!" he shot back at me. He opened the door and slammed it behind him before I could say another word. I opened it and yelled behind him.

"What are you trying to say? I'm not a good mother to my children? You got some nerve!"

Sydney didn't break his stride as he got into the car and backed out of the driveway faster than a convenience-store thief being chased by a cop. I was pissed but determined to find out where he was going and what Suzetta looked like.

"Let's go, y'all," I said a second time to my sons, who were glad to ditch their homework for a car ride. "We'll stop by McDonald's and pick up something."

"Yay!" they cheered in unison, then started their own specialized McDonald's chant.

I whipped the car into the drive-through line, then sped straight to the Raleigh Marriott City Center.

"Help me find your daddy's car," I instructed the boys, pulling into the parking lot and circling the lot. Carlos took one side and Casey scanned the other as I drove, row by row, through the lot. I didn't see Sydney's vehicle, however. I had to bite my tongue, wanting to cuss but not wanting the boys to hear me.

"Y'all stay here for a minute." With the car parked right at the hotel's main entrance, I walked inside to check the conference rooms, just in case the three of us couldn't see his car in the dark, but sure enough he wasn't there.

"Can I help you, ma'am?" a young lady standing behind the registration desk called out to me, noticing my random wandering through their facility.

"Where is your next closest location? I was looking for a business meeting tonight and I thought it was here."

"We don't have anything going on here tonight, but it maybe at our Crabtree Valley location." She pulled a slip of paper from a box and jotted the address down for me. "Do you need directions?"

"Just the address will be fine."

"It's only about ten minutes away. Good luck," she added, handing me the paper.

"Thanks." Within minutes I was headed down 401 on a mission. This time, when we scanned the lot, we did spot Sydney's car. I had Carlos and Casey wait on a sofa in the hallway as I entered the rented ballroom and visually zoomed across heads looking for my husband. There was a projector set up displaying a company logo against a screen, and several people were moseying around the room, as if they hadn't gotten started yet. I didn't see Sydney right away because he'd been stooping at eye level to a table looking like he was sorting some papers. Beside him stood a slim woman, who had to be six feet tall, with the deepest, darkest complexion I'd ever seen in my life. Her skin tone contrasted to her stark white teeth, which were on prominent display. Her hair was cut and brushed into a neat Caesar, and hanging diamonds flanked her strong facial features. She wore a pair of black slacks, which showcased a round, firm butt, and a sparkling silver knit top embellished with brilliant rhinestones, which caught and reflected every glimmer of light in the room. She shone so brightly she almost looked like a Christmas tree. As if she needed the additional height, she wore four-inch black stilettos. I had to give it to her—the woman was gorgeous, stylish, classy, polished, and professional.

Sydney rose to his feet and, for a quick moment, slipped his hand casually around her waist with one hand and pointed toward the papers with the other. She nodded with understanding, rested her hand on his shoulder, and smiled.

Sucking my stomach in and tugging at my sweater, which was a bit too snug, I pasted a fake smile on my face and walked to the front of the room, where they both stood.

"Hey," I greeted, bouncing my eyes back and forth between my husband and this woman.

"Hello!" she responded, smiling welcomingly, and reached for me to shake my hand. "I'm Suzetta, and you are?"

"Kareese. I'm Sydney's wife."

"Oh," she said, looking quickly at Sydney. "I didn't realize you had a better half. It's nice to meet you."

That's what I thought.

Sydney had his hand conveniently pushed into his pants pocket, hiding the fact that he'd taken off his ring. My quick glance at Suzetta's hand revealed that she was single.

"Likewise," I returned.

"So what do you think of the business?" she asked.

"Well, Sydney has tried so many, it's difficult for me to keep them all straight. He's always looking for the next big thing," I answered, not caring that Sydney scowled with embarrassment.

"Really?"

"Oh yeah! He's been trying to be successful at this for years. But I don't think he's putting any true effort in it. How's his downline looking?"

"Sometimes it takes a little time to get started and see the results that are necessary, but I tell everyone in my downline, consistency is key and 'success' only comes before 'work' in the dictionary. Excuse me for just a minute," Suzetta said, stepping away, discerning that there was definitely some negative energy between me and Sydney.

"Why are you here, Kareese?"

"Oh, I just wanted to see you at work, that's all."

"You need to take the kids home."

"No, I don't. I'ma stay here and just check out things."

I turned on my heels and sat midway in the room, flanked now by Casey and Carlos, whom I had called in from the hallway. I counted the number of women who came up and greeted Sydney with a hug that was a bit too close, and a tad too long for my liking, or a kiss on his cheek. Every one of them was slim, curvaceous and attractive. I said nothing, but saw how nervous Sydney seemed to be.

Once the presentation started, Sydney moved to the door like he was an usher at church, shaking people's hands as they came in, and pointing them toward chairs. He disappeared with a young lady for several minutes, but he made his way back before I got up to find out where he'd disappeared to. The actual presentation was pretty boring, but watching my husband flounder around and try to avoid the women he probably flirted with, at least once a week, was entertaining.

"And now I'm going to have someone come up who is just absolutely blowing it up in this business. He's taking his efforts to another level and is just on fire with his strategies that have got him out of the gates and making money like crazy!

"He's the strongest leg on my team, and I am so glad to have him as one of my leaders," Suzetta declared. "Sydney Christopher, come on up here and let us glean from your wisdom."

What? What money is Sydney making? Sydney cut his eyes over at me but looked away just as quickly.

Let him tell it, and he was still trying to find the right people and still trying to get things off the ground. But let this woman tell it, and he's the strongest person on her team and making money. I folded my arms across my chest and listened intently.

"First I want to welcome y'all to a fantastic opportunity tonight, and tell you that you have the power to change your life. I want to thank my wife for coming out here tonight. She normally stays home with the boys, but she's here this evening. So I gotta give my baby a shout-out."

Sydney was smooth with his cover-up. That was his way of telling all his chickenheads to back off for at least tonight. I could feel several pairs of eyes stare in my direction.

"If you are looking for a great business to get started with and to change your life, I'm telling you right now, this is it. I know what some of y'all are thinking. 'Well, Sydney, I tried this and I tried that, but they didn't work for me.' Well, let me just tell you, this ain't that!" There were a few whoops and claps from the audience, co-signing on what he'd just said.

"My wife and I decided to come into this business after we were approached by Ms. Suzetta Franklin one night out at dinner."

Sydney was up there lying his butt off. I'd never met Suzetta before in my life. Sydney might have gone out to dinner with her behind my back, but we hadn't met her together.

"She just kinda stopped by our table, and she had on these real fly shoes." He chuckled, looking over at Suzetta, who'd begun to giggle. "I didn't say nothing to my wife. . . ."

Because I wasn't there, but anyway.

"But I was like, man, that lady got on some bad shoes! I mean they was like . . ." Sydney motioned with his hands what his mouth couldn't describe, but ultimately he said nothing. "They was just real nice, and I wanted to get my wife a pair because her birthday was coming up. So I had approached her and was like, 'Excuse me, miss, that's some real nice footwear you got on.' And I'ma tell y'all, this woman right here? She don't mess around! That is all she needed me to say to her. She whipped our her business card and an application so quick, I didn't have no choice but to start filling out the paperwork!" The crowd laughed. "Now, at first, I was fillin' it out kinda slow, right? Because, I mean, I didn't wanna be selling no ladies' shoes and stuff, but then when Suzetta started tell me how much money she made just by walking around in her own shoes, I started writing faster." There were more chuckles from the crowd. "Then I was like, how I'ma set up here and tell my wife that she married to Al Bundy from the *Married with Children* show."

It would be better than telling your wife that all you want to do is work fast food.

"But then Suzetta showed me about five of her paychecks. After that, it was a wrap! She told me how much it was to get started, and I told her, 'Hold on, I'm going to the ATM. I'll be right back.' I ain't never drove to the bank so fast in my life. Now, all of us know women like to look fly and they love them some shoes. Am I right?"

"That's right!" a woman behind me shouted like we were in an old-timey church testimony service.

"And everybody wears shoes, right? Look at the person sitting next to you and see if they got some shoes on their feet. If they do, I want you to tell them, 'This business is for you.'" The woman beside me complied with Sydney's directions. "Now, if you see anybody who don't have any shoes on, I want you to look at them and say this business is *definitely* for you!" The group erupted with laughter again. "Now, Suzetta is gonna come back and show you how you can start making money tonight in this business, and then when she is done, if you ready to get started, make sure you talk to the person who invited you out here tonight so we can get you making money right away."

So how much money had Sydney made sitting on the floor and fitting women's feet into a variety of shoes? I was going to have to steal one of his bank statements again and find out what was really going on. According to him, the budget was tighter than a high-school snare drum.

I lingered after the meeting and again watched as a crowd of women flocked around my husband, some modestly dressed and others dressed like stank hoochies who were looking like they were about to be out on the stroll. Now that it was time to collect money or whatever it was he was doing, he let those women hang on him like clothes in a closet. He seemed less nervous but still looked around to see just how closely I watched.

I did end up leaving before they finished for the night and walked away with two things: Sydney was making a lot more money than he pretended, and Sydney was presenting himself as a single and available man.

I had no solid proof, but I fully believed Sydney was cheating on me. And I've heard it said that if you think your man is cheating, he's cheating. It wasn't my style to hound him on his cell phone. I pretty much only called if I needed something. And with me working so many hours, a lot of times I was too consumed with trying to excel at work than chase and keep up with Sydney. I probably made it so easy for him to start cheating.

I should have started following him around, but I just never had the energy or desire to do that, nor would I have known where to go to start spying on him. I could see now how people say, "You see what you want to see."

When he came in that night, I had questions, of course.

"So how much money do you actually make, Sydney?"

"I ain't making nothing," he commented. "You just gotta say that stuff to hype people up."

Knowing I wouldn't get the truth out of Sydney, even if I tortured him with a hot poker, I left it alone. I would just have to sneak his next bank statement.

Chapter Fifteen

It was Keith and Stephanie's wedding day, and despite our challenges and setbacks, I had awoken with high expectations. I had this lofty, romantic fantasy of falling in love with my husband all over again, sparked from seeing this new union come together. Instead, all I felt was isolated. Sydney and the boys had to be at the church, two hours before the wedding actually started, to help his brother do groomsman stuff. Instead of us arriving as a couple, it was just me showing up like an abandoned spinster. I never even saw my husband until he entered the sanctuary from a side entrance, went to the front of the aisle and waited on bended knee, with a single rose for the bridesmaid with whom he'd been paired, to approach him with a smile. I now understood why so many people, particularly women, cried at weddings. It had to be the emptiness and lack of love they felt in their own relationships.

That's what it was for me, anyway. Before I could stop myself, tears were rolling down my face. This bronzed beauty approached a smiling Sydney, and he presented her with the rose, kissed her hand, stood to his feet, placed a hand on her back, and led her to a spot where they stood together, hooked up like they were a couple. I was hurt and jealous. Jealous of a woman who had just flown into town the night before and had met Sydney less than twenty-four hours ago. Jealous of the way he looked at her, although it was all staged. Jealous of the rose he gave her that he didn't even buy. Jealous that they looked happy together.

Stephanie looked so incredibly stunning when the back doors opened and she made her appearance. Her gown reflected light as if it had been made entirely of crystals, and it fit her body like a glove. She didn't have a single bulge anywhere, except where womanly bulges belonged. I would almost give my right arm to have her body. In awe of her beauty, every eye was on her as she absorbed every moment of her glory during her walk, escorted untraditionally by both her parents. I stood, batting and swiping away tears, wishing it were me. My life was so jacked up.

When the ceremony ended, I stayed in the sanctuary with random other people as the pho-

tographer captured shots. After I congratulated
Keith and Stephanie, I stood nearby trying not to
get in the way, but trying to get close to Sydney.
I longed for my husband to break away from the
bridal party for just a few seconds to kiss me,
hug me, or at least acknowledge me. He didn't.
I may as well not have even been there. Hurt
and embarrassed, I slunk back a few pews, took
a seat, and watched the shoot. Even when it was
over, Sydney never came over to where I sat,
but instead, laughing and chumming it up with
the other groomsmen, he strode out toward the
limo, jumped inside, and rode off. I should have
gone home right then, but the fool in me thought
that we surely could have some rekindling moments at the reception.

The one thing that I didn't like about the
seating at Stephanie and Keith's reception was
Stephanie had the entire bridal party sit at the
head table, but didn't include seating for their
spouses. It left me and a few other husbands
and wives looking like members of the lonely
hearts club. At least, I felt alone. All of Sydney's
family was in the wedding; even Carlos and
Casey served as junior groomsmen, escorting
junior bridesmaids. I barely knew anyone else
there. It would have been great for Sydney to sit
with me, but what could I do? I poked around

in my plate of wild rice with mushrooms, glazed pork tenderloin with grilled apples, roasted baby carrots topped with butter, and a hard cold roll, trying my best to look pleasant, like I was having a good time. I couldn't have been more glum. I was desperate for love. Desperate.

"I just want to say to my brother, Keith, and his lovely bride, Stephanie, I wish you many, many years of wedded bliss, and, man, I'm so happy that you finally found someone to make you happy, make you horny, then make you breakfast in the morning." Sydney toasted the couple with a gleaming smile, looking so handsome and somehow revolting at the same time.

At Sydney's not-so-tasteful toast, hoots of laughter erupted from the reception crowd, mostly the men, while we clinked glasses of champagne. Stephanie turned a shade of red as she giggled, then kissed her new husband on the lips before sipping from her glass. She looked so beautiful and happy; ironically, it made me sad and miserable. Not miserable for her, but miserable for me. I couldn't remember the last time I'd felt so giddy about my marriage, or any time, for that matter. No one could deny the love Keith and Stephanie had for each other. It was in their eyes, the several mini kisses they shared, their touches and their smiles.

Sydney never looked at me or touched me that way. Even now, being at this wonderfully romantic event, he was way across the room, skinnin' and grinnin' in every other woman's face, not paying me any attention. When they opened up the dance floor, I hoped that he'd come take my hand, but instead, my husband mingled around the room, drinking. After about thirty minutes, he made his way over to me and tapped me on the shoulder from behind. I hadn't even seen him coming, so I broke out into a welcoming smile.

"What time you planning on leavin'? The boys need to go 'head home with you. We gotta pack these gifts and stuff."

"After I dance with you," I suggested.

"I don't feel like dancing. You know I don't like that kinda stuff."

"Why not? It's a wedding. I'm your wife." Al Green's voice came through the speakers, crooning "Let's Stay Together."

"Come on, babe, please?" I pleaded, tugging on his hand. "We can at least pretend for a minute that it's our own wedding, since we didn't have one."

"Don't start that mess here," he said, pulling away. "I need to go support my brother. Take the kids with you when you leave," he finished, walking off. The words cut slow and deep as I was forced to accept his rejection.

I constrained additional tears as I watched other couples swiveling, rotating, and circling each other on the dance floor. My feelings were more crushed when, at the bride's command, the entire wedding party engaged in some kind of group Chicago Step dance. The moves were clean and in no way inappropriate, but it did involve some holding of hands and woman twirling, which Sydney skillfully did with his bronzed-beauty partner for the day.

The angry black woman in me wanted to go out on that dance floor and slap the skin off Sydney, but the civilized woman in me wouldn't let me do it. Before the presentation ended and while everyone's attention was captured, I slipped out the side door, leaving Casey and Carlos behind. They'd be just fine with Sydney's family.

Emotionally dazed behind the wheel, I drove toward home, but I didn't want to go. I wanted to run away from the world. Or maybe not the world, but from my life. It was crystal clear to me now that Sydney had no love for me at all. Suppose I had no connections to Sydney Harris Christopher. What would my life have been like if I would have done what Andra did and ended my pregnancy? I'd have my degree. I probably could have nailed down better jobs and gotten

promoted several times over. Maybe I would
have moved to Atlanta and started my own business and flown to Paris at least once. Or maybe
I'd know what it felt like to choose a party with
girlfriends over dinner and dishes. Spend a night
enjoying a good book and a bath instead of doing
laundry. I wished I had somewhere else to go,
but out of the boredom of my life, it seemed like
my car just automatically drove home.

I turned my key in the lock, went inside, and
collapsed on the couch, where I sat paralyzed
for more than an hour. Across from me on the
wall was a family photo of Sydney, the boys,
and me, taken when the boys were just toddlers.
I'd never noticed it before, but my face looked
so tired, although I was smiling. Sydney hadn't
smiled at all, as if smiling was a sin. All these
years, I'd always viewed his expression as firm
and assertive, in a sexy, manly way, but now he
looked completely stoic and empty. The boys, at
least, looked happy—I think.

I decided to run myself a hot bath and take
advantage of the silence, no matter how somber.
Over the years, I'd collected so many bath and
body products, which were just waiting for a moment like this. In a few minutes, my bathroom
was filled with a sweet, flowery fragrance, and
India.Arie's voice reverberated against the walls,
which helped my mood to change. The water

hadn't even begun to cool before I heard the sound of the front door opening and my family coming in. I vaguely could hear the TV in the den pop on, rattling in the kitchen and the boys talking, laughing, and playing on their way to their bedroom to change clothes. I prepared myself to ignore Sydney when he came bursting into the room with a lot to say about me leaving the boys with him, but he didn't come in.

Cool, I thought. I wasn't going to complain. I didn't want to hear his mouth, anyway. Convinced that he was going to let me finish my bath in peace, I relaxed and let my thoughts randomly circle my head, but they all seemed to center around one thing. How sorely disappointed I was with the day. What else could rekindle romance like a wedding? Was I that unattractive that my husband couldn't even bear the thought of dancing with me? Roberta Flack and Donny Hathaway's "Where Is the Love?" floated into my head, and I found myself singing that same line, over and over again. I was being foolish, but I still replayed the fantasy of my husband holding me in his arms, suited in that handsome tux, and dancing with me. We were laughing, and he would whisper what I'd heard called sweet nothings in my ear. I probably wouldn't know what a sweet nothing sounded like if it came blaring through a bullhorn.

Maybe Sydney didn't know how much I needed him today. He couldn't have been so cold and callous to deny me such a simple pleasure as a dance. Now that I had a chance to think and calm down my emotions, I could have a heart-to-heart with him and just let him know how much I was starving from the lack of true affection.

Having warmed the water four times, and now waterlogged, I finally emerged from the water, toweled off, lotioned my body, slid into a pair of satin pajamas and wrapped my hair. I tried to work out in my mind what I was going to say, but premeditation wasn't going to work. It would have to come straight from the heart, straight off the top.

I padded through the house, peeking for Sydney in the living room and kitchen, then in the den, where I only found the boys.

"Where's your daddy?"

"He dropped us off and left," Carlos answered. "He said we could play PlayStation for a little while, since we don't have school tomorrow."

"Where was he going?"

"I don't know," they answered in unison.

A slow stream of air left my cheeks as I pushed it through my lips, turned on my heels and headed back to my bedroom to dig my cell out of my purse to send a text.

Where r u

He didn't respond. Seven minutes later, I sent the same message, followed by two exclamation marks, to which I received no response. I waited a few minutes, then sent:

> Y r u ignoring me!

Ten minutes went by.

> U can't answer your texts?

Ten more minutes went by.

> U that busy that u can't answer ur wife?!

Two minutes went by after this last one before his number popped up on my screen.

"What do you want? You know I'm here tryna do stuff and you blowing up my phone like you crazy! What!" he yelled as soon as I answered.

"Where are you at?"

"What you mean, where am I at? You know exactly where I am! And why you ain't take Casey and Carlos with you like I told you! I turn around and they running all over the place and you ain't nowhere to be found. You know goodness well they didn't need to be here with all this drinking and stuff going on, and you just gonna leave without telling nobody. Then you got the nerve to be asking me where I'm at? Pssssh! Bye!"

Just like that, he clicked off.

He didn't come home until one o'clock the next morning.

Chapter Sixteen

Unfortunately, things between Sydney and me got worse. He spent more and more unaccounted-for time away from home, changing network marketing businesses every few months. Our heated sex spree hadn't lasted longer than three months, and we were back to a hit-or-miss schedule, but I was having full-blown cybersex with Quinton. Plus, I learned the secrets of pleasing myself; thus, I was less concerned with Sydney and his whereabouts.

While I was able to cover up my virtual indiscretions, Sydney's found him out. He'd come in the house one afternoon with a slight limp.

"What happened to you?" I asked.

"I had to get a shot."

"A shot? Why?"

"You remember when we was having all that wild and crazy sex?"

"Yeah, and?"

"Well, one of them nights I had slipped on a condom because I didn't want to come so fast, but the condom was old and I ended up getting gonorrhea from it."

"You got gonorrhea," I repeated stoically.

"That's what the doctor said."

"And you want me to believe that you got it from a condom?"

"Either that or I got it from you," he accused.

"You ain't got it from me 'cause I ain't got it."

"How do you know? You might not have symptoms. Almost fifty percent of women with gonorrhea don't have symptoms."

"And what is the percentage of men that get it from using an old condom?"

"Well, I musta got it from you, then!"

"I don't have gonorrhea, Sydney."

"I don't believe you."

"Just because you don't believe me don't mean it's not true."

"I shoulda known when you came in here all ready to have sex every night that something was up."

"Whatever. You better go let those heifers you been doing in the streets know that they need to go get a shot."

"I want to know why you ain't going down there."

"Because I don't have gonorrhea. We haven't had sex in weeks, and you didn't get it from no condom," I said with assurance. "Your mess done caught up with you."

"You probably had it and gave it to me, then went ahead and got treated for it," he charged.

"You're just gonna try to pin it on me any way you can, huh?"

"You the one brought it home!"

"Whatever, Sydney."

Strangely, I didn't feel as badly as I thought I should have felt for my husband telling me that he brought something home that he hadn't left with. Honestly, I felt indifference. It was proof of what I'd overlooked for a long time. Sydney was cheating on me. I just couldn't figure out why he'd been so forthcoming with it. He could have said anything to hide a limp. It wasn't like we were sexing on the regular, so he could have taken the prescribed treatment and gotten it all cleared up without me ever knowing. Even if I did fall into one of my horny moods, he wouldn't have had any problem refusing me.

For the sake of my own safety, I called my gynecologist the next day and asked for a quick appointment to be tested, just in case, and was relieved when she gave me a clean bill of health. I was glad to tell Sydney.

"That don't mean nothing but you got rid of yours before I knew about it," he snarled.

"No, it means you got it from one of them hooker-shoe-wearing hoes you mess with in the street. And I'm so done with you, Sydney, it don't even make no sense. You might as well go and be with them, because it ain't nothing left for you here."

Sydney got dressed and left without a word. They always say be careful what you ask for.

I turned over and squinted at the clock, which read 1:14. Where was Sydney? His side of the bed was cold and empty. Reaching over to my nightstand, I checked my cell phone for a missed call or text. As I suspected, Sydney had been silent regarding his whereabouts. This was nothing short of ridiculous and unacceptable, but it was becoming more and more typical. I started to text him an angry message, but who was I kidding, thinking he would actually respond? Sadly, it wasn't the first time he'd pulled this kind of stunt, and exemplified this level of disrespect. I'd been foolish to accept it all this time.

I did manage to drift back to sleep, but, of course, I had an ear to the door listening for what time he would come in. It was a little bit after four, and he tiptoed into the bedroom and tried to slide out of his clothes as quietly as possible. As he undressed, though, I sat up.

"Where've you been?"

"I was at the beach."

"At four in the morning?"

"I had a lot to think about, so I just went there to think."

"Guess you just lost track of time, huh?"

"No, not really. Just had a lot on my mind."

"And I'm just supposed to believe and accept that?" Sydney hated the beach. It was one of the many places he never wanted to take me, as much as I'd begged over the years to go together, always complaining that he didn't like the feel of sand beneath his feet or between his toes. "So, all of a sudden, the beach is where you go to think. You must think I'm a fool, Sydney."

"I'm just answering your question. I told you, I got a lot on my mind."

"Like what?" Or *who* would have been a better question.

"Suicide," he said, pulling on a pair of pajama pants.

Suicide? Hmm. Suicide was a new trick that I wasn't ready for. I gave it a few seconds of thought. Maybe I was being crass and heartless, but I didn't believe Sydney. He'd stayed out too late with some woman and needed a really good excuse for coming in at four o'clock. A really good reason. So this is what he picked. "Whatever."

"You don't have to believe me," he commented quietly as he got on his knees and reached under the bed for a small portable safe. Sydney dug around on the nightstand drawer on his side of the bed for a small key, unlocked the safe and pulled out a small handgun, then left the room.

I waited a couple of minutes before I followed him out, finding him silently seated on the couch in the den, with the gun in his lap. "What are you doing, Sydney?"

"I told you, I'm thinking about suicide," he calmly responded.

"And?"

"I'm going to sit here and think, and if I decide to, I'm going to take this gun right here"—he lifted the gun to his head and pressed it against his temple—"and pull the trigger."

I didn't know what to make of that, but the thought of it scared me. I still couldn't help but think he was just trying to get himself out of hot water. "Why are you going to do that? That's stupid." That probably wasn't the smartest thing to say to a man with a loaded gun, but it was all I could think of on the fly.

"So I'm stupid?" he asked mordantly.

"You must be, if you think I'm falling for this shenanigan."

"Just leave me alone, Kareese."

I turned on my heels, leaving him there and trying to determine if he was serious or not. And if he was, what should I do? I wouldn't be able to live with myself if I let that man sit in there and shoot himself. Not more than two minutes passed before I was back in the den with Sydney.

"Why don't you just come to bed, Sydney?" I suggested, releasing my disapproval of the fact that he was just cracking the door at four in the morning.

"I need to sit here for a while and think this through."

"So you're gonna let Casey and Carlos come in here tomorrow to find you with your brains splattered all around the room?"

"If it comes to that—yeah."

I sat silently for a few minutes on the opposite end of the couch, having no idea of what I was supposed to say.

"You don't have to sit in here with me," Sydney stated.

"I thought you might be able to use a listening ear."

"Ain't nothing to talk about. You haven't been interested in listening to me all this time. I don't know why you're acting so interested now."

"We have our disagreements, Sydney, but I still love and care about you." It took a lot for me to say that, not that I was making it up; I just didn't feel like saying it with all the other stuff Sydney had put me through, including bringing home an STD. Maybe he had to share that news with whoever he was sleeping with and she got mad and went off on him, which led to him sitting here with a gun in his hand. If he came home and told me, he had to tell her.

He let out a sardonic chuckle. "Yeah right, Kareese. Don't nobody care."

"How can you say that? You don't think those boys love you? If I didn't love you, I would have been gone by now, but I've stuck by you and with you," I said in an attempt to be comforting.

"That ain't what you were saying a few hours ago."

"I was upset a few hours ago."

"I don't know how you're gonna be upset with me over some mess you brought up in here."

I winced at his accusation.

"I'm sitting up here thinking you love me and all that, and you out here sleeping around and burning me. Then you're gonna tell me to get out of my own house." He shook his head sadly, but all it did was make me angry.

"Okay, well, I'm calling the cops to get you some help. I don't want to see you die tonight." I stood, walked quickly to the kitchen and just rattled the phone against its base, challenging him.

Sydney immediately jumped to his feet. "All right, all right. I'll come to bed."

That's what I thought. I should have just laid into him about wherever he'd been, but I couldn't ignore the fact that he was acting crazy, and he had a gun.

He followed me to the bedroom and we both got in bed, but I found out quickly that it was much more harrowing having him there than leaving him in another room where he could have played his crazy game by himself. I had lain down, but Sydney sat up against the headboard, gun still in hand, which made me panicky. I started thinking about how many stories I'd heard of a man killing his wife or girlfriend and then himself. Or sometimes his entire family. I couldn't do anything but pray. Well, maybe I could have, but I couldn't think of anything else to do besides act unfazed but pray as hard as I could.

Sydney must have stayed posted up for about twenty minutes before he spoke. "You asleep?" he whispered.

I didn't answer, pretending that I was.

"Kareese," he called out louder.

"What?"

"You asleep?"

"Yes, I'm asleep! You come in the house from who knows where at the crack of dawn, then expect somebody to stay up with you?"

"You don't even care, do you?"

"Go to sleep!" Keeping my back to him, my eyes chased around wildly, hoping that my false lack of concern would show him that he was just wasting his time. It worked. About two minutes later, he put the gun back into the safe, slid beneath the covers and went to sleep.

I'm not sure who won that night. Him, for getting away with his unexplained whereabouts and four o'clock entry time, or me, who got away without being shot or him shooting himself? I didn't bring it up later. I just started thinking about living on my own.

While Sydney spent the morning doing yard work with the boys, I spent time online looking for a place to live so I could leave my husband. My marriage wasn't much to hold on to, never had been, but I'd been hesitant to let go. Sometimes it was out of my naïve thinking that things would get better. Other times I felt like I shouldn't quit on us just because we were going through tough times. Disagreements were a part of any marriage relationship, and anyone who was married would tell you that. Calling it quits felt like a cop-out to me.

I should leave. Other than the boys, I had no real reason to stay with Sydney, and I was only fooling myself trying to pretend that there was no way he wasn't somewhere creeping. I guess I'd given him the benefit of the doubt because I'd never seen anything with my own two eyes. But did I actually need to see it to be convinced? Up until this point, I'd pushed out of my mind all of the indicators that clearly pointed to infidelity, not wanting to believe and accept it. There wasn't any getting around an STD, though. Then, that whole thing with the gun?

Peering outside, I could see Sydney and the boys busily raking leaves and trimming hedges. As if Sydney could hear me, I tiptoed to our bedroom and pulled out the safe, curious about whether there had been any bullets in the gun. Just before I picked it up, I thought I should have gloves on, not that I knew how to check for bullets in the first place. Pulling on a pair of winter gloves, I carefully handled the firearm, turning it over in my hand and trying to figure out how to open up or detach the magazine or clip or whatever it was called. I had no clue what

I was doing and didn't want to mess around and shoot myself. There were a few bullets rolling around in the bottom of the safe, which were probably the ones that were loaded in the gun last night, if it had been loaded at all. I really felt like the whole thing had been an act and a game to manipulate me and redirect the heat that he knew was coming from staying out all night. It was hard to believe that Sydney would have actually shot himself.

But I couldn't be too sure. I locked the safe, pushed it back under the bed, then wrapped the key in a wad of tissue and flushed it down the toilet. After it disappeared in a swirl of water, I flushed again with more tissue to make sure it was gone.

Chapter Seventeen

Suzetta moving to VA in 3 weeks and want me to help her—you mind?

I sat frozen in place for a few seconds, thinking about how I could best answer Sydney's question other than just saying, *Hell yes, I mind!*

It had been a month since he'd pulled that gun trick, and not much had happened since then. He still came home at varied hours without saying where he'd been, but never again as late as four. Most nights lately, he was in by nine, but we were kind of just coexisting at this point. He wasn't saying too much to me; I wasn't saying too much to him. We slept sexless in the same bed, managing the other pieces of our lives like we'd always had—him doing whatever the hell he wanted to do and me going with the flow, making no moves on my own to change my situation.

I re-read his text. First of all, I couldn't believe that he even had the audacity to ask me, and did he really expect me to give him my stamp of approval? The sad part was, he did. I'd been so passively accepting all this time, why would he expect anything different?

When I thought of my best response, I began to text back:

> If I say yes I mind, u will try to make me feel stupid, n if I say no I dont mind Im not being honest w/ u or myself. U decide which 1 is more important to u – how ur wife feels or helping her.

A few seconds later, my phone buzzed back with his response, which simply read:

> Ok.

Okay? What did that mean? Okay, as in he was going to help her move; or okay, as in he was going to respect my feelings? I waited a few seconds for clarification, but he said nothing more, which made me wince. I decided that I wasn't going to say another word about it; I was just simply going to wait to see if he brought it up again, or what he decided. Even still, it bothered me. I hated my marriage, and it was time for me to stop sitting by idly and letting stuff happen to me.

Over the next week, I could hardly think about anything else but ending my marriage. I was sure I wanted a divorce, but I wasn't sure that it was the right thing to do. God hated divorce, and I didn't want to make God mad at me. At the same time, this mess couldn't have pleased God. I pulled out a sheet of paper and made three columns in an attempt to deal with my reality.

Stay	Leave	Fears
Pays rent	Cheating	Insecurity
Good sex when we have it	Gonorrhea!!	Finances
Made life long vows	Don't love me	Used to being here
Casey and Carlos	Playing with gun!!!	Scared to venture out
Keep my family together	Won't get a real job	Self-esteem
Sydney could change	LaRowe	Family will say "I told you so"
We could get counseling first	Manipulating (gun, bracelet, STD)	Failed marriage
I should trust God	Peace of mind	Single parent

The fact that my columns were evenly bal-
anced across the paper made me more confused.
Before I started, I expected to see one column
heavily outweighing the others. Since no column
prevailed, I had to dig deeper, starting with my
fears. I didn't want to focus on staying, and I
knew I had plenty of reasons to leave. So what
was stopping me? I looked at every reason on my
paper and gave it hard, honest thought.

Insecurity? So what? Sydney paid the rent
and a few of the bills; I was responsible enough
to prioritize my spending and could find an
affordable place for me and my boys. I put an X
by it to signify to myself that it was just an excuse
and moved on.

Finances? I'd been wasteful over the past
few years, spending money on all kinds of stuff.
Clothes, shoes, hair, nails, eating out. Even the
money I'd won at the casino had trickled through
my fingers in the form of frivolous spending. I
was going to have to do better with my money
if I was going to live alone. Sydney did always
manage to pay the rent; then we worked the
other bills between us. My salary would support
me doing it on my own if I just became more
disciplined, which was worth peace of mind any
day.

I needed to save up some money. Rent amounts
were no joke, and needing to pay security deposits,
lights, cable, in addition to my car payment, insur-

ance, and credit card bills, and then the price of raising two kids, made me feel defeated before I even got started. It would take me at least three months to get myself together financially to make a move.

Used to being there? That one was really sad. Who had I become that I had become comfortable and content with someone mistreating me? I'd been too forgiving, too excusing, too accepting. I couldn't believe that I'd actually accepted everything in my "Leave" list as my normality, just living in hell on autopilot. I marked it with an X.

Scared to venture out? X.

Self-esteem? That was something Yalisa had pointed out to me years ago. I didn't believe her then, but she'd been so right. I realized that I really didn't have a positive image of myself. I felt underachieved, having never completed my degree; I had issues with my body, and two kids on my back. Somewhere in my mind, I didn't believe anyone would want me besides Sydney, but that couldn't be true. There were plenty of women just like me who were living life to the fullest, whether they had a man or not. And if they could do it, why couldn't I? And even if nobody in the world wanted me, I had to love myself more than to let anybody just run all over me and treat me any kind of way. I was worth so much more than that. X!

Family? X. Forget them. It wasn't like I'd had a great relationship with them over the years, anyway. They could say what they wanted. Besides, if my momma knew half the mess I'd been through with Sydney, she would have told me to leave him a long time ago. I so should have listened to her.

Failed marriage? So I'd be a divorce statistic. So what? X.

Single parent? Hmm. Now, that was truly one I wasn't looking forward to, especially with boys. I couldn't just X that one out, but at least I'd weeded out the ones that were dumb excuses, and now my "Fears" list was much shorter.

Pushing back from my desk, I decided to head out for lunch with Yalisa if she could get out. My entire afternoon was booked with conference calls for a new Consumer Advocate Associate role I was in training for, so this was my only chance to escape midday.

"Let's go to lunch." I popped into her cubicle and took a seat at her desk. "I need a break."

"Hold on a minute." She tapped her fingers against the keyboard, finishing up an e-mail.

"I'm leaving Sydney," I stated, fiddling with a knickknack on her desk.

"Whatever." Yalisa didn't even look up. She'd heard me say that a million times before.

"I'm serious this time."

"What happened this time?" she asked, pulling her purse from her bottom cabinet drawer, then rising to her feet.

"Do you have to say it like that?"

Yalisa ignored my last statement. "What do you have a taste for?"

"Fresh air," I said, pouting.

"Great, we can get fresh food to match."

On the way to Souplantation & Sweet Tomatoes, a soup and salad bar restaurant, I shared my latest nuptial drama. As usual, Yalisa listened wholeheartedly, but she was careful not to advise. Sometimes I hated that about her. I wanted her to respond, but just take my feelings into consideration when she did. She only nodded, and commented "hmm" intermittently.

I opted for the chicken pot pie stew and a salad, paid for my meal, slid into a booth and waited for Yalisa to join me. She meticulously picked over the salad bar vegetables, inspecting every single leaf, vein, spot and blemish before putting it on her plate, but finally she took a seat across from me.

"So what are you going to do about your situation?"

"I already told you. I'm leaving Sydney."

"Just like that, huh?"

"Not just like that. It's taken me seven years to get to this point."

"Have you tried going to counseling?" I didn't dignify her question with a response. My rolled eyes said it all. "Well? Have you?" she repeated before filling her mouth with a forkful of loaded baked potato.

"What black man do you know who is willing to sit up in some office and tell somebody all his business *and* pay for it?"

"Lots of men do it, I'm sure."

"Black ones?"

"I don't have any statistics or records, but I'm positive that a ton of black people get marriage counseling."

"Yeah, if they are interested in working on their marriage," I flippantly added.

"You don't want to save your marriage?"

I paused momentarily, too embarrassed to admit what I thought my heart felt. "I don't know." That was easier to say than just a flat-out no.

"So, if you went home right now and said, 'Sydney, I'm leaving you,' and he fell down on his knees and said, 'No, baby, please don't do that. I love you. I love the kids. I know I've made some mistakes, but I'm sorry and I'm willing to do whatever it takes to keep our family together,' what would you say?"

"First of all, Sydney wouldn't say that."

"How do you know?"

"Look how he's acting right now!" I said a little louder than I meant. "He's not acting like a man who wants to be married, coming in all hours of the night and creeping with his so-called friend." I fingered quotation marks around "friend" to emphasize my point.

"How are you going to accuse the man of creeping if you haven't at least tried to find out what he is really doing?"

I hadn't told Yalisa about the STD package he'd brought home. "I did that once," I admitted. "He said he was going to be at the bowling alley, and I showed up, and there he was—with a group of guys—bowling. But I'm still not convinced that he's not sneaking around, screwing someone behind my back."

"Well, confront him."

"For what? He's just gonna lie. What man in his right mind would look his wife in the face and just confess flat out to cheating?"

"True, true. But if you don't confront him, what are you going to tell him when you announce that you are taking your stuff and his kids?"

"I don't owe him any explanation. He knows he ain't livin' right."

"Kareese, you just don't up and take a man's kids away without saying a word, especially when he is present and active in their lives. Do you know how many mothers are out here just *wishing* their kids' fathers were even remotely around?"

"Don't try to make Sydney look like some kinda knight in shining armor. He might be an active part of their lives, but what kind of example is he setting for them as a husband?"

"You have a point there, but still they are getting something positive out of his presence; I mean, he ain't beating on you or nothing like that."

She didn't know about the gun thing either. I was too embarrassed to tell her and then follow it up with the fact that I was still there.

"Where are you thinking about living? Are you going to rent a place, move back home with your parents, what? What about child support and visitation?"

"You're asking too many questions." I sighed and stared up at the ceiling, not having figured out any of that stuff. It was starting to sound complicated and overwhelming. But wives left husbands all the time, with kids in tow, so it couldn't be *that* hard. Then again, maybe it would be easier and more cost effective just to accept that my marriage was a bust and for us to just live like roommates.

Lucky for me, I had my "Stay, Leave, and Fears" chart to snap me back to reality.

Chapter Eighteen

Sydney got up without saying a word and began to get dressed, pulling on a pair of tattered jeans and an old sweatshirt.

"Where are you going?" I kept my tone even and nonchalant, although I knew his answer would be unacceptable.

"I decided to help Suzetta," he announced.

"So you care more about her than you do me," I stated, more than asked.

"She has a boyfriend."

"It's not about what she has—you're my husband. If she has a boyfriend, he needs to help her. You had ample enough time to tell her no."

"You just need to trust me."

Trust him? After he had to be treated for gonorrhea? Was he kidding me? I'd already prepared myself for anything I thought Sydney might say, so I didn't have the need to raise my voice. "I want you to know, Sydney, that if you leave here today to help that woman move, when you get back, there will be repercussions."

"It ain't nothing going on between us," he said, referring to himself and Suzetta. "We're just friends."

"Okay," I said dismissively. "I just want you to be able to make an intelligent decision about how you want to spend your day. I don't want you to come back thinking everything's okay, because it won't be." I turned over and nestled into my pillow.

"I don't even know why you acting like that, Kareese. I'm just helping the girl move."

"Well, don't worry about it then. It's your choice."

He stood staring at me momentarily, looking as if he was trying to discern my level of seriousness. "I'ma go ahead and help her."

"Okay, see you later. Just be ready to be accountable for your actions when you get back."

No sooner than Sydney pulled out of the driveway, I hopped out of bed and began gathering his things, stuffing them into trash bags. It was D-day.

"What are you doing, Ma?" Casey asked, pulling away from his Saturday TV programming after seeing me drag three bags through the den and into the garage.

"Nothing. Watch TV."

"You need some help?"

"No, but thanks" tumbled out of my mouth before I remembered how Sydney had used the boys against me in that whole dinner-and-bracelet shenanigan. But still, I had more character than that.

An hour later, our closet was completely devoid of Sydney's belongings. I wasn't quite sure how things would go down, but I knew by the end of the night, one of us would be leaving.

When Sydney returned late in the evening, the boys were already in bed, and I was more than ready to turn him around on his heels.

"Hey, babe," he said, entering our bedroom and finding me relaxing and reclining on the bed, watching *Grey's Anatomy*.

"Hey," I responded without looking his way. "I put all your stuff in the garage."

"What stuff?" he asked, peeling out of his jacket.

"All your stuff. Your clothes, your shoes, coats, jackets, suits—all of it is ready to be put in your car and moved to wherever it is you're sleeping tonight."

Sydney sighed first, then spoke. "Look, Kareese." He lifted a hand to his head and rubbed pensively. "I made a mistake."

"I know you did. Don't even worry about it."

"Will you just listen, please?" He waited for me to turn my attention away from the TV, which I did when a commercial came on. "After I left, I realized I shouldn'ta done that and how disrespectful it was, and I'm sorry."

"Apology accepted, but you still need to get out. You knew what you were doing before you left. You chose to leave. Now you don't have a choice—leave," I ordered.

"I'm not leaving my house," he affirmed.

"Fine, then I will leave. It doesn't matter to me, but one of us will not be living here after tonight." I scooted from the bed and started pulling my things out of the closet. Sydney walked up behind me and placed his hand over mine as I grabbed a few more hung garments.

"Kareese, stop. Just stop. Let's talk about it."

"There's nothing to talk about, so move."

"So you're just gonna leave me?"

"Yep, just like you left this morning."

"That's not right; I was helping a friend."

"And helping her meant more to you than respecting me, so move." Yanking away from him, I threw more clothes on the bed.

"Okay, but before you go, I have something for you."

"What is it, Sydney?" I huffed, throwing my hands on my hips.

"Come here." He tugged on my arm, coaxing me to sit on the bed, although he remained standing and began looking a bit nervous.

"Well, I was thinking about what you were saying about us renewing our vows, since we didn't have a wedding. And I know I have always said no, but, baby, you deserve to have what you want, and I want to give you the wedding of your dreams." He dug into the pocket of his jeans, pulled out some kind of ring, and dropped to one knee, holding the ring between his thumb and forefinger. "I already picked a date."

"Wow," I responded with little enthusiasm. I couldn't describe to anyone what the ring looked like, because I only glanced at it.

"Will you marry me? With a real wedding." He pushed the ring on my finger, nestling it over the tiny speck of a diamond he'd bought me when we'd gotten married.

This time I did look down at the ring. I didn't know how to estimate stone sizes, but if I had to guess, I would say it was maybe a quarter of a carat solitaire set in yellow gold—not the biggest ring in the world, but much larger than what he'd given me eight years before. I guffawed.

"I love you Kareese, and this is something that I should have given you a long time ago."

"Yep, you should have, but since you didn't, who's leaving—me or you?"

Sydney focused his eyes on me, looking as if he was thinking of what he should say next. "Did you hear what I just said?"

"I sure did." I shrugged. "And?"

"I just asked you if you will marry me."

"I heard you," I responded without batting an eye. I folded my arms across my chest.

"Baby, I've spent my entire life making bad decisions, but I really didn't realize how bad they were until they were mingled with the love I feel for you. I guess it's like thinking that driving with expired license plates will just get you a ticket, then finding out that it's a felony and you actually gotta do some time. You know it's wrong, just not how wrong." He paused, waiting for more of a reaction from me than my eyes rolling. "I pray that God forgives me, and I know He does. I know you are not God, but you are my angel from heaven and I love you. You've been nothing but good to me, and I don't need even a whole chance, just half a chance to prove that I can change . . . that my love for you has changed me. For all the bad I've done, I just want half a chance to do good—that's all I need. I love you more than life itself, and without you, I have no life. It's *your* time, baby; your time to get the good out of this, to be treated like the queen that you are. That's why I want us to renew our vows. Let me serve you, my queen."

Pulling my left hand away from my chest, I held it up in front of me and tilted my head from side to side, studying the ring. "No," I stated concretely, twisting the ring off my finger and slapping it into Sydney's palm. "Want me to help you put your stuff in the car, 'cause it's getting late and I'm 'bout ready to go to bed."

Sydney looked down at the ring in hand, biting his bottom lip and avoiding eye contact; then he shook the ring in his hand as if he was about to roll a pair of dice.

"You know what? Since I was nice enough to bag it up for you, you can put it in the car yourself. I'm about to take a shower." I maneuvered around him, went into the bathroom and started my shower, leaving Sydney standing in the middle of the bedroom. Standing under the water, I thought about Sydney's poor attempt to manipulate my feelings with his proposal. What had really happened was Sydney had snapped to his senses. His little heifer friend just moved out of state—if he was telling the truth about that—and his fling had come to an end. He had long quit his jobs running behind Suzetta, no longer had money in savings, and knew that he needed me financially to survive. He didn't have a choice but to come home and act like he suddenly wanted our marriage to work, but I was no longer buying wolf tickets.

I didn't know what Sydney was doing, but it sounded like he was banging something against the dresser. I could hear him striking something, over and over, which made me peer around the shower curtain. I couldn't see him, but the sound made me nervous.

"What are you doing?" I called out.

"Don't worry about what I'm doing. You just take your shower." His tone had changed from sincere pleading to menacing.

A few seconds later, Sydney came into the bathroom and started banging. Pulling the curtain back, I saw him standing there, hammer in hand, and striking things on the counter, starting with the cup we used to rinse after brushing. With two hits, it was smashed to bits. Then he moved to the soap dish.

It scared me, but I refused to show it. He had to go to manipulation plan B. He probably had tried to dig that gun out again, but since the key was gone, he couldn't get to it.

"Don't break up anything of mine," I said, snatching the curtain closed. He didn't say anything, but he kept hammering, and suddenly I had a fear of him smashing through the shower curtain and knocking me in the head. I kept silent but began to hurry. Before I finished, Sydney left the bathroom, relieving my fear of a blind attack.

However, the noise didn't stop, and I didn't know what Sydney was thinking or planning. Quickly I stepped out of the tub, wrapped a towel around my body, and looked out into the bedroom to make a quick assessment. He was pacing the floor, randomly hitting the top of the dresser, then bouncing the hammerhead off his palm. I couldn't tell what else he'd broken up, and despite my fear, I rolled my eyes, and turned back to the bathroom sink when he looked at me.

I took my time brushing my teeth, but my eyes focused on the telephone that sat on the night-stand on my side of the bed. It was a straight path from where I stood to the phone, although it was several steps away. Feeling that Sydney had become unpredictable, and maybe even dangerous, my plan was to jet for the phone, dial 911, and end this potentially volatile situation.

"You done? We need to talk," Sydney said, appearing in the bathroom door's entrance.

"It's not gonna work, Sydney. One of us needs to leave," I said, looking him dead in the eye. "Tonight." He turned his back, moving away from the door, and I made a mad dash to the phone.

"What are you doing?" Sydney dashed across the room, snatched the phone from my hand, and pressed the hook before I had a chance to dial. Immediately he unplugged the phone and wrapped the cord around the handset and base.

"Calling the police," I answered adamantly. "I don't know what you're planning to do with that hammer, but if you think I'ma just let you smash up stuff, you crazy." He turned the corners of his lips down, scrutinizing my face, but I refused to show intimidation. On the contrary, I put on my best *I ain't playing* expression. "So when are you leaving?"

"I told you, we gotta talk first." He left the bedroom with the phone and I followed him out, but I tried not to make my concern so conspicuous by going to the laundry room and stuffing some clothes in the washer. I couldn't give him any indication that he was setting fear in my heart. He would have used it against me. When I did pass Sydney a few minutes later, I saw that he'd collected every phone in the house and was taking them to the garage. My cell phone included. I tried to pay him no mind, but my head was beginning to spin.

Think, Kareese, think! Okay. If I just shut up and went to bed without saying anything else, he would feel like he got away and would eventually go to bed; then I'd just leave in the morning. In the bedroom, Sydney had unplugged the lamps and the alarm clock. I wasn't sure what had happened to the hammer. I moved the clothes I'd thrown on the bed to an armchair, then climbed into bed, trying to act unfazed by his behavior. In my heart, mind and spirit, though, I began silently praying.

Flicking the switch on the wall, he turned the overhead light off and begin pacing back and forth at the foot of the bed in silence; then he said, "So let's talk."

"There's nothing to talk about," I said, blinking quickly to get my eyes to adjust to the sudden darkness.

"Yes, there is," he insisted. "Let's talk about you."

"What about me?" I asked with indifference.

It wasn't funny, but I had to fight back a giggle when he pulled the trigger on the long lighter I used instead of matches for igniting candles. He was keeping it lit while he talked.

"Let's talk about what you do when I'm not around," he suggested. The flame went out. "Anything you need to tell me?"

"Nope."

He approached my side of the bed and flicked the lighter again about a foot from my face. "You sure about that?"

"Get that mess out of my face," I ordered, slapping it away.

He fell silent, probably surprised that I wasn't falling for his act. "How is it that you're just so perfect?" he asked cynically. "You just don't do anything, huh?"

"Nope." I wasn't concerned; he had nothing on me.

"And you think I believe you." It was a statement. He flicked the lighter on and off intermittently as he talked.

"I don't care what you believe. Believe what you want." My hand flung away his implied accusation.

"Oh, it's funny how you believe something and you want me to get out, and I believe something and all of a sudden you don't care. But guess what? I'ma get some answers tonight."

"Why can't you just leave? You know you're wrong. You don't want to be here. You'd rather be with Suzetta. So what's stopping you from just calling her and going over there? Oh, I know what it is—she don't want your broke behind." I had said too much.

From seemingly nowhere, Sydney had pulled out an aerosol can and began to spray. I didn't know what it was, but it smelled like hair spray. Whatever it was, I knew it was flammable. "Keep right on talking."

Oh, Lord. Oh, Lord. Oh, Lord. Don't panic, Kareese.

"Who are you seeing at work?" he asked, confident in his assumption.

"You're so stupid," I shot back. "What are you tryna prove?"

"If I gotta get held accountable for my actions, you're gonna be held accountable for yours." He sprayed more of the substance into the air and on the covers. "So you actually think you gonna put me out my own house."

"You put your own self out when you decided to disrespect me."

"But you're not being disrespectful when you come in here insulting my manhood, and acting like you working all day and half the night. That ain't disrespectful, though, huh? Because you're so perfect. You don't make mistakes," he said sarcastically.

I didn't have time to think about Sydney's idiotic questions. I had to try to discern if he was playing with my head or if he was really planning on setting our bedroom on fire. It was barely two months ago when he scared me to death by threatening to commit suicide. I wasn't sure what to think. It was too serious to ignore, and too manipulative to take seriously.

Lord, do you see this man? I prayed. *What in the world is really going on here? I'm scared and I aint tryna die in here tonight like this.*

Sydney kept on asking stupid questions, and spraying spray, and I kept on praying and thinking of how I could best escape. As more seconds passed by, the more I felt threatened. *Let me get up and use the bathroom and move around a bit,* I told myself. Maybe I could find something in the bathroom or somewhere that I could use for *something.* It would at least give me a chance to dash for the door, which Sydney had closed and locked at the beginning of what was turning out to be a most frightening ordeal. I threw my legs over the side of the bed, but Sydney wasn't having it.

"Where you think you going?" he asked, charging toward me.

"To the bathroom. Move!" I stood, toe to toe with him, not hiding my scowl.

"Naaaw," he drew out. "Why don't you just hold it," he said, blocking me from moving.

"What? Boy, move!" I pushed past him, ignoring his orders.

"All right, that's fine," he stated serenely. "Go on ahead to the bathroom, one more time."

One more time? My head was swirling not knowing what to do or think. Once in the bathroom, I regretted making the mistake of turning on the light, which meant my eyes would have to readjust to the darkness. I emerged from the bathroom, trying to figure out how I could dash for the door. There was no way I'd be able to beat him to the door, especially not being able to see clearly. Needing more time to think and strategize, I got back in bed.

Help me, Lord, I pleaded silently. *Help me.* As soon as I got under the cover, Sydney began his goading again. *How can I get out of here?*

"You comfortable?"

"Yep."

"You sure?" he mocked.

"Yep."

"Good." At that, he sprayed the bed for a full thirty seconds, lighter in hand.

"Why don't you stop being so ignorant!" I yelled, jerking the covers up in the air a few times to fan away the cloud of spray he'd created.

"That's right. Just let it soak in there, real good."

Oh, my God. Is he for real? Is he serious?

"You make me sick!" I screamed.

"You won't be sick much longer," he said, not changing his tone. "This is gonna be a night of destiny for you and me."

In all my days of praying and asking God to speak to me, He came through that night. Just as clear as birds singing first thing in the morning, I heard Him say:

"Don't you lay up in this bed and get burned up."

That was all I needed to hear. At that moment, I knew that it wasn't some manipulative "flip the script" game anymore. I was in serious danger if I didn't take action. I jumped up from the bed and darted for the door, but Sydney, who was already standing, was three times quicker than I was. He met me at the door and covered the knob with his own hand.

"No, no, no! Where are you going? Don't try to leave now!" he teased.

"I'm getting out of here because you're not gonna burn me up."

"I'm not gonna do that," he said, sounding snidely sweet. "Why would I do that?"

"What are you gonna do then?" I demanded.

"Oh, you'll see. You'll see."

"Give me that lighter." I had nothing to lose by challenging him. Surprisingly, he put it in my hand. The bad part was, he picked up the hammer again. I didn't get back in the bed, but this time I sat in the armchair, burying the lighter in the clothes beneath me. Now that I knew without a shadow of a doubt that this was no game, I began to cry silently. Sydney was busy entertaining himself with the hammer, while I thought about how much my life had just changed. If and when

I made it out of our bedroom alive, our marriage was absolutely over and I was leaving with my two boys. I didn't know where I was going to go, or work, or live, or anything, but what I did know was I was out.

Sydney began to pace again, then pulled his cell phone from his hip and glanced at it. "Oh, it's almost time," he stated.

I didn't know what he meant, but I didn't plan to be around to see it come into fruition. Still trapped and endangered, I kept praying, while I thought about the conversation I was going to have to have with my boss to see if I could be transferred to another location. There was no way I planned to stay anywhere that Sydney could get ahold of me, but I still needed my job. There were Freedom Federals in several locations, and I'd always been a model employee, so I didn't foresee it being a barrier.

"So who have you slept with on your job?" Sydney asked.

"Nobody." I sat still, almost numb, trying to figure out my next move. It would be impossible for me to open and get through a window, but there had to be a way out.

"Nobody? Not one person?"

"No." My answers were stoic. My eyes fell on the security system panel, just inside my bedroom door, and I recognized it as my way out.

"I'm going to see how you answer that question by the end of the night."

"You know what, Sydney. Whatever you're gonna do, you better do it right now," I said, locking in on my strategy.

"What are you talking about?" he taunted further.

"Whatever it is that you plan on doing, you better do it right now!" I repeated boldly.

"Don't worry about what I'ma—"

Before he could finish his sentence, I sprang up from the chair and bolted toward the door. Just as I anticipated, Sydney dived for the doorknob, but I targeted every panic button on the alarm control panel, and I quickly pressed all three emergency buttons, triggering a blaring alarm throughout the house. It caught Sydney completely off guard and broke his level of control over the room. With him stunned, I was able to flick on the lights and open the door.

"What did you do that for?" he asked, feigning confusion like I'd sounded the alarm for no reason. He pressed the appropriate buttons to silence the alarm.

"Oh, I thought you were crazy. You mean you've come back to your right mind?"

"Ma, what's wrong?" Rubbing their eyes, both Casey and Carlos stood in the hallway. Both were dressed only in their white briefs and T-shirts.

"Nothing. It's just the alarm on the house. Go back to your room."

"Oh." They both padded back to their bedrooms, while I went to the living room and peered out the window, waiting for the police to arrive.

"All right. I'ma just leave. You said you wanted me out, so I'ma just leave. Can you move your car out the way?" he asked.

"What are you leaving for now? Don't get scared. Your friends are on the way."

"Where're your car keys?" he asked, planning to move my car himself.

"I don't know.'" I shrugged, unconcerned.

Sydney started scouting around, looking for my keys. Before he could locate them, I could hear the sound of sirens in the distance. In a matter of seconds, three fire trucks and an ambulance rounded the corner, expecting to put out a fire and save our lives. Apparently, the fire button was the first panic button my fingers found. I snatched our front door open and walked out across the lawn to meet the crew that wasted no time jumping off their emergency response vehicles. Sydney followed a few steps behind me.

"Are you all okay, ma'am?"

"I'm fine, but y'all need to take him"—I pointed behind me at Sydney—"because he was just about to set our whole house on fire."

I guess Sydney expected me to say that the alarms were set off in error, but when he heard what I did say, he went in the house, grabbed a jacket, and began walking down the street. Not even missing a beat, the fireman spoke into his radio receiver, communicating in coded numbers and a few words what the situation was, then followed with:

"The suspect is a black male, six feet, dressed in black jeans, dark-colored jacket, leaving by foot, headed east on Santana." He looked back at me and allowed me to share more details as I led him inside the house, stopping just inside the front door. I saw a police car pull up with a detained Sydney in the backseat, and another vehicle followed, in which were Sydney's mother and his brother, Keith.

"Kareese, are y'all all right?" Keith asked, dashing across the yard, his mom following closely behind.

"Yeah." I nodded, confused about how he knew to come over. "Come on in."

"I thought I had lost y'all! The people called and said the house was on fire and they called and didn't get a response," Keith said, still a bit panicked.

It was then that I realized that Sydney's unplugging all the phones in the house had backfired on him. When they couldn't get ahold of us, they called Keith, who was first on our emergency contact list. His mother had just happened to be visiting.

"What happened? Where is Sydney?"

I pointed to the police vehicle, but before I could start with the story, the fireman interrupted me.

"Ma'am, you're going to have to stay out of your bedroom until the fire marshal gets here, because it's a crime scene. I've pulled the door closed."

"What? A crime scene?" His mom could only shake her head as I described to her, in short, what had happened. "I need to sit down," she puffed out. She grabbed her chest in pain. "Lawd, ha' mercy."

"Calm down, Ma," Keith encouraged, patting her shoulder while my mother-in-law took a seat on the couch.

"My pressure going up." With the medics standing nearby for a false alarm, they quickly turned their attention to Ms. Patricia. "I'm so sorry, Kareese," she offered, panting. "Sydney knows better than this."

With all the commotion and voices in the house, Casey and Carlos wandered out of their room one more time, confused, but happy to see their grandma.

"Gee-Gee," Carlos called, walking over and hugging her. Casey, instead, came and wrapped his arms around me, scared and seeking answers.

"Ma, is Daddy gone to jail?"

"No, babe. Listen, I need you and Carlos to go back to your room for a little while, okay?" They were reluctant but obedient.

"He ain't never seen his daddy do no mess like this." Ms. Patricia nudged at a tear, while the medic took her blood pressure. "I don't know why he acting like this, Kareese."

"Mrs. Christopher, I'm going to need you to write a statement for the police report," a female officer said, handing me a form and a pen. Between police officers, medics, firemen, family and the marshal, I didn't know who walking through my front door, but as long as it wasn't my husband, I was fine.

The fire marshal took a quick walk through our bedroom, which was heavily permeated with the aerosol scent of hair spray. He collected the lighter, the can of spray, the hammer, and a few of the smashed items as evidence. He then radioed to the officer outside to take Sydney to jail with a charge of threatening to bomb or burn.

I didn't feel one bit sorry for him, although I did feel bad for Ms. Patricia, who began to pant and cry all the more.

"Ma'am, I'm glad you got out of this alive. I'm going to have the courts grant you an emergency restraining order. It will only be good for three days, so you may want to think about getting a full order within that time."

"Yes, sir, I will." There was no way I could let Sydney walk back in this house. "Where do I go to obtain one?"

"The Juvenile and Domestic Relations building."

I had no clue where that was, but I was intent on being there first thing on Monday morning. At some point, the fire trucks eased away; the paramedics ended up assisting Ms. Patricia into the ambulance and taking her to the hospital, when they couldn't get her pressure down; and the fire marshal asked for my signature on a document and left. I finished my statement, handed it to the officer and saw her to the door.

Finally the house was silent again. I leaned against the door and blew out a sigh, thinking about the past few hours, and waited for a sense of sadness to wash over me, but it didn't come. Wasn't I supposed to start crying or something? My emotions surprised me. There was no sadness, no wishing things had gone another way, no desire to make up. I was done.

Chapter Nineteen

The boys were crushed when I told them Sydney was in jail. It was a hard conversation to have. I didn't want to tell them all the details, because it just wasn't their place to know. First they cried, then they moped around the house while I changed the locks on the doors. Like that would be enough to keep Sydney out if he really wanted to get inside. It would at least give me time to call for help.

Video games would do little to soothe the boys emotionally, but they gravitated to them in their boredom and mixed emotions, which gave me a chance to call my mother.

"Hey, Ma, it's Kareese. Sydney and I broke up," I announced as soon as she answered.

"Kareese?" she confirmed. "What do you mean you broke up?"

"He tried to kill me, Ma." It didn't sound right leaving my lips, but I'd thought about everything that Sydney had done and said, and I narrowed it down to two things: A) He really was going to set the bed or room on fire to hurt, if not kill me; or B) He really wanted me to think that, so I'd forever be afraid of him. Either way I looked at it, there was no justifying his behavior.

She gasped. "Tried to kill you? When? What happened?"

"It's a long story, but let me just tell you—he's in jail right now."

She gasped a second time. "How are you doing?"

"I'm fine." I quickly shrugged. "Glad I'm alive."

"Where are the kids? I'm coming over there," she insisted.

"I'll make some coffee."

My mother had made her visits scarce over the years, and I'd pretty much limited my visits to holidays and an occasional and quick drop by. It had kept me from oversharing about my marriage, but had also kept the boys from having a little more than a cordial and respectful relationship with her. Somewhere in my heart of hearts, I knew my mother cared about and loved me and the kids, even if it stayed hidden under layers of lack of communication. I really hoped that today would be one of our better days and she would be sensitive to all I was prone to share with her regarding my and Sydney's relationship.

Thirty minutes passed before my doorbell rang, and my mother was standing on the other side. She grabbed me in a bear hug as soon as I opened the door.

"How are you holding up, Kareese?" She held me by my shoulders, studying my face.

"Ma, I'm fine. Really."

"You've got to be feeling something. After all, it is your husband," she said, trying to dig deep into my feelings.

"Please. Trust me, I'm fine. Carlos and Casey, your grandma is here."

"I thought she was in the hospital," Carlos said, running to the living room, where we still stood.

"Patricia's in the hospital?" Momma asked. I didn't know what the answer to that question was. I should have called and checked up on her, but I was too consumed with my side of things.

"Oh! Hey, Grandma," Carlos said. "I thought you were my other grandma. The ambulance took her to the hospital last night," Carlos volunteered.

"She was over here?" My mother's eyes bounced back and forth between Carlos's face and mine.

"Hey, Grandma," Casey greeted, coming into the living room.

"Hey, baby. You all right?"

"I guess." He shrugged, quickly hugging her upon his approach, then returning to the den, with Carlos following.

"Did you tell them?"

"I had to tell them something, for all the commotion that was going on over here last night."

"So what happened?"

Starting with my near-death experience, I recapped the past four or five years of my marriage as we sipped from coffee cups. She couldn't help interjecting every other sentence how much she never liked Sydney in the first place. It was her way of saying "I told you so," but right now, I was fine with it.

"Well, it's over now."

"You're not going to take him back?" she asked. "I know you love him."

"It takes a fool to learn that love don't love nobody," I said, quoting The Spinners, as I got up to answer the ringing phone. "I've been a fool long enough. Hello?" I spoke into the handset.

"Mrs. Christopher?"

"Yes?"

"This is Walter Robinson. I'm the bail bondsman for your husband, Sydney Christopher, who is being held in the Raleigh City Jail."

"If you are calling to ask me to bring you money, I'm not going to do that," I said flatly.

"No, ma'am, I'm not. And I'll be honest with you, after reading the police report, I don't blame you. But I was calling because I had a chance to talk to Mr. Christopher and he's saying that his wallet is there at the house, and he has cash in it that he needs in order to be released. Would you be willing to bring his wallet to my office, or if that is asking too much, I will be glad to pick it up."

"I don't know where his wallet is, and I'm not looking for it. He better be glad that I don't take that money and pay next month's bills with it."

"I understand, ma'am. You have a good day."

"He must be crazy," I said aloud. "Anyway."

"So what are you thinking about doing?"

"Ain't nothing I can do but move on. I got a good job, we have a house, so all I have to do is pay bills and live. And I've been paying bills all this time, so that is no big deal."

"What are you going to do when he comes back after you? Because you know he is coming."

"How do you mean?"

"I mean, if he threatened you once, what's going to stop him from doing it again?"

"I think he was halfway playing mind games."

"What about the other half? The half that you say the Lord warned you about."

"I don't know, Ma. You think I should get a gun?"

"You got one here already, don't you? The same one he said he was gonna shoot himself with."

"Oh yeah—there is one here, but I can't get to it. It's locked up. Besides, I don't know. I don't know if I can shoot anybody."

"I bet you could if your life depended on it."

"Well, I don't want to think about that, Ma."

"You better think about it, because you know he's coming back either to finish up what he tried to start or get you to take him back."

"That definitely ain't happening. Ma, this marriage has been nothing but hell from that day that I announced our engagement. And I feel like Mary J. Blige when she says she should have left his ass a thousand times."

"I'm sorry you had to go through this by yourself."

"It's all right. I needed to go through this by myself so that I could make my own decisions and not be influenced by you or Gene or anyone else. I do know I'm going to be filing for a divorce," I announced.

"Good for you," she said, sipping from her cup. "You're gonna have to be strong, Kareese, regardless of what he says."

"Ma, Sydney don't want me. He never did. This is a free pass for the both of us."

"He might didn't want you then, but he might want you now. If he wanted to leave you, he would have done that by now, but he was holding on to something."

"Well, it wasn't love, that's for sure," I said, standing to answer the doorbell.

Yalisa came in and wrapped her arms around me. "Giiirl!" she drew out. "I am so glad you and the boys are okay."

"Thanks. Come on in, my mom is here in the den."

"Your mom," she whispered.

"Yeah. I told her and she came over."

"Oh, okay." Yalisa walked in the den and took a seat. "Hey, Mrs. Watson."

"How are you doing, Yalisa? It's good to see you."

"You too. I'm glad my friend is alive and well."

"I'm glad too."

For the next few hours, I talked openly about specific points of marriage, everything from Sydney hiding money to trying to convince me that he got gonorrhea from a condom.

"Lawd, child," Momma said. "He don't deserve you, Kareese."

"I know, Ma. It took forever to realize it, but I know it now."

***

On the next business day, I called in late for work to go down to Juvenile Domestic Relations and file for a temporary restraining order, and while I was down there, I went ahead and filed for child support and alimony, killing three birds with one stone. Sydney wasn't going to be happy about me demanding money from him, but so what? Who cared about him and what made him mad? He didn't even have a job, but he'd be forced to get one now.

Sydney had gone to stay at Keith's house when he was released on bail, and Keith came by to pick up his things. I hadn't talked to Sydney, and I didn't want to. I let the boys talk to him every day, though. The question that I'd heard them ask most often was:

"When are you coming home?"

I hated that. Knowing Sydney, I knew he put all the weight on me. All the weight, all the blame, all the reasons why he wasn't home. He'd just say it was my fault. I was fine with that for now. I didn't have time to think about Sydney's tricks. I had to focus on making sure I provided as a single parent for my boys. Being the only provider meant I had to think differently; I had to work longer hours to stay on my A game and make more money. I had to go harder, go faster, become more efficient, dot every *i* and cross every *t*.

***

It had been months since I'd talked to Quinton. I'd blocked him from my chat contacts when I was trying to behave myself. And with all the drama Sydney kept piling on me, I didn't have time for it, anyway. Quinton had sent me a couple of e-mail messages trying to spark up conversation, but I'd kept our interaction extremely short. He caught me by surprise when I walked in to work one day and found him strolling the back hallways.

"Hey, Mrs. Christopher," he called from behind me.

I turned around and smiled in surprise. "Quinton." We greeted each other with a hug, and although we'd pretty much had sex with each other over the Internet, I felt nothing when our bodies met.

"What's going on with you? You just cut a brother off." He grinned.

"Nothing and everything," I answered, shaking my head. "How about you?"

He bit his bottom lip and just stared at me. "You look good, Kareese."

"Thank you. So how long are you here for?"

"Couple of weeks. We're opening the new branch next week."

"Oh. I didn't know you were a part of that launch."

"That's because you've been ignoring me for months now." Quinton folded his arms across his chest and leaned against the wall.

"I'm just in a different place. Trying to get some things done and stay focused."

He nodded his head toward my hand. "So what's going on with that?"

"With what?"

"That empty ring finger."

"It is what it is." I shrugged.

"So you're single now?"

"Something like that."

Quinton studied me silently, probably looking for a hint of sexual interest, but I just didn't have it in me.

"Well, I need to get started with my day, so I'll see you later. It's good seeing you," I managed to say.

"Likewise," he stated. "Lunch later?" he tested me.

"My day is pretty booked. I'm sorry." I scooted past him, leaving him looking a little put off.

He looked really good, but I didn't have time for distractions. Not while I had court dates coming up and had to take care of all the bills. And not just that, but I really didn't want to get caught up again in uncontrolled feelings of lust. My bumping and grinding with Quinton was a long time ago, and I was so over the thought of sleeping with him. He probably had had it on his mind as soon as he found out that he would be coming to North Carolina. That's typical male behavior for you, though. Always thinking about what they can get.

Quinton and I did share a couple of cups of coffee in the employee break room for a few mornings. We used that time to catch up just a bit. In actuality, I never really knew that much about Quinton and his personal life. Other than the fact that he had a corporate position, he lived in Maryland and we had a bit of a fling, I had nothing. On the other hand, he didn't really know much about me either.

"So you and Mr. Christopher called it quits?"

"Yeah. That's the end of the story."

"What happened?"

"Things just weren't working out, and through the years, we just kind of had the Gladys Knight and the Pips thing going. You know, neither one of us wanted to be the first one to say good-bye."

"So who ended up saying good-bye first?"

"Umm. It's kinda hard to answer that exactly, but I guess you could say I did."

"So what happened that you just got to the end of your rope and you decided to pull the plug?"

"I really don't want to go into it, Quinton, but it was just getting to be more than I wanted to deal with."

He nodded. "Well, if you are happy, I'm happy for you."

"I am happy," I confirmed.

"Do you miss him?"

I pressed my lips together and shook my head. "It's kinda sad, but no, I don't. You would think that I would for the years that we were together, but it was just really time to end it."

"Well, that's good."

"So what about you? You were seeing some girl who wasn't the one, but she was good enough."

"There's nothing going on with that," he said dismissively. "I told you, we were just kicking it, to begin with."

"Mmm," I responded nonchalantly.

"So what's up with me being able to redeem my lunch you promised me? You can't say you're tied up with your husband."

"No, I'm not tied up with him, but I am tied up with other things and I just don't need to be distracted or introduce other things into my life that could potentially be disastrous."

"Do you think I would be a disaster in your life?"

"Potentially, yes."

"Why would you say that?"

"Because we both know you don't want any-thing, Quinton. I mean, after we finish rolling around on a mattress in a hotel room, what would we have?" I paused to give him a chance to answer, but he didn't. He only looked at me blankly as if to say, "What could you possibly be expecting?"

"Right now where I am, I just need to be focused, and I don't have time for additional drama," I declared.

"Well, go head-on, soul sista."

"Thanks. I'll talk to you later. Maybe we can have lunch here in the break room or something."

"No, you go ahead and focus on what you need to get done. I can appreciate and respect that."

After that conversation, Quinton didn't have too much to say to me for the rest of his visit, which actually made me want him. I wanted him to flirt with me a little bit, just so I could turn it down. He did circle back around on his last day at our branch.

"So, am I gonna get my promised lunch, or are you going to send me back home with a promise unfulfilled?" Quinton had sneaked up behind me in the break room and pressed into my backside.

"If anything, you should be taking me to lunch," I countered. "You better get your little weenie off of me before somebody sees you."

"Little weenie? I got your little weenie." He took my hand and pressed it against his crotch, then made his manhood pulse forward. "Does that feel like a little weenie to you?"

I snatched my hand away like he'd stuck it in a fire pit. "What is wrong with you!" I laughed, mildly turned on by the thrill of our inappropriate acts.

"I'm just saying. If you scared, then say you scared."

"Ain't nobody scared of that little mess. You're probably a minute man."

"I'll tell you what, let's meet up after work. We'll have dinner and we'll see what happens from there."

"Outback. Seven o'clock."

"See you there."

My womanhood twitched and flinched for the rest of the day in anticipation of getting a piece of Quinton. Right at six, I rushed home and showered, straightened up my bedroom; then I slipped into a hot pink knit minidress with black accessories.

"Y'all ready?" I called to the boys. Sydney was keeping them for the weekend, like he did most weekends, but I'd always offered to drop them off, not wanting Sydney anywhere in the vicinity of the house.

"Where you going, Ma?"

"To a work function," I lied. Had I said out on a date, or with a friend, they would have spilled it to Sydney, and it was none of his business.

I got to Outback just two minutes before seven, and rushed inside trying to be on time, and was glad to see Quinton had beat me there and already had us on the waiting list.

"Sex-ay, Sex-ay!" he whispered in my ear in his best E.U. "Da' Butt" voice; then he kissed my cheek.

"Hey, Quinton."

"Mmph, mmph, mmph!" His eyes traveled down my body as he licked his lips.

Our table was ready in fifteen minutes, and Quinton took me by the hand, leading me there as he followed the hostess. We sat across from each other, looking at both the menu and at each other.

"I'm glad you came, Kareese. You're great company."

"Thanks. You don't do so bad yourself." I smiled. "I'll be right back." I stood to go to the bathroom and smoothed my hands over my dress, to get him to look at me again.

"Mmph!"

"It's just a dress!" I waved his attention off. "Be right back." In the bathroom, I washed my hands, puckered my lips to myself, then returned to the table. Quinton had changed his seat to sit adjacent to me rather than across from me. When I sat down, he rested his hand on my thigh.

"You look good, girl."

"Thanks." I cleared my throat, a bit uncomfortable with him having his hand on my lap. But Quinton and I had been flirting around with each other so long, this was nothing. He drew little circles on my leg, turning me on. Tonight it was gonna be time to do it or stop dreaming about it all together.

I ordered roasted pork tenderloin, with a sweet tangy glaze, and a side of garlic mashed potatoes and fresh steamed French green beans. Quinton picked tilapia, which was crowned with a crab stuffing, then topped with pure lump crab meat and sliced mushrooms, drizzled with a light lemon butter Chablis sauce, and accompanied by a serving of zucchini and squash.

Quinton sampled from my plate and I sampled from his as we laughed, talked and made all kinds of sexual comments, building the tension throughout the meal.

"So what's up?" he asked after he'd paid the bill and walked me out to my car.

"I've got to get out of these shoes," I said as an excuse to get him over to my house. It sounded less trampy that way. "You can follow me there, if you want."

We got in our cars and took a short drive to my home. No sooner than he was inside, he pinned me against the door and pushed his hand up my dress and kissed me.

"I've been waiting to do that all night," he panted, grinding his pelvis into mine. "You feel that?"

"Mmm-hmm," I moaned, which was all I could do, since my mouth was filled with his lips.

He broke the kiss for two seconds. "Does that feel like a little weenie to you?"

I only giggled as I broke away to lead him to the bedroom Sydney and I used to share. On the way, he pulled my dress up to my waist and cursed under his breath when he saw my cheeks separated by the tiny strip of material of my thong. We entered my bedroom, keeping the lights off, and went at it like there was no tomorrow. What he had was way more than a weenie, and he knew how to use it. He used his tool, his hands, his lips, his mouth and even the prickly hair that grew from his chin to spin me out of my mind.

When Quinton and I finished, I definitely was ready to sign up for the subscription. Yeah. It was just that good.

Just as I was about to nestle into his chest, he shifted his weight and turned his back to me. Not a problem. I scooted forward and pressed against his back, instead, and slid my arm beneath his, fitting my hand inside of his. He grunted a bit, kissed my fingers, and gently pushed them away.

"Your arm is uncomfortable right there," he mumbled.

I didn't comment, but a little put off, I retracted my arm and backed up a bit. I wanted him to feel my pulling away and say, "Where're you going?" but he said nothing. I flounced around a bit, hoping that he would turn over and wrap his arms around my body and hold me. Quinton didn't budge.

"Quinton?"

"Hmph," he mumbled.

"Why are you turned that way?"

"That's how I sleep," he uttered.

"Can you turn this way toward me?"

"For what?"

"Just to hold me."

He grunted as he turned over and dropped his arm over me. It felt nothing like I wanted and needed it to. His arms were empty and I felt nothing. Nothing warm, inviting, or affectionate. He was just there.

"Remember that time you said, 'Oh, I could hold you in my arms all night,'" I lowered my voice an octave to sound more like a man's.

"Not really."

His words stung. "But you did."

"I don't think I did, because that's uncomfortable to me." He began to snore a few seconds later, disrupting the spooning and cuddling I craved.

"Quinton?" I nudged him with my elbow.

"Hmm! What, honey?" he answered, sounding delusional. "What time is it? I gotta go in a few minutes."

It was almost midnight. Where was he planning on going?

"Go where?"

"I gotta pack. My plane leaves tomorrow."

"I thought you had an afternoon flight."

"Yeah, I do, but I got some stuff I need to take care of in the morning and I don't want to be rushing around."

Still lying against him, empty and dissatisfied, I let my eyes roam around the room. I could have kicked myself for being so stupid, expecting him to act like he really felt something for me. What in the world made me think that Quinton wanted something other than sex? And now that he got it, he was ready to jet. How many times had I heard women complain, cry, and talk about how they had their hearts broken over this very thing? Just the way Quinton and I got involved in the first place ought to have told me everything I needed to know. Once he found out I was married, that should have been it. There should have never been any dinners and casinos, and huckin' and buckin' on the couch of my hotel room. A real man would have respected the fact that I was married. I'd heard it a million times before—men were dogs.

Then again, I guess I couldn't be too mad at Quinton without being mad at myself. I was the one who had made the vows to be faithful and true, and I was the one who'd shown a lack of respect for my own marriage, as awful as it was. I knew better than to go out with him; I knew better than to let him in my room; I definitely knew better than to be having cybersex with a man I wasn't married to. There was no getting around it—I'd played myself. I wished I'd never met Quinton, but little good that did, now that I'd let him in my sacred place.

The only good point I could find about this was I was the one that wasn't going to have to get up, get dressed and get out. I poked Quinton in his shoulder.

"Quinton, get up," I ordered.

"Hmm, what?"

"It's time for you to leave." I clicked on the light and poked his shoulder harder. "Get up."

"What are you talking about?"

"It's time for you to go. Now!" I snatched the covers away from where he lay and wrapped them around my body. "Get out of my house."

Quinton sighed as he sat up, his eyes still squinting from the light. I didn't hear it quite so clearly, but it sounded like Quinton called me the *B* word. I kicked hard into his back, making him stumble to his feet.

"Get the hell out!"

Quinton pulled his clothes on without a word and left my bedroom, with me close behind looking like I was on my way to a toga party, still wrapped in a sheet. I followed him down the stairs and to the door and locked it as soon as he was on the other side.

Chapter Twenty

I wasn't the one on trial, but I was extremely nervous getting ready for court the morning of Sydney's trial date. It had been three months since Sydney and I'd broken up, and I'd thought a lot about his future. I had mixed feelings about what I wanted to see happen in court today. In my opinion, Sydney needed to be held accountable for his actions, but I didn't particularly want to see him go to jail. I didn't want it for him, and I didn't want it for the boys. At the same time, he didn't need to get off scot-free, like it was perfectly all right to make someone fear for his or her life.

Dressed in a black sweater, a zebra print skirt, black tights and black shoes, I looked smart and sassy. Maybe the skirt was too edgy for a court appearance, but I kept it on, anyway. It made me feel good, not to mention I looked amazing, which is how I needed to look for seeing Sydney for the first time in over three months.

I got to the courtroom first and took a seat midway in the room. It was pretty empty, only court-related employees were there, wandering in and out. It was quiet enough for me to think. If Sydney went to jail, how was I going to tell the boys? I don't know what Sydney had said to them over the past few months, and I'd never mentioned to them that he was at risk of going away. It was probably something I should have done.

Fifteen minutes passed before Sydney came in with his attorney, a homely-looking black woman with hair that looked like she drove there a hundred miles an hour with the windows down. She was dressed in a conservative long gray A-line skirt and an off-white turtleneck sweater whose sleeves were too short. I wasn't sure what kind of lawyer tricks she had up her sleeves, but intimidation through the image of high-powered attorney was certainly not it.

When I was called to the stand and explained what had happened, she seemed not to have a questioning strategy, asking if Sydney swung the hammer out of nervousness. Excuse me? Nervous about what? That I was putting him out? Whatever. She asked me a few more questions, which really didn't amount to much, but I guess they were effective. In a matter of minutes, the judge ruled in Sydney's favor, saying he didn't see how Sydney's actions suggested he was going to do harm.

What? What kind of cockamamy trial was this? We were barely there twenty minutes! Sydney didn't get called to the stand at all, and there was no prosecuting attorney who could come up and magnify Sydney's behavior as threatening, or ask me in front of the judge how very afraid I was. Shouldn't there have been some presentation of the police report and the fire marshal's report? I'd seen TV judges dig more into a case about damaged cell phones than what this judge did. He had to be kidding me. How could a man make me feel like I was about to die, and the judge simply excuse it with a wave of his hand? Sydney pretty much sprayed me down with a flammable substance while he held a lighter in his hand! If that is not a threat on someone's life, I don't know what was. The judge must have been some kind of woman beater. And now that I thought of it, how could a woman attorney have even taken his case? She must have needed the money. From the looks of her outfit, she did, and I guess she earned her keep today.

I walked to my car, feeling totally dejected and worthless. The judge's decision brought tears to my eyes. Did my life have any value at all? I could see Sydney celebrating right now. Laughing at me. Planning his move back home, as the judge's ruling made my restraining order null and void. He could have at least given Sydney community service or something. You mean to tell me he wouldn't even make Sydney pick up trash off the street on Saturday mornings after he almost took my life? There was no sense in me thinking that he wouldn't move back into his own home. Back to square one—I was going to have to move.

Two days after court, Sydney called me and I answered. We did have business to discuss, after all. "Will you at least meet me for lunch?" he asked.

I rolled the thought around in my head. I needed to know what he was thinking so I could get my own plans together. "Where at?"

"How about T.G.I. Friday's," he suggested.

"What time?"

"In an hour, if that works for you."

I chewed on my bottom lip. "Make it an hour and a half," I said, wanting to keep him on my time. And it would give me a chance to pull it together and look like a million bucks. I was a different person than I'd been a few months back. Not only had I weighed more, but my clothes then were so drab and motherly. I'd

updated my wardrobe to be more fashionable
and youthful. I pulled on a pair of boot-cut
jeans that showed off my twenty-pounds-lighter
figure, a black-and-gray striped sweater, with
matching knit skullcap. Hoop earrings framed
my face, and heeled boots gave me a height that
demanded attention. I felt good, powerful, and
in control. It was what I needed for this meeting.
Especially since I was going to spring on him
that I was filing for a divorce.

I made sure I showed up fifteen minutes late,
and when I got there, Sydney was already seated
in a booth and sipping on a glass of tea. He
looked nervous, instead of confident, which is
what I'd expected, and he had the unmitigated
gall to have on his wedding band. I chuckled.
More tricks and games.

"Hey, Kareese," he greeted.

I barely spoke back as I took my seat. We sized
each other up on the sly. I caught him looking at
me, and he caught me looking at him.

"You look good," he uttered, then pretended
to study the menu.

"Thanks." I didn't look at him.

"What can I get you to drink, ma'am?" The
server was a young man with smooth, thick locks
pulled away from his face and hanging down his
back. I raised a flirtatious eyebrow at him and
ordered a soft drink.

"Were you two ready to order, or did you need a few more minutes?" he asked, licking his lips. I don't know what he thought the dynamic of my and Sydney's relationship was, with me not having on a ring and Sydney wearing his.

"I'm ready," I answered, not waiting for Sydney. I ordered golden brown chicken strips, coated with Asian panko bread crumbs and topped with toasted sesame seeds, tossed in a tangy Jack Daniel's glaze, along with a side salad.

"And for you, sir?"

"I, uh"—Sydney quickly glanced over the menu—"I'ma have this." He pointed to a dish of sautéed garlic-marinated chicken and shrimp tossed in a bruschetta marinara with onions, peppers, and mashed potatoes. It was all served on a platter of melted Mexican and American cheeses.

"I'll have that out for you in a little bit."

"What's your name?" I asked, smiling.

"Malcolm."

"Thank you, Malcolm."

"No problem." Malcolm turned and left, and I purposely let my eyes follow.

"What's that all about?" Sydney asked, annoyed.

"What?" I closed my menu and slid it behind the condiment bottles on the table.

"That with you and Mr. Waiter-man right there."

"I don't know what you're talking about."

"I'm talking about you sitting here, right in my face, flirting."

"Whatever, Sydney. Why did you ask me here?" I laced my fingers and set them atop of the table, making sure that my empty finger was clearly visible.

"Where's your ring?" he asked, almost demanding.

"Who cares? What do you want?"

He searched my face for a few seconds, then cleared his throat. "I've been doing a lot of praying since I've been gone," Sydney started.

Here we go.

"I did a lot of fasting and just asking God to help me."

"Help you what?"

"Help me be a better husband and better father." He paused to give me a chance to respond, but I said nothing. "He told me that I owed you an apology."

"Mmph," I huffed through pressed lips.

"He showed me so many things I did wrong and how bad I treated you and how I was not a good example for how Casey and Carlos should treat their wives, once they grow up and get married."

"Well, good. I'm glad you and God got to have some conversations. So tell me—what exactly were you trying to do that night, Sydney?" I couldn't resist confronting him.

"I wasn't tryin'a do nothing," he commented.

"Yes, you were. You were either gonna kill me or you wanted me to think that so you could control me. Which one was it?" When Sydney didn't answer, I took my voice up an octave. "Which one?"

"I'm sorry, Kareese," he said, almost choking, just as Malcolm came back and set our food on the table.

"Mmm! This looks so good!" Ignoring his apology, I looked at Malcolm. "Thank you so much. Can you bring me just a little more Jack Daniel's sauce, please?"

"Sure. Does everything else look okay?"

"Yeah, man, yeah—yeah," Sydney answered, rushing him off, then looking at me. "Did you hear what I said?"

"Yeah. You said you're sorry; I heard you." I stuffed my mouth with a chicken tender and shrugged.

Sydney looked taken aback. I know he didn't think that weak apology was gonna fly. "He also told me that I needed to put on my wedding ring because our marriage isn't over."

I couldn't help but giggle out loud. "For real?"

"I'm being serious," he said, toying with his food.

"Okay. Just don't expect me to take you seriously."

He looked crushed. "That's fine. God told me you weren't going to be open to hearing me."

"Oh, I hear you just fine."

"Well, you know what I mean, Kareese."

I rolled my eyes.

"God is going to prove—"

"Listen," I said, cutting him off. "I'm filing for a divorce, Sydney." I didn't want to hear another word about all this talking he was suddenly doing with the Lord.

Sydney fell silent and stared at me. "I'll be right back." He got up and meandered toward the men's room. I tasted his food while he was gone.

"Okay, I only have this one request before you file," he said, sliding back into the booth minutes later.

"What did you do, go pray right quick?" I mocked. Although I fully believed in the power of prayer, I could hardly believe Sydney's sincerity and felt that he was using faith as a smoke screen to attempt to manipulate me.

Sydney didn't laugh. "We've been through a lot, Kareese, but I refuse to let our past drama dictate our future. Will you just give me three months? Three months to prove to you how much I've changed," he stated.

"You can't show me that you've changed in three months. All you can do is treat me well for three months. Anybody can do that. And if you think I'm going to trade three months of you acting like you got some sense for the rest of my life in hell with you, you must be crazy."

"Well, let's not set time limits or boundaries, then. Just agree to uphold the vows that you made when we got married. To be with me through sickness and health, richer or poorer . . ." He paused to think of more of the vows we both took. "For better or for worse, to have and to hold, till death do us part." He paused again. "Did you mean those words when you said them, Kareese, or were you just saying stuff? As much as you talk about honoring God, don't you know that the Bible says it's better for a man not to make a vow than to make one and not keep it? Now, I may have made some mistakes, but I have never once tried to leave you."

Malcolm appeared to get our plates and placed the check folio on the table. "I'll pick that up when you're ready."

I grabbed it right away, glanced at it and handed it back to Malcolm. "Two checks, please."

"Oh. I'm sorry," he said, glancing at Sydney, who looked a bit stupefied.

"No apology necessary."

"You won't even let me buy you lunch?" Sydney gaped.

"Nope. I don't want you to do anything for me but sign the divorce papers when they arrive."

"I'm moving back home next week," he said flatly.

"Thanks for the heads-up. I'm moving out then," I countered. I dug in my wallet, pulled out a ten and a five and slid out of the booth as Malcolm was approaching. "Here you go," I said, handing Malcolm the money.

"See you in court, Sydney."

On my drive home, I thought about where I wanted to live; I was definitely moving out if Sydney moved back home.

When I got home, Casey and Carlos greeted me at the door with long faces and tears on Carlos's part.

"What's wrong?" I questioned.

"Daddy called and said that you were breaking up our family, even though the judge said he could come home now," Casey answered.

Immediately my blood began to boil. And he wondered why I didn't want to hear anything he had to say this afternoon!

"Your dad and I need to spend some time apart. I know you don't understand it right now, but it's what needs to happen."

"But why, Ma?" Carlos whined. "We supposed to be a family because God honors marriage."

"Who told you that, Carlos? Because I know you haven't been reading your Bible."

"Daddy told us to remind you of that."

"Of course he did." Tossing my purse on the couch, I moved on. "So what do y'all want to eat?"

"I'm not hungry," Casey said. "I'm just going to my room."

"Can we have pizza?"

"Sure, go start the order online," I answered, following Casey to his bedroom.

"Casey," I called from his doorway.

"Ma'am?"

I didn't know what to say after that, but I knew I was doing the right thing by separating myself from Sydney. How could I say that without making it sound so harsh? "Look, I know this is hard for you and Carlos because you two are used to having both of us around, but what I want you to realize is that no matter what happens, we both love you very much."

"Ma, I need the password," Carlos said from behind me.

"I'm coming." I knew better than to just fork over my Pizza Hut profile password. Those boys would have pizza and breadsticks coming to the house every night.

"But don't y'all love each other?"

I hesitated. I couldn't say yes. Anything close to love that I had for Sydney had completely fizzled out that dangerous night a few months back. Maybe I had a little lust for him, but whatever it was, it couldn't rightfully be described as love. I answered as best I could. "Well, we will always care about each other because we have you and Carlos," I answered. It sounded weak, like I should have just said no, but I couldn't bring myself to confess that to my kids.

"Do you care enough even to try to work it out, because Daddy said you won't even try?"

Sydney made me sick!

"I'm not sure what we're going to do right now," I lied. I knew full well what I planned on doing. "But first I have to make sure that I'm safe, and you boys are safe, and that means your dad and I will be splitting up for at least a little while."

Casey's eyes randomly circled his room.

"We will probably be moving really soon, but you will get to see both of us. You will still have both parents, and we still love you. That's not going to change."

"All right, Ma," he said, more out of exasperation than acceptance.

"It'll be all right." I turned to leave his room. "Make sure you eat something before you go to sleep, okay?"

"Yes, ma'am" he said dolefully.

When the pizza arrived, we sat together in the den and watched the different generations of *Shrek* and tried to make the best of the evening. Sydney did call during the movies, and as much as I wanted, I didn't stop the boys from talking to him. If I had, they would only hate me for it later.

Sure enough, just like he'd said, Sydney moved back in the house. He did it without telling me that day, and while I was at work. I guess to keep the drama down. Maybe that was smart on his part, because it wouldn't have been a pretty sight, had I been there. Although, there was really nothing I could do to stop him.

He called me just as I was getting off work to announce that he had moved in.

"Hey," he started as soon as I answered.

"Yes, what is it, Sydney?"

"You on your way home?"

"Yeah."

"Okay. I'll be here when you get here."

My stomach dropped. I knew it was coming, but I didn't want to face it. I'd started my search for a place to live, but I hadn't secured anything just yet. I was just going to have to pray my way through and sleep in the extra bedroom.

When I walked in the house, Casey and Carlos seemed happier than they had been in months, bouncing up and down like two rubber balls.

"Hey, boys," I greeted with quick kisses on their cheeks, but I rushed past them, needing to relieve myself. In our bedroom was where I found Sydney. He was beside the bed on his knees, with his hands raised high in the air. Donnie McClurkin's "I'll Trust You, Lord" was playing from the stereo, and Sydney had tears streaming down his face.

"Hallelujah," he cried repeatedly. "Thank you, Jesus."

I found it unimpressive. I couldn't say whether he was having a moment with God or not, it was just mighty funny how he timed it around the same time I was due to come home. I never even broke my stride to pay him any attention but instead beelined it to the bathroom. I came out, whizzed past him, as if he wasn't there, and closed the bedroom door behind me.

Grateful that the kids had already eaten, I reclined behind the closed door of the guest bedroom, which would just have to be my bedroom until I transitioned to a new residence. I just wished it had its own bathroom, but under the circumstances, I was willing to share with the boys.

I'd just begun to doze off when Sydney tapped on the door.

"What?"

"Can I come in for a few minutes?" he asked, sniffing.

I got up and allowed him entrance, pointing him to an armchair, but he sat on the side of the bed, instead. I kept my position by the open door, just in case I needed to make a quick move.

"I know you are not going to want to hear this from me, but as I was praying, the Lord told me to tell you something."

"And what is that?"

"He said that you weren't leaving because he told you to. You're leaving because you want to, and you are walking out from under your umbrella of protection."

No comment.

"I know you don't want to hear that from me, but God told me to tell you, anyway."

"Well, thanks for doing what the Lord told you to do. You can get out of my room now."

Sydney looked deflated as he stood. "You know, you could pray and ask God yourself if you don't believe me."

"Thanks. I will do just that." I nodded my head toward the door, indicating it was time for him to leave. He walked out in silence, and I closed and locked the door behind him.

I didn't believe a word of what he'd just said, and as far as I was concerned, he only said it because he knew I'd always encouraged him to lead the family in worship. Now all of a sudden, he had a hotline to heaven. Yeah right.

Or did he?

Suppose I was wrong? Suppose God really did speak to him and wanted to heal our marriage and I wasn't listening. I lay back on the bed and wondered if what Sydney said had any truth to it at all. It probably didn't, but just suppose it did.

"Lord, speak to me regarding this situation," I prayed out loud, afraid that I would miss God's will. After all, how many times had I heard God hates divorce? That was one of the "Stay" reasons I'd listed on my paper months ago. It wasn't enough to make me reconcile right away, though. The best thing I could think to do in the situation, just to make sure I wasn't wrong, was to pray and ask God for a sign. But in the meantime, I found a two-bedroom town house not too far from the house that was available for rent, which I wasted no time submitting an application for. When it was approved, I counted that as a sign to leave. I did a walk-through of the

property, and while it was not as large as the house
Sydney and I rented together, it was perfect for
what I needed for the moment and, luckily, it didn't
require that Casey and Carlos change schools. I took
that as "Leave" sign number two. The driveway
pulled right up to the front door, so I'd be in the
house within seconds; it had a spacious master,
which I'd give to the boys, and a smaller second
bedroom; a front and a back door, just in case I
needed to escape; and, most of all, it had a security
system already installed. A third sign. As far as I
was concerned, this was a done deal. Since I had
the money to cover the security deposit and first
month's rent, I whipped out my checkbook and
signed the lease in a matter of five days.

I left with nothing more than my clothes, my
kids, and a single TV for their bedroom. Anything else could easily be replaced and wasn't
important to me, so Sydney could have the entire
house and everything in it.

I grinned as I wheeled my car in my parking
spot, right next to my new neighbor's car. I felt
proud of myself. It was my very first place out on
my own.

"What do y'all think?" I asked, smiling at the
boys, opening the door and letting them walk
through. "You two can have the big room, since
it's two of y'all and only one of me. And I got
cable."

"It's all right," Casey said, shrugging. I knew they weren't happy, by any stretch of the imagination, but they had no choice. They weren't too vocal about their feelings, but I knew if they had a choice, they'd much rather Sydney and I stayed together. Back at "home," they'd be sleeping in their beds rather than on two air mattresses, and now they had to watch a TV that sat on the floor, for lack of a table or stand. Other than that, the house was completely empty. Empty, but peaceful and safe. Before I turned in for the night, I checked the locks on the doors three times and set the alarm.

I hadn't been able to get an air mattress for myself yet. So, wrapped in a sheet and nestled against a body pillow, I drifted off to sleep, with a smile.

Chapter Twenty-one

"The North Carolina law states that you can't file for a divorce until you and your husband have lived separate and apart for a year." Steven Cole pushed his framed specs up on his nose and sat back in his chair. "You can't do it before that, unless he abandoned you or made the home unsafe for you to live there."

"He did make it unsafe," I explained to the attorney, who sat across from me. I was ready to start my divorce proceedings. "I was scared for my life."

"That's what you're saying," he responded, "but with the case being dismissed in court, I'm not sure if you can use that as reasoning to move forward today. You may just need to wait a few more months before you file."

That was almost enough to bring tears to my eyes. I felt like he wasn't hearing me or feeling my pain. But then again, if he handled divorces, he probably saw people all the time who were desperately trying to get out of their situations. I was probably no different than any other client he'd taken on.

"Now, are you filing contested or uncontested?"

"What's the difference?"

"Is your estranged husband agreeable to this divorce?"

That was a good question. I really didn't know what kind of trick Sydney would try to pull.

"If both of you are agreeing to divorce, then it would be uncontested, which is going to cost you about five hundred dollars. If he is going to fight you over it, then you will have to sue him to get a divorce, which would be contested. That's going to run you about two thousand."

"Two grand?" I gasped.

"Contested takes more time and more court visits," he explained.

I pondered the thought and cost for a few seconds and thought it best that I filed contested. Knowing Sydney, he would refuse to sign the divorce papers and I'd be stuck being telling people that "we're married, but we're not together" for the next thirty years.

"I better file contested." I sighed at the thought. I had to trust that the money spent would be worth it in the end. We worked out a payment plan so he could get started on my case, and I felt one step closer to my freedom.

Bit by bit, paycheck by paycheck, over the next six months, I furnished my home and turned it into a haven that my boys and I could enjoy. I especially loved my bedroom. It was small, but I'd finally gotten a bed, a luxurious comforter set, with matching curtains, and a few accents to pull the room together. I had framed pictures of things that I felt expressed woman empowerment on the walls, placed a few candles, and stacked a few journals and books on a foot chest at the end of my bed. There was no television in my bedroom, only a small stereo, which I kept on a smooth jazz station twenty-four hours a day, maintaining a calm and peaceful ambience. It was warm and inviting and, best of all, drama free.

So this is what it felt like to be single. Life was great, and I had a newfound appreciation for it. Now that I didn't have to be accountable to anyone, I could enjoy my evenings in the way I liked best. Reading a book, enjoying a candlelit bath surrounded by rose petals and sipping on a hot cup of peppermint tea, working out to put more effort into shedding my extra weight. It felt good just to enjoy my own time. I didn't miss Sydney at all. I wasn't wondering where he was, what he was doing or whom he was doing it with. And I didn't care.

"Let's go out," I said to Yalisa when she answered her phone.

"Go out where?"

"I don't care. Somewhere. Let's go get something to eat." Yalisa sighed. "Come on, please," I whined. "You know I haven't done anything but sit up in the house for the last eighty-seven years," I exaggerated. "I'm ready to get out and live life a little bit. We can go to Sullivan's Steakhouse and get dessert or something."

"All right," she puffed in reply. "I guess I could throw something on right quick and go out for a little while. Can you pick me up?"

"Why can't you just meet me there? I'm gonna have to drive twice as far to pick you up, then drop you back off."

"All right, all right. I'll meet you in an hour."

A quick shower, followed by a slathering of lotion and a few spritzes of body spray, a little black halter dress, adorned with ruffles, and a pair of peep-toe pumps had me looking like a diva. I kept my jewelry simple, with a pair of rhinestone earrings and a matching floating necklace. With glossy lips, smoky eyes, and extended lashes, I told Casey and Carlos that I'd be back in a bit.

"Where are you going dressed like that, Ma?" Casey asked. "Just out with Yalisa."

"'Like that'? What's wrong with this?" I spun in a circle.

"Nothing. You look great," he complimented. "I'm just wondering who you going out with."

"Too bad I ain't married to you, or else I'd tell you."

"Don't make me have to punch nobody," he teased.

Yalisa and I pulled up at Sullivan's at the same time and had our cars valet parked.

"Why didn't you tell me you were putting on something cute!" she fussed.

"You know how we do!" I giggled. "You say that like you look bad." Yalisa was dressed in a mauve silk drawstring Capri jumper, and had on a pair of black stiletto studded ankle boots, which matched her purse. Her long hair was gathered in a ponytail, swept to the left side just behind her ear, and large gold earrings hung from her lobes.

"Yeah. We're too fly," she bragged with puckered lips. "Come on."

The ambience in Sullivan's was incredible. It had an upscale jazzy feel; its lighting, shiny cherry wood décor, black-and-white photos on the wall and live music made it a perfect adult fine-dining atmosphere. It was one of the places I'd asked Sydney to bring me, and he never would.

We took a seat at a small table and decided to split a tempting sweet potato casserole and sparkling cosmopolitans from the bar.

"So what's up with your boy?"

"Nothing. We did it the other night."

Yalisa frowned. "Why?"

I shrugged. "I don't know. I got horny." I'd been driving home and Jill Scott's "He Loves Me" played on the radio. I remembered how Sydney and I loved to make love to that song, and the more Jill sang, the more I started craving Sydney's sex. I knew I didn't ultimately want Sydney, I just needed a little maintenance.

"So! You should have gotten a toy."

"I don't have any toys, but I do have a husband."

She frowned even more.

"What? We are still married," I said, responding to her facial expression.

"So he's conveniently your husband?" Her tone was sarcastic.

"Not conveniently, legally."

"You ought to be ashamed of yourself." She shook her head.

"Well, he is. We're not divorced yet," I said, forking the combination of sweet potatoes, brown sugar, butter, pecans, and cinnamon into my mouth. "I still got rights to that if I want," I mumbled. "So I called Sydney and we hooked up." Yalisa only blinked at me. "It was good too."

She couldn't help but smirk at that. "Did you spend the night?"

"Girl, please, I can't close my eyes around that man. Suppose I fell asleep and he decided he wanted to get revenge for sending him to jail, getting him put out the house, and then leaving him. I ain't that crazy. It wasn't all that. As soon as it was over, I got up and left."

"Y'all did it at the house? In the same bed that he tried to take you up outta here in?"

"No, we went and hooked up at the Marriott."

"Ugh! That's just nasty."

"What's nasty about that? People have sex in hotels all the time. Besides, it was safe. You know they got cameras there when people walk in the lobby, and as many people stay in a hotel, I could have done a whole lot of screaming and hollering if something went down."

"I wouldn't have done it."

"Don't sit up here and act like you were in love with everybody you shed your panties for."

"I was!" she exclaimed. "Well, at least I thought we had a relationship. I wouldn't have done it after somebody put my life on the line. Anyway, you just used Sydney for sex."

"So what? Men do women like that all the time. You don't think Sydney did me like that? Do you honestly think he loved me when he was creeping around town with whomever?"

"What did he say when you left?"

"What could he say? He thought I was going to lay up there in the bed with him and cuddle and spoon and whatnot." I rolled my eyes. "Our spoonin' days are over. He had the nerve to say I made him feel cheap. It was just sex. He knew that when I called him."

"No, he didn't, Kareese."

"Why would he think it was anything else? He knows I'm divorcing him."

"Yeah, but you know that he's hoping to work things out."

"Who cares what he's hoping for! I don't. I hoped for a lot of things when we were together and I can't even tell you how many times he disappointed me, broke my heart, and didn't care. So, all of a sudden, I'm supposed to be sensitive to him and want what he wants to do? I don't think so."

"Yeah, but you knew his emotions were involved and he was expecting more."

"And my emotions didn't matter? I didn't expect more out of my marriage? I didn't expect more of him as my husband? I didn't expect him

to come home at a reasonable hour?" I don't
know why Yalisa was making such a big deal out
of this and defending Sydney. It was pretty much
a one-night stand with the man I was still married to. Nobody told him to bring his emotions
to the table.

"I'm just saying, you're playing with his head."

"It ain't nothing he ain't ever done to me. He
was the master of playing head games. Anyway,
I don't agree. I didn't say, 'Let's do it, and I
promise we can work on our marriage,' or 'If we
have sex tonight, then that means I'm moving
back home.' He knew what it was when I called.
You mean to tell me he don't know what a booty
call is?"

"I'ma just leave it alone, because I think you're
wrong and we're not going to agree on this at all."

"I can't believe you are taking up for Sydney."

"It's not that I'm taking up for him, but we all
know what that feels like, when you really want
somebody and the other person just uses you for
your body."

I knew exactly what that felt like, but this time
I also knew what it felt like to have sex with no
emotion attached—like men did all the time. It
was surprisingly easy to shrug the escapade off
as 'just sex' regardless of how Sydney felt. My
only concern was that condoms were involved.
"Let's change the subject," I suggested.

"What's going on with Quinton?" she asked. I did eventually tell her about our little thing after we'd slept together.

"Excuse me," I heard come from behind. I turned my head to see a vaguely familiar male face looking down at me. "Forgive me for interrupting your, uh, girlfriend time, but I just wanted to come over and say hello. Do you remember me?"

"Mmm," Yalisa hummed, with raised brows.

"Yeah, I do. You work at T.G.I. Friday's, but I don't remember your name."

"Malcolm," he reintroduced.

"Oh yeah." I nodded. "How are you?"

"I'm fine," he answered. "I saw you over here, and I hope you don't mind me coming over to say hello, and, uh, I wanted to know if I could give you my number."

"Mmmmm!" Yalisa hummed again, then yelped when I kicked her under the table.

"I'm not really in a position . . ." Yalisa kicked me back, but I ignored her. "I really don't call guys."

"Are you seeing someone? I'm sorry, I should have asked that first," he checked.

"Not exactly. I've ended something with someone and I'm not really up for anything new right now."

"Who, that dude you were with the other day?"

"Mmmmmm!" Yalisa moaned even louder.

"Please excuse her," I chuckled. "She's never seen a man before."

"I'm Malcolm." He extended his hand toward her.

"Yalisa." She accepted and shook quickly. "Kareese, give him your number."

What? She just had all this moral concern for me sleeping with Sydney but now wanted me to start cheating on him—go figure!

"Kareese is a beautiful name," Malcolm complimented, reaching for his wallet. "I tell you what. Just take my card, and if you call, I'd be delighted to hear from you. If you don't, then at least I asked."

I smiled. Couldn't help it. "Okay," I accepted.

"You lovely ladies have a good night."

"Are you gonna call him?" Yalisa asked, barely letting the man get out of hearing range.

"I know you are not encouraging me to cheat on Sydney after all you had to say, not even two minutes ago, about him getting his feeling hurt over some cheap sex."

"I think you should call him."

"I think I should get a divorce first. You just got finished being so concerned about Sydney's emotions being involved, and now you've turned your back on him. Not that I care."

"So call Malcolm. You don't have to date him—just be friends."

"We'll see," I said, glancing at the card, which only had his name—Malcolm L. Vincent—and number on it. I tucked the card in my purse.

"What man were you hanging out with at Friday's?"

"Sydney. Remember, I told you we met for lunch after we'd gone to court, and he was sitting there with his wedding band on, talking about how God said our marriage wasn't over? Well, Malcolm waited on us."

"You should call him."

"I'll let Sydney know you're not in his corner anymore."

"It's not about me being in his corner. It's about not doing people wrong," she said, defending Sydney again.

"Let me see if I'm understanding you. If I have sex with my husband, I'm doing him wrong. But if I call old dude who was just at the table, while I'm legally still married to Sydney, that's okay. That's what you're saying?"

"You know what—just forget it."

We were silent for a minute.

"It was good too, girl. Sydney put it *down!*"

Chapter Twenty-two

"Hello?"

"Let me speak to my kids," Sydney snarled. I didn't waste my breath to respond to him.

"Casey and Carlos, your dad is on the phone! Take it up there!" I yelled in the stairwell. A few seconds later, they picked up the phone.

"We got it," Carlos yelled down.

Normally, I would hang up, but tonight I pressed the mute button on the cordless handset and locked myself in the downstairs bathroom to listen to what Sydney had to say.

"How y'all doing?"

"Fine."

"Everything okay?"

"Yes."

"Your momma still going out?"

No, he wasn't trying to dig into my personal life. It wasn't any of his business whom I went out with.

"Not that much. Sometimes she goes out with Ms. Yalisa."

"Did y'all get the shoes you wanted?"

"No. Ma said she didn't have the money."

"What? What does she mean she didn't have the money?"

"That's what she said. She said she had to pay rent and bills."

"All that money I give her every month, it ain't no reason in the world why she shouldn't be buying y'all anything y'all ask for."

What! All what money? All Sydney was paying in child support was a whopping $225 a month, because he'd only had a minimum-wage job when we had our child support hearing. I couldn't believe Sydney was filling their heads with that garbage. But then again, yes, I could.

"Y'all need to be asking her, what is she doing with the money I give her for y'all?" Sydney continued. "What did she buy you this month?"

"She just took us to Wal-mart and got us some school supplies, a coupla pairs of jeans, and some shirts, but that's it."

"She need to take both of y'all to the mall and let y'all pick out some real clothes. It don't make no sense!"

"How much money do you give her, Dad?"

"Both you and Carlos should be getting at least two-hundred-dollars' worth of stuff every single month." Two hundred probably sounded like a million dollars to the boys. "See. You gotta watch your momma. She is greedy and she is after that dollar."

It took everything I had not to unmute and go off on Sydney, but I couldn't blow my cover.

"Ask her what she does with the money I give her. I give her that money for y'all, not for her to go out with. She had the money to get y'all the shoes y'all wanted."

"Carlos, Dad said he gave Ma the money for our school stuff and we need to ask her, what do she do with the money?"

"He did!" Carlos exclaimed.

"That's what he just told me, and that she shoulda took us to the mall instead of Wal-mart."

"I'ma get on her about that too, 'cause that ain't right!" Sydney added.

I twisted my lips. Sydney knew goodness well that he wasn't about to call me asking me what I did with the few dollars he gave me in child support. He knew better, but the boys didn't.

"Let me talk to Dad?" Carlos asked.

"Dad, Carlos wanna talk to you. Here he go."

"Dad, can we come over on Saturday?"

"I'ma be outta town this weekend, Carlos, so we gonna have to hang out another time."

The boys hadn't been to Sydney's since I moved out. They missed him desperately, but I'm sure he was out living his new single and child-free life. I'd never say that to them, though. They talked trivially for a few more minutes, then ended the call. Once they hung up, I threw the phone in the cabinet under the sink, flushed the toilet, and came out of the bathroom to find Casey practically standing outside the door.

"Ma, can I ask you something?"

"Yep."

"Why can't you buy us the Nikes we wanted if our dad is giving you child support money?"

"Because child support money is for taking care of the child, not buying the child whatever he asks for."

"Dad said he gives you more than enough money, and we should be able to get whatever we want."

"That's because your dad doesn't pay bills over here. Taking care of you and Carlos is not free."

"He said he gives you more than two hundred dollars a month for us."

"And how much do you think it costs to take care of the both of you. To make sure you have a roof over your heads, food in the refrigerator, lights, water, cable, school lunch, toilet tissue and toothpaste, and everything else y'all need?"

"I don't know."

"Go get a sheet of paper," I instructed. "And while you're getting it, think about how much it cost. And think about how much that book bag costs that's holding the notebook with the paper in it; then think about how much that notebook cost. And while you're at it, grab a pencil and think about how much that costs too."

For the next hour, I tried to make both Casey and Carlos understand income and just how little $225 was in the whole scope of my monthly budget and commitment to take care of them. In the end, they still wanted new high-priced sneakers.

Chapter Twenty-three

I did end up calling Malcolm. Not that I was super interested, but I think I was just bored and needed something to do. I found out that he wasn't a server at the restaurant. He actually was the manager of T.G.I. Friday's and just happened to be out on the floor the day that Sydney and I had eaten there.

"So who was it that you were with that day?" he pried.

"My soon-to-be ex-husband." I didn't mind sharing.

"I know the feeling." He nodded, sitting across from me at a table in the café at Borders bookstore. I had agreed to meet him for a hot chocolate date, just to talk.

"You're divorced, then, I take it?" I asked.

"Yeah."

"How long were you married?"

"About four years. I got a beautiful daughter out of it." He smiled as he pulled out his wallet and turned to a photo of an adorable little girl.

"She's cute. What's her name?"

"Syrena. She's my pride and joy. So you have two sons, huh?"

"Yeah, Casey and Carlos."

"Twins?"

"No, they are two years apart. I don't have any pictures of them," I said, responding to his outreached hand. "So what happened to your marriage?"

"It's hard to say, really. We dated for about four years, and as soon as we said 'I do,' it just seemed to go down from there. Like we grew apart, instead of growing together."

"Did you leave her, or did she leave you?" I asked frankly, trying to figure out what kind of man was sitting in front of me.

"We just both agreed that it was for the best." He paused with a reminiscent but sour expression on his face. "I think we just got to the place where our interests were too separate, so we started spending more and more time apart. That left the door open for other things, which just weren't conducive to a successful marriage." He motioned as if to say at this point he was over it and it was no big deal. "What about you? What kind of battle scars did you walk away with?"

"A couple of wounds, but nothing that can't be healed or hasn't already scabbed over. I made the decision to leave, so he took it kind of rough."

"Yeah, that's how it happens—the one that gets left is always the one that gets mad."

"You got that right. Where does your daughter live?"

"She lives in Costa Rica with her mom. She comes to visit about twice a year. I wish it were more, but I have to take what I can get."

"So this is your boyfriend?"

I jerked my head up, and there stood Sydney, snarling down on us. I felt my heart nearly stop in my chest.

"Excuse you?" fell from my lips, with a strong neck roll.

He threw up his hands in mock surrender. "I don't mean no harm; I'm just asking, since you still married last I checked. I'm just wondering how long you been doing this. Probably for a few years now, huh?" He looked over at Malcolm. "I'm sure you won't mind if I sit down beside my wife and see what it is the two of you got to talk about." Sydney pulled out a chair, but before he could sit, Malcolm stood to meet him, eye to eye.

"Look, man, why don't you—"

"Malcolm, don't even worry about it," I said, reaching for my cell phone. "This is about to be resolved in just a few minutes." Assuming I was calling the police, Sydney changed his mind about lingering at our table.

"You two go ahead and enjoy your little date," he said, backing away. "Kareese, I'll call you later."

Malcolm watched Sydney's back as he left the store, then looked back at me.

"I'm sorry about that," I said, slightly embarrassed.

"No apology necessary. It wasn't your fault. Yeah, he's pretty bitter." Malcolm nodded.

"Don't pay him any attention."

"How long were the two of you married, again?" He looked toward the door and then behind him to check his surroundings.

"A lot longer than we should have been." I blew at my cup of hot chocolate and sipped to avoid saying more.

"Would you get married again?" He stared me straight in the eyes, which made me a bit uncomfortable. I felt like he was trying to pick me apart.

"Where is that question coming from?"

"I'm just asking, for conversation sake." A quick rise and fall of his shoulders suggested his question was trivial, but it was a bit heavy, if you asked me.

"I don't know. I guess I would if I found the right person who loved me and was in love with me. I don't believe Sydney was ever in love with me." I should have kept that last sentence locked in my thoughts.

"He must have been at some point; he married you," Malcolm suggested. "Most men won't marry someone they aren't in love with."

"I don't know why he married me, but it wasn't for love." I shook my head. "It couldn't have been that. But listen—let's talk about something else other than our broken marriages." I didn't know Malcolm well enough to be transparent and vulnerable. Nor did he need to know my life story.

"You like Mexican?"

"Mexican is okay."

"Come on." He stood and pulled my chair out and helped me with my coat. "You're gonna love this place."

Malcolm and I drove separate cars to a small spot off Capital Boulevard in a strip mall. The atmosphere was quaint and authentic; painted in shades of rust and pale yellow; woven blankets, feathers, and the like adorned the walls; and the sound of horns, maracas, and castanets filled the air. There was a dance floor near the bar, and booths and tables filled with people who seemed to enjoy their food and the company they were with.

"It's always crowded here. The food is really good, though," Malcolm explained. I watched inconspicuously as he scrunched his brows and licked his lips. His hands were tucked into his jacket pocket as he looked around, hoping to find a free table. He was so easy on the eyes, but I made myself look away. "They really need a hostess here to do seating, because sometimes it can just be a free-for-all." Without any warning, he grabbed my hand, slightly jerking me to the left. "There's one." Once we were seated, I chose a taco salad, while Malcolm rested on fajitas and something from the bar. "You want anything?" he asked, offering me a drink.

"No, I have to drive home, and I don't drink and drive."

"Do you eat and dance? Salsa starts in about thirty minutes." He bobbed his head toward the dance floor.

"I haven't before, but there's a first time for everything."

"Do you know how to salsa?"

"Nope, but I've always wanted to learn. How about you? Can you work the dance floor?"

"I know a few moves," he bragged, grinning and winking. "I can show you a step or two."

After our meals, Malcolm led me to the dance floor, which was already filled with other couples. He put one of his hands on my hip and took my hand into his other.

"Put your hand here on my shoulder," he instructed. "Now what you're gonna do is a rock step, with your right foot to the back, like one, two three, then forward with your left the same way." He looked down at our feet while I followed his lead into an easy rhythmic pattern. "Now relax it just a bit, you feel so tense and stiff."

"Sorry." I giggled. "I've never done this before." I collapsed my shoulders while I kept my feet moving.

"There you go!" He nodded. We went another minutes or so, him allowing me to get a feel for what I was doing. "Now sync with the music and then put a little hip in it." He looked down again and let go of my hand to place it on my other hip, to further guide me into the step. I didn't need any help in making my hips work, but I had to admit, his hands felt good right where they were. "That's it," he coached.

I felt so alive and sexy out on that dance floor with Malcolm. I felt like a desirable woman.

"So how long have you been dancing?" I asked, letting my eyes meet his.

"Since I was a kid. Grew up doing it." He did some kind of hand switch and guided me through a clumsy turn, which made me laugh out loud. "You're a pretty good dancer."

"Yeah, if I can stand up," I replied, teasing myself.

"Just make it a three count; you'll get it." Malcolm spun me again, "Ba, ba, bah," he puffed, enunciating the rhythm. "Ba, ba, bah. Okay, now come back in," he coached, reeling me toward him. I landed against his chest, while his arm wrapped at my waist, and he took my hand again. My sexual blood pressure shot up as I felt his hips circle and gyrate in a risqué Latin dance way, rather than a nasty club floor bump-and-grind way. It did make me a tiny bit uneasy, but it was so sexy, I couldn't help but blush and enjoy it.

I watched the other couples around us, some more skillful than others, whipping, turning and stepping. They all looked happy, beautiful and sexy; they challenged me to join them. I accepted the challenge and worked a little harder at staying on beat and swaying my hips.

"That's it, you got it!" Malcolm smiled. He turned me twice more, which made me laugh like I was watching BET's *ComicView* or Katt Williams or somebody. I was having a fantastic time and didn't want to leave the dance floor. It didn't matter that I'd broken out into a full sweat. I needed the exercise, anyway.

By the time we did leave the floor, I was out of breath, but I felt exhilarated and young again. I didn't have a care in the world.

"That was fun!" I panted as I took a seat at the bar, as our table had long been cleared and taken by other patrons.

"You've never done that before?"

"No. I've always wanted to, but I don't know, I guess I never took the opportunity."

"Well, you did great. You're almost a pro," he complimented before ordering a drink.

"Do you give lessons?" I asked, and then flagged our server for a glass of water. I patted my face and neck with a napkin.

"Used to. Not so much anymore. I don't have time." He tapped his fingers on the table as he looked out at the dance floor.

"You should. You're great at it."

"You want to be my student?" His hand reached across the table and grabbed mine, then tickled my palm with his fingers.

"I wouldn't mind taking a class."

"We'll have to see what we can work out."

We sat another half hour chatting; then Malcolm walked me to my car, pecked my cheek, and watched as I pulled off. I wore a huge smile on my face all the way home, replaying the evening in my head. I'd actually been on a date. The thing was—I wasn't ready to start dating yet.

"I'm on my way to pick up the boys." I'd dialed my mom's number once I got settled in the car.

"Oh, let them spend the night, Kareese; they having such a good time in there with Gene watching the football game." I could hear the three of them cheering and chanting in the background.

"You sure, Ma? I don't mind coming to get them."

"No, no, don't worry about it. We needed a little youth in this house."

"Okay, well, I will be at home."

"You make sure you call me when you get in, since you gonna be home by yourself."

"I'm always home by myself, Ma. Casey and Carlos don't offer much protection."

"Still. You make sure you call me."

"I will."

I'd gotten in the house and started to run some bathwater and danced my newly learned salsa steps in my bedroom as I looked for something to slip into after my bath. Settling on a pair of burgundy satin pajamas, I poured myself a glass of mixed-berry Pinot Noir, retreated to the bathroom and immersed myself in a tub full of hot water and bubbles.

I liked Malcolm. Well, I liked his company tonight; it was fun. He was amazing, and he did nothing that was sexually suggestive or disrespectful. He didn't try to read me, analyze my situation, or take advantage of any hint of vulnerability that I might have displayed.

And he knew how to salsa dance. His arms were strong and sexy; his lips, framed by a goatee, were inviting; but I refrained. His smile was electric, his hair soft and touchable, even in locks, his skin smooth, his demeanor pleasant. I probably could go on for the next thirty minutes recapping what I saw in Malcolm. Yet and still, I felt it was too early for me to delve into another relationship. The last thing I wanted to do was jump out of the frying pan and into the fire.

Just as I pulled away from the water and slipped into my pj's, the phone rang. It was Sydney's number that popped up on my caller ID. A sigh preceded my decision to answer.

"What, Sydney?"

"I just called to see if you were home or if you were still out ho'ing in the streets."

I hung up the phone. I wasn't going to let Sydney ruin my night. The phone rang a second time.

"Be sure you tell your divorce attorney that you—"

I hung up a second time. When the phone rang for a third time, I let it ring.

"Whatever." It rang back once more and I snatched it up.

"What?"

"Kareese? Is everything okay?" Of course it would be Malcolm.

"I'm sorry, Malcolm. I thought you were someone else. Everything's fine."

"Okay. Just wanted to make sure that you made it home safely. I thought I'd let you get in and get settled first."

"I did." I smiled.

"Okay. Have a good night."

"You too."

"Are we on for a dance lesson next week?" he tested.

"Umm. Let me give you a call back on that." I'd wanted to say yeah, but thoughts of Sydney stopping our divorce ran through my head. I didn't need that. But then again, if I cheated on Sydney, that was grounds for divorce.

Chapter Twenty-four

I knew I shouldn't have, but I just couldn't help eavesdropping on the conversations Sydney had with Casey and Carlos. Most of the time, they talked about nothing. Sydney made promises to come pick them up and take them out on the weekends, or they talked about the game or school, but every now and then, I would catch Sydney bad-mouthing me.

"Dad, can we come live with you?" Casey asked.

"Yeah, you can," Sydney answered, but he didn't stop there. "What's going on over there that you don't wanna live with your mom?"

"We just don't like it here," he complained.

"Why not? She be having dudes stay over?"

"No."

"So what is it?"

"We would just rather live with you. Ma be making us clean up and take the trash out and stuff like that."

"Y'all were doing that, anyway."

"I know, but it's just different." Casey stressed.

"And then we can't even be comfortable in our own rooms, 'cause Ma won't let us shut the door unless we just got out the shower or something."

"What else?"

"I mean, it's hard to explain, Dad."

"Is she feeding you?"

"Yes. We take turns cooking most of the time, or we go out."

"Well, I'ma talk to her and see what's going on."

That was his way of getting out of it. He was not at all interested in taking primary custody of the kids, and why would he? He was free to live his life without restrictions and limitations. He had no one to answer to, and he had to be loving every minute of it.

"Did y'all get the money I gave to your momma for you?"

"No."

"See, you gotta watch her because she's very slick and sneaky," he said again.

Casey didn't comment.

"See, this is some of the stuff that used to happen when we were married. I'd give her money to pay the bills and whatnot, and she would just do whatever she wanted to do with it. It don't make no sense."

"So when can we come live with you?" Casey wouldn't let Sydney off the hook so quickly.

"I'ma talk to your momma first and see what she gotta say about it. Knowing her, I'm sure she's gonna try to make you and Carlos stay there so she can keep on getting child support payments."

"Can you just tell her that we want to come live with you?"

"Did y'all tell her yet?"

"No. We didn't want to tell her."

"Okay, I will tell her and see what she says."

Now that was a setup against me if I ever saw one. He was going to pretend to talk to me, then go back and tell the kids that he would have let them come live with him, but I said no. He'd make up some crap about if he had pressed me about it, I would have sent him back to jail, so it was just better if they continued to stay with me a little while longer. Well, I was going to have a trick for that.

I waited a half hour after the boys got off the phone; then I called them down for dinner, which was homemade cheeseburgers and sweet potato fries.

"We're going to sit down and eat together tonight," I announced. They weren't suspicious, which was perfect.

"I've been thinking about something," I started to say, "and I want to see what you two think about it. . . ."

"What's that?"

"I thought it would be a good idea to let you boys go live with your dad." I watched their eyes light up like Christmas trees.

"Yay!" Carlos cheered.

"You would like that, Carlos?"

"Yes!" he answered, looking back and forth at me and Casey.

"Well, I was just thinking, since y'all are boys, it would be better if you were around your dad so you can learn how to do manly things, and you don't have to hang around here for girly stuff. What do you think, Casey?"

"I think it's a great idea," Casey said, grinning.

"Really? I thought you boys would be really sad about not living with me."

"Well, we are a little bit sad," Carlos said, trying to make sure my feelings weren't hurt. "Because you are our mom and we love you, but I think you are right about since we are boys, we should live with Dad."

"How about you, Casey?"

"I don't mind living with either one of you, because both of y'all are my parents, but I would like to go live with Dad too."

"Wow! If it sounds like a good idea to all of us, then all you have to do is ask your dad. If he says yes, then I guess you two will be moving out."

They both looked at each other, about to burst, while I smiled smugly to myself. I hoped that I'd done enough to make whatever Sydney had up his sleeve backfire.

"Suppose we ask Dad and he says it is up to you."

"That's fine. Then you can tell him that you already talked to me about it and I'm fine with letting you live with him."

"Yay! Yay!" they both cheered. "Can we call him now and ask him?" Casey added.

"Sure, after we finish our family dinner."

Those boys couldn't scarf down their burgers fast enough. This time they called Sydney in front of me so I couldn't sneak on the phone to hear his response.

"Hey, Dad," Carlos started, "we talked to Ma about coming to live with you, and she said yes." After that was a series of yes and no responses, but I could see Carlos's face dropping. Man, I wish I could have heard the other half of the conversation. "All right. Okay. Love you too. Bye."

"What did he say?" Casey asked before I could.

"He said we shouldn'ta asked you, because he said he was going to take care of it, and since we didn't wait for him to be the daddy and take care of stuff, that he wasn't going to let us come, because he needed to be able to trust us when he tells us something."

"Did you tell him you didn't ask me, but I asked you?"

"No. He wouldn't hardly let me say anything because he was fussing," he responded, sulking.

Casey just stood and walked upstairs, clearly disappointed.

Hmm. How could I have made this turn out differently? All I had done was make them more loyal to Sydney now. The next time he told them something, they would be more likely to keep it to themselves. *Sigh.*

The sadder part was how far Sydney would go to play with anybody's mind. He knew he was wrong. If he really wanted his kids, he would have been just as happy as they'd been. But he would rather make those boys cry, and make it look like my fault. He ought to be ashamed of himself.

Malcolm and I had been seeing each other for about six months now, and I was having the time of my life. I still wasn't ready to say that we were dating, but seeing him was pleasant and easy. He'd been right about me falling in love with the little salsa corner he'd taken me to. We frequented there so much that the staff knew us by name. He would twirl me around for at least two hours at a time, and I loved every minute of it.

It was after one of our nights of seductively swaying in each other's arms at different speeds that we ended up back at his candlelit living room to continue the dance party. He had been teaching me how to dance the *bachata,* which involved a sexy tangle of our legs lifting every four counts. When it was done right—which Malcolm knew how to do—it sent a fire up my spine that had to be doused by a cold shower every time. Tonight I wanted to let the fire burn.

My divorce had yet to be finalized, so I did feel a sense of guilt in coming closer and closer to my decision to make love to Malcolm. I felt silly about trying to be loyal to a marriage that only existed on paper. In reality, my marriage to Sydney had long been over. And Malcolm had been better to me in six months than Sydney had been in ten years. I laughed at myself on both counts of trying to be faithful *not* to Sydney *but* to the sanctification of marriage, and then trying to justify how it would be all right to sleep with Malcolm.

"What's so funny, babe?" Malcolm whispered. I could feel Malcolm's breath softly on my ear, which enhanced my desire to have him, and to let him have me. I closed my eyes.

"Nothing," I answered.

He pulled back a bit to look into my eyes; then he moved in for a kiss. It wasn't the first time our lips had met, but his kiss, along with the ambience of his home, mixed with the feeling of his body against mine, was more than enough to sway my decision to indulge.

Our tongues circled each other and I gave more lift to my leg as we continued to dance. Malcolm's hands caressed my thighs, then my back, then my breasts. He began to dip and circle his hips slowly, bringing mine with him. After a few dips, we ended up on the floor of his living room, him on top of me. We kissed again, before he suckled at my neck, then made his way lower, slowly and carefully unbuttoning my blouse, but seemingly attentive to whether I had any reservations. And while his lips were warm and wet, tantalizing and sweet, my mind was consumed with the wrinkled skin of my belly, which he was about to find under my blouse. Suppose he became repulsed and awkwardly backed away? I'd be so embarrassed. I didn't know how many sex partners Malcolm had had, but somewhere in his life he had to have seen stretch marks.

"Malcolm," I whispered, pulling him back toward my face.

"Yes," he panted, still planting kisses.

I didn't say a word, because I didn't know quite what to say: *Please don't look at my stretch marks?*

"What's wrong, babe?" He studied my face for a few seconds, which made me look away. "Hey." He nudged my chin to face him. "What's wrong, Kareese?"

"Nothing is wrong; I'm just a little uneasy."

He shifted his weight a bit and rested more on his elbows.

"What's making you uneasy?"

I shrugged, feeling a bit foolish.

"What is it?"

"I'm just not sure that I'm ready to go further than where we've been." We had done some bumping and grinding before, but I'd never let him undress me.

"What is it that you're afraid of?" he asked. This time he shifted over to rest his head on one hand and traced a finger down my face. "Are you afraid that we might mess up a good thing?"

"I guess," I agreed. "I've just never been big on sharing my body with other people. I have some insecurities about it," I admitted.

Malcolm nodded. "So what could I do to make you more secure?"

"I'm not sure if there is anything you can do. It's probably all me."

"No, babe, whenever a woman is insecure, it's because her man has not secured her. He hasn't made her comfortable. If you're not secure, then there is something that I either haven't done yet, or I've done to make you insecure or question my intentions."

"What are your intentions?" I asked.

"Kareese." He paused for a moment. "Kareese, you might not believe this, but I love you."

I bit into my bottom lip.

"I loved you when I first saw you."

I took his words as a trick to get inside my panties. After my mistake with Quinton—although he'd never said he loved me—I just didn't want anything like that again. I felt Malcolm trying to read my expression.

"I got something for you." He lifted his weight, padded to another room and came back with a small bag from a jewelry store. I sat up as he opened the bag and presented me with a small box. I wanted to be excited, but it reminded me of that awful trick Sydney had played a few years back with the bracelet. Malcolm sat beside me and watched my expression as I opened the box to find a necklace with a diamond heart pendant.

"Wow. This is nice," I commented, but my enthusiasm was missing.

"You don't like it?" he asked, picking up on my tone.

"It's beautiful, but why did you get it for me?"

"I told you." He paused. "I bought it a month ago, but I wasn't sure when would be a good time to give it to you. I don't want to pressure you, and I know you're going through a lot. At the same time, I can't hide my feelings toward you, Kareese."

I took the necklace out of the box and held it in my hand, thinking over Malcolm's words.

"Here." He took it from me and placed it around my neck, then kissed my cheek. "Listen, we don't have to make love tonight, or any night until you're ready, if ready ever comes for you. If it never comes, then I will deal with my emotions another way."

We sat on the floor for another ten minutes, practically speechless. I didn't know what to say, and I guess he didn't either. Malcolm finally moved to kiss me on the mouth and I obliged.

"I'll take you home if you're ready."

"Yeah. I think I am."

He heaved himself up, then extended his hands to me to help me to my feet. When I stood, he wrapped his arms around me tightly and held me for nearly a minute. His embrace felt so good. It felt warm and genuine, like love.

After Malcolm dropped me off, I spent a lot of time just sitting on my bed, thinking. I felt miserably confused. I was scared to think that Malcolm could actually love me. Had Sydney messed up my head so much that I couldn't recognize love? I thought of the many ways Sydney had hurt me, tricked me, manipulated me and controlled me. I thought about how he never loved me, although I thought he did, and how I was so afraid of making that same mistake again—of letting my emotions and desire to be loved get the best of me.

Quinton popped in my mind too, but I had no one to blame for that but myself. I realized in retrospect that Quinton had never expressed more than wanting to have sex, and I'd only tricked myself into believing that it could be more. But truthfully, I don't think I expected Quinton to love me; it just would have been nice to have been held and adored, if just for a few minutes. Quinton just showed no regard for the emotional side of what we did. Maybe he didn't owe me that, but still it would have been nice.

And now here I was with Malcolm, and I liked Malcolm a lot, but I couldn't discern whether his intentions were true or just a lie. I couldn't tell if he really felt something genuine for me or not. I wanted to believe I felt it in his hug, in his kiss, in his embrace, but suppose it really wasn't there. I'd been so desperate for love and intimacy in the past, I overlooked the obvious, accepted the unacceptable and turned the other cheek when I should have slapped back with such force that I knocked somebody down. How could I know?

I grabbed at the heart pendant on my neck and right then my mind flashed back to the day I married Sydney. I remembered how my neighbor Miss Hazel clasped the heart pendant she wore around her neck from her one true love. It made me smile.

Chapter Twenty-five

"Kareese, I'm just calling to let you know that I got the letter in the mail about the final deposition, and I am not going to sign it. I love you and I want my family back. I'm willing to fight for it, so I will not be signing any divorce papers."

"That's fine, Sydney, you don't have to. I knew you were gonna try to pull some kind of game, so I filed contested divorce. That means you don't have to sign anything. I'm divorcing you, whether you like it or not."

"Don't do it, Kareese. Please. I don't want to live without you."

"I don't know why. It's all you have ever tried to do. You've always tried to live without me. I don't know why you're trying to hold on so tightly now. You may as well give it up."

"Kareese, I swear if you divorce me, I'm going to kill myself."

"For real?"

"I'm serious. I don't want to live without you."

"If you kill yourself, I hope you got some money saved up so we can put you in the ground just like you want to be put away, because you know insurance companies don't pay out money for suicide," I stated calmly.

Sydney didn't respond right away, probably not knowing how to respond to what I'd just said. "I can't believe you are so cold and mean."

"Oh, well, you will get over it. I gotta go. Bye." I hung up the phone, smiling smugly. That extra money that I'd paid in attorney fees had come right in handy.

The next day, my mother came with me to the deposition appointment as my witness, prepped on the type of questions that would be asked. Sydney sent the same homely-looking female lawyer to sign the paperwork on his behalf.

The first part of the deposition went smoothly as the court reporter started recording, and the lawyer verified the identity of everyone present. Where it began to go sideways was when my mother was asked information about my and Sydney's union and breakup.

"Mrs. Watson, what is your relationship to the plantiff, Kareese Christopher."

"She's my daughter," she stated with ease.

He next asked about when Sydney and I got married, and like a whirlwind, my mind flew back to the small room just down the hallway where

I'd stood what now seemed like a lifetime ago, promising that only death would separate us. Well, it wasn't quite death, but it came close to it.

"To this union, how many children were born?" he asked.

"Two."

"Please state their names."

"Casey Christoper, who really wasn't born into their union because my daughter had him before she married Mr. Christopher; and Carlos Christopher, who she had about two years after she married."

"And how old are the children?" was his next question.

"Let's see . . . Casey is, um . . . don't know. I think he is about eleven or something like that, and I guess Carlos is about nine . . . ten."

She knew goodness well how old my boys were. I pressed my lips together, becoming frustrated with whatever my mother was trying to pull. I wanted to kick her under the table. Why would she get in here and start acting clueless? Again the lawyer raised his brows, looking like he was seriously questioning the validity of her answers.

"Are you okay?" he asked.

Oh, my God. She was about to mess me up.

"Yes, I'm fine." She nodded, folding her fingers together on top of the table.

"Can you confirm that your daughter lived separate and apart from her husband for at least a year, prior to seeking divorce?"

"I guess she did," was her answer. "I think she lived in their home for a little while, but then she moved out."

What the hell? Why couldn't she just say yes! Had Sydney been there, he probably would have been gloating and laughing at me.

"Can you confirm that she lived separate and apart from Mr. Christopher for at least a year?" he asked again.

"Yes, I'm pretty sure she did."

The lawyer had to be thinking, "Where did you get this witness from? Is this really your mother?" If he was thinking that, I couldn't blame him. I couldn't even look at my mother right now. I let out an inaudible sigh when he stopped asking her questions and moved on.

After an hour of making a recorded statement and signing documents, all that remained to be done was the formal filing with the courthouse, which would take about thirty days, and I'd be officially divorced.

I confronted my mother as soon as I got her alone in the hallway. "Ma, why were you answering the questions like that? It's not like you didn't know the answers."

"I didn't want to make it sound like we practiced."

So you'd rather sound like an idiot and cost me my divorce? I thought. I couldn't say that without being disrespectful, so I kept it to myself. "Ma, the attorney would expect my mother to know the answer to those questions. Why would I bring a witness who couldn't answer questions?"

"I just thought it would sound more real if I acted like I had to think about it."

It felt like she tried to sabotage my proceedings, but I didn't comment further. At this point, it didn't matter, now that it was over. I simply made the decision to continue to handle my mother with a long handled spoon. Maybe one day we'd get past our differences. Just not today.

I just about skipped to my car that day, feeling very different from the day I left court a year ago when Sydney's case was dismissed. I called Sydney just to gloat.

"Thirty more days and I'll be single!" I sang.

"I can't believe this is something you're really happy about, Kareese."

"Just because you don't believe it, doesn't mean it's not true!" I laughed. "I can't wait! But you know what, you ought to be doing a happy dance yourself, because you never wanted to be married to me at all, Sydney. Admit it."

"I don't know why you think I never loved you. I did love you and I want you to know that I've never cheated on you."

"Whatever, Sydney. Right now, it doesn't matter to me whether you did or you didn't. Let's talk about something that *does* matter. When are you going to let the boys come live with you? You know they want to."

"Long as I'm paying child support, you gonna take care of them."

"Okay, I'll let them know that."

"No! Don't tell them that."

"Why not? That's what you just said." Oh, this was so much fun.

"I'm just saying if they come live with me, I'm not going to still be giving you money every month for them."

"Fine by me." I shrugged. "I'll drop them off to you tonight."

"Wait a minute!"

"Wait for what? They want to come; you already told them that they could; I'm in agreement, so it's a done deal."

"Are you gonna start paying me child support?

"I sure will, and you're gonna start paying me alimony," I countered. "So I think it will pretty much be a wash."

"You know what, Kareese, you make me sick!"

"Great! So you should feel better about our divorce, then. I'll talk to you later."

***

Carlos and Casey were excited about gathering their belongings and moving out to live with Sydney.

"We'll come visit on the weekends, Ma," Casey promised.

"Sounds good." I kissed my babies on their smiling faces as they piled their bags and then their bodies into the car. "Y'all sure y'all want to move out?"

"We're sure," they answered in unison.

"Well, I will miss you."

"We'll miss you too."

I pulled up in front of my old marital home and saw that Sydney was indeed home, as indicated by his car in the driveway.

"Go knock on the door and make sure he's there," I instructed. With a bound, my boys sprang from the car, knocked a few times, then returned for their things once Sydney opened the door. "Love you,"

"Love you too!" they both sang together before slamming the car doors.

Once I dropped the boys off, I headed back down to the Juvenile Domestic Relations building to enter my request to cease child support payments. Fair was fair, and Sydney and I both knew that cash didn't replace having to see after and take care of two boys. I didn't file an alimony request just yet, figuring Sydney and I would work that detail out later, but kept it in my mind as an option if I needed it.

Malcolm rang my cell as I drove home to enjoy the rest of my day off.

"How's your day going, love?" he asked.

"Pretty good," I shared. "Everything's going as planned. I'm headed home now."

"Do you mind if I swing by for lunch? I'll bring it with me."

"Not at all."

"What would you like?"

"Anything you bring will be fine."

Malcolm rang my doorbell forty-five minutes later, toting a bag from Jason's Deli and a bouquet of mixed flowers. He lightly kissed my cheek as I let him in.

"You look beautiful," he commented, handing me the flowers.

"Thank you, and thank you." He kissed me again and allowed me to play with his locks. "You look great yourself."

He put two huge baked potatoes, loaded with grilled chicken, cheese, sour cream, and *pico de gallo* on the table, while I put the flowers in water and centered them on the table. Like a gentleman, Malcolm pulled a chair out for me and seated me.

"You don't mind taking an UNO beat-down today, do you?" He pulled a deck of UNO cards out of his pocket and began shuffling them without looking at me, so he didn't notice my gazing right away. When I didn't answer, he shifted his eyes up to mine. "You okay, baby?"

I nodded silently.

"What's wrong?"

This time I shook my head.

"Everything went okay at your deposition?" He put the cards down and took my hand.

"Yeah, everything went fine."

"What are you thinking about?"

"Nothing in particular," I shrugged. "Deal the cards." Malcolm kissed the back of my hand, then distributed cards between us while I thought about everything, actually.

What I'd actually been thinking was how giddy and wonderful I felt whenever Malcolm was around. And how he brought me flowers every time he came over. How he always asked how was my day, and then took the time to listen, no matter how long I rambled on. I thought about how Casey and Carlos took a liking to him when we'd strategically set up a chance meeting on a basketball court. And how many nights we'd just spooned on the couch, watching movies and sharing tender kisses. I thought about how amazing and incredible he was. He'd come into my life so gently and easily, it couldn't have been more perfect.

I shared all those thoughts with Malcolm as we mildly competed with each other to get rid of cards. Some things I mentioned, we laughed about; some things we smiled about; some things evoked sadness. We never finished our game, because by the time I finished sharing my thoughts, Malcolm laid his cards on the table and wiped my tears away, instead.

We held each other for almost ten minutes. "I love you, Kareese," he whispered just as he kissed me good-bye.

After he left, I lay on my couch and clutched my pendant. There was no way I could see Malcolm. Not now—not yet. He would make me fall in love with him, and in love was the last place I needed to be right now. I realized through my struggles and heartaches with Sydney, somewhere along the way, I'd forgotten how to love myself. I wondered if I'd ever even known how. I couldn't invite or ask Malcolm, or anyone for that matter to embrace the shattered pieces of my heart until I was able to embrace, appreciate, and love myself first.It had been a long, hard journey, but I'd made it. I survived. And now—alone—I just needed to heal. I needed to rest.

Other books by Kimberly T. Matthews:

ORDER FORM
URBAN BOOKS, LLC
97 N18th Street
Wyandanch, NY 11798

Name (please print):_____

Address:_____

City/State:_____

Zip:_____

QTY	TITLES	PRICE

Shipping and handling: add $3.50 for 1st book, then $1.75 for each additional book.
Please send a check payable to:
Urban Books, LLC
Please allow 4-6 weeks for delivery